TARO AND THE OF DOOM

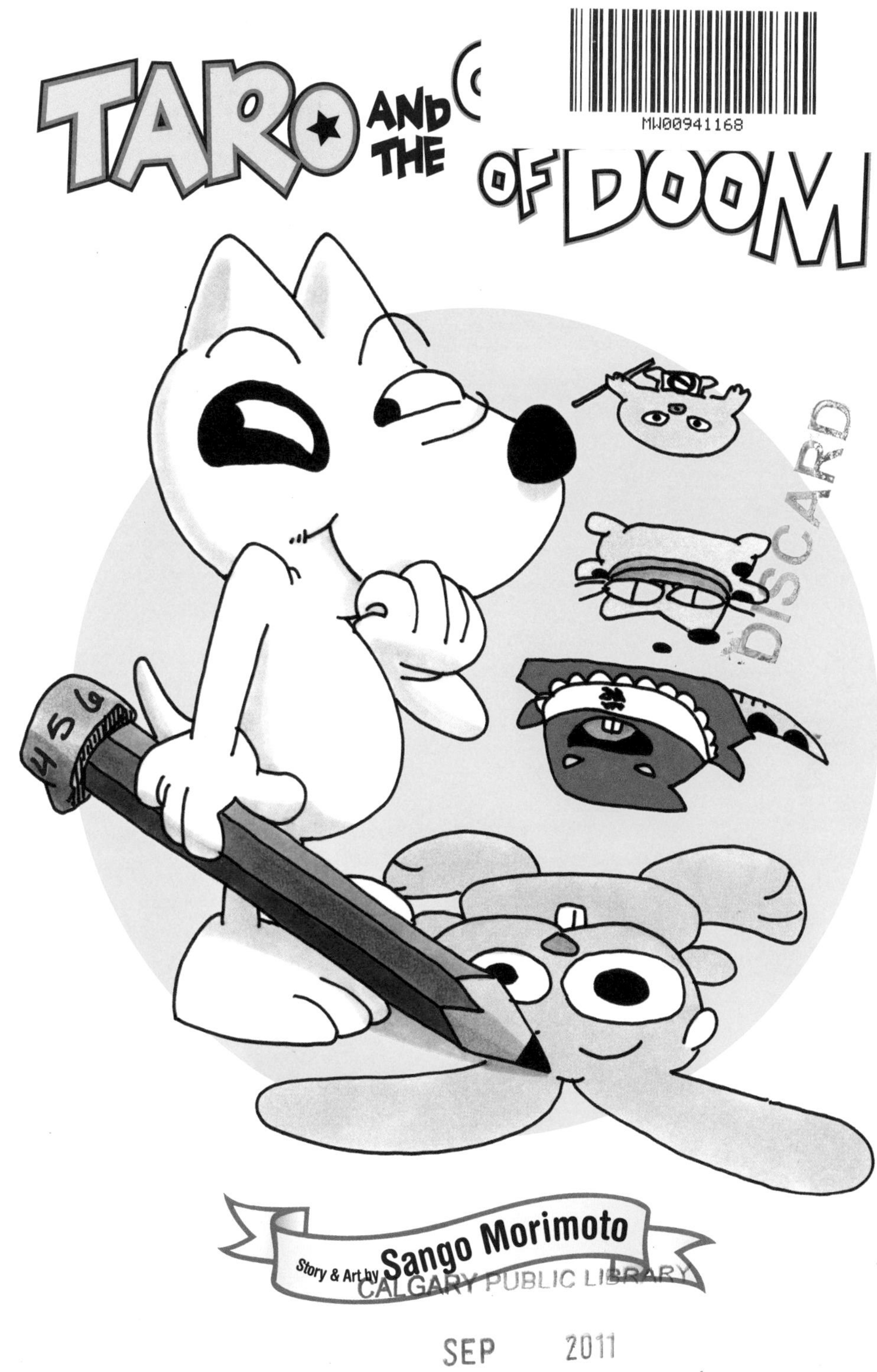

Story & Art by **Sango Morimoto**

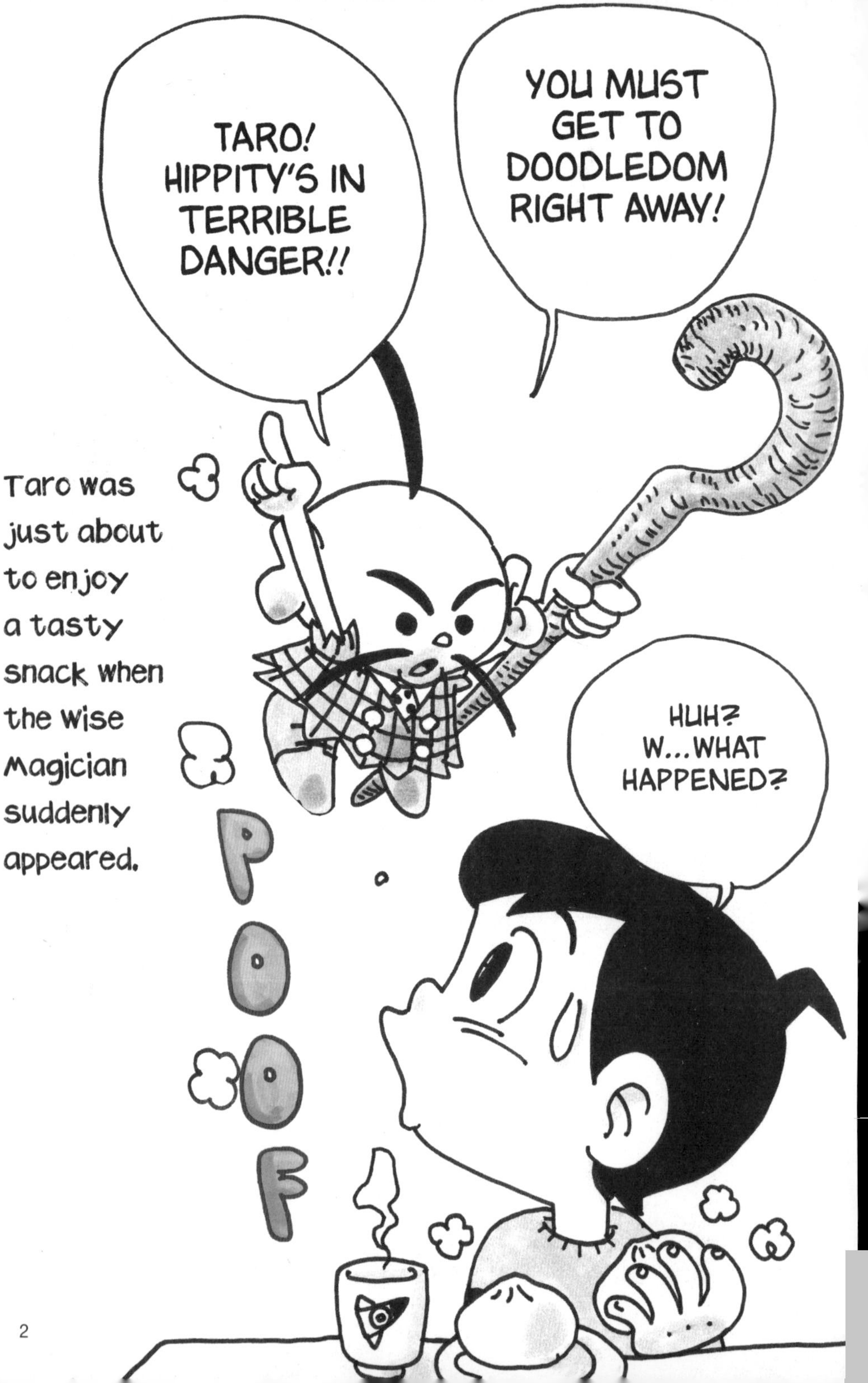
TARO! HIPPITY'S IN TERRIBLE DANGER!!
YOU MUST GET TO DOODLEDOM RIGHT AWAY!
Taro was just about to enjoy a tasty snack when the wise Magician suddenly appeared.
POOF
HUH? W...WHAT HAPPENED?

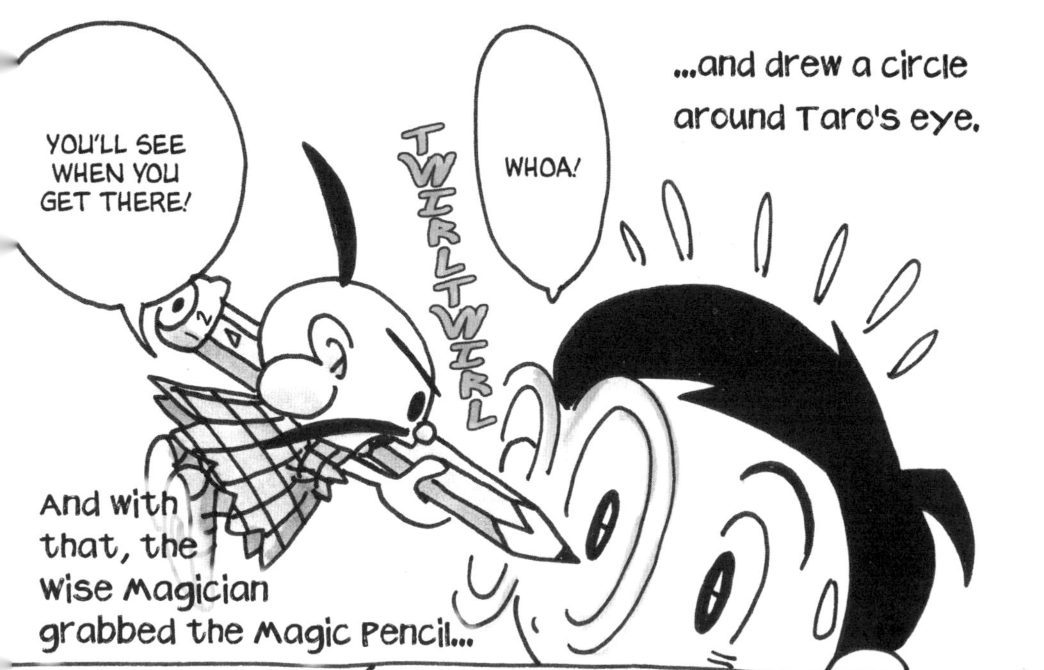
YOU'LL SEE WHEN YOU GET THERE!
TWIRLTWIRL
WHOA!
...and drew a circle around Taro's eye.
And with that, the Wise Magician grabbed the Magic Pencil...

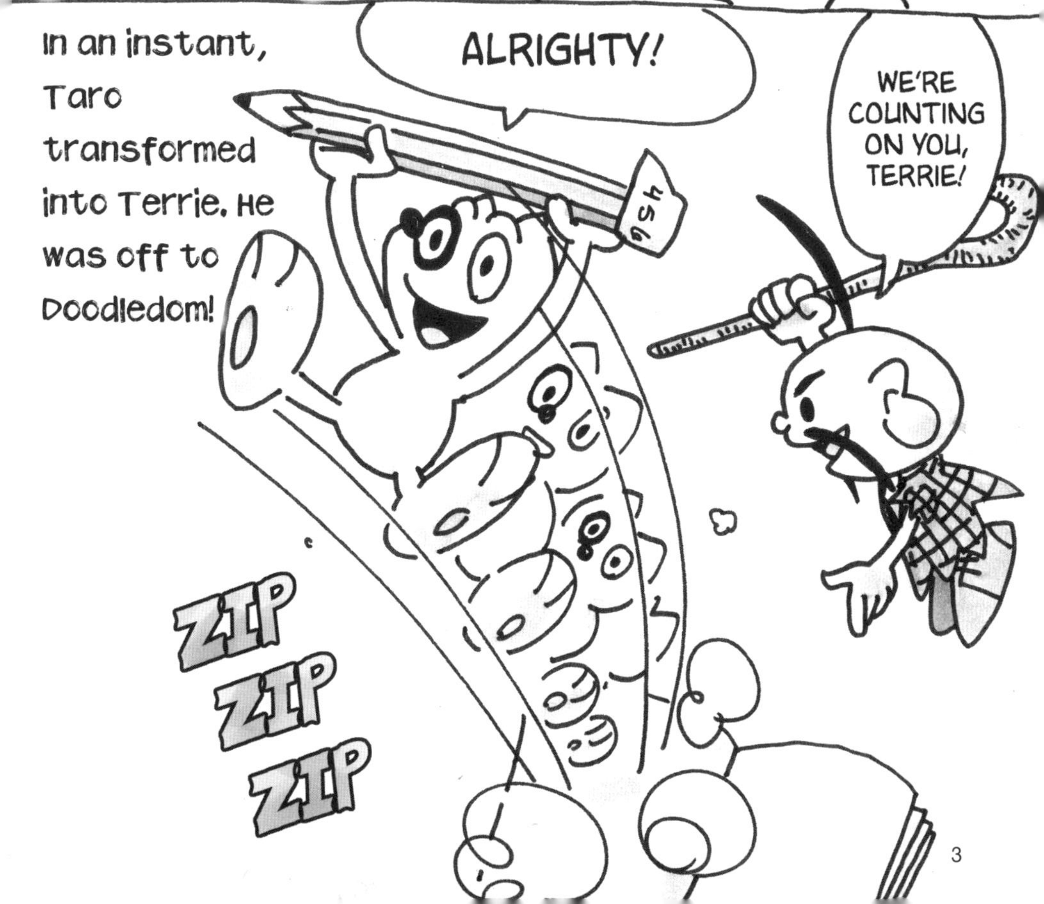
In an instant, Taro transformed into Terrie. He was off to Doodledom!
ALRIGHTY!
WE'RE COUNTING ON YOU, TERRIE!
ZIP
ZIP
ZIP

As soon as he arrived in Doodledom, Terrie saw what the Wise Magician was talking about. Hippity was being chased by a flying creature with a butterfly net!

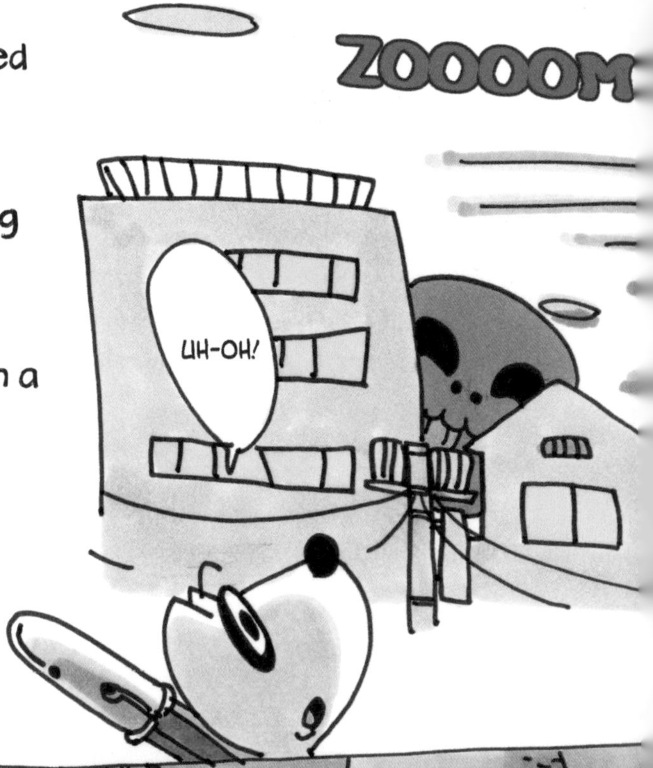
ZOOOOM
UH-OH!

Before Terrie could do a thing, the creature scooped Hippity up!

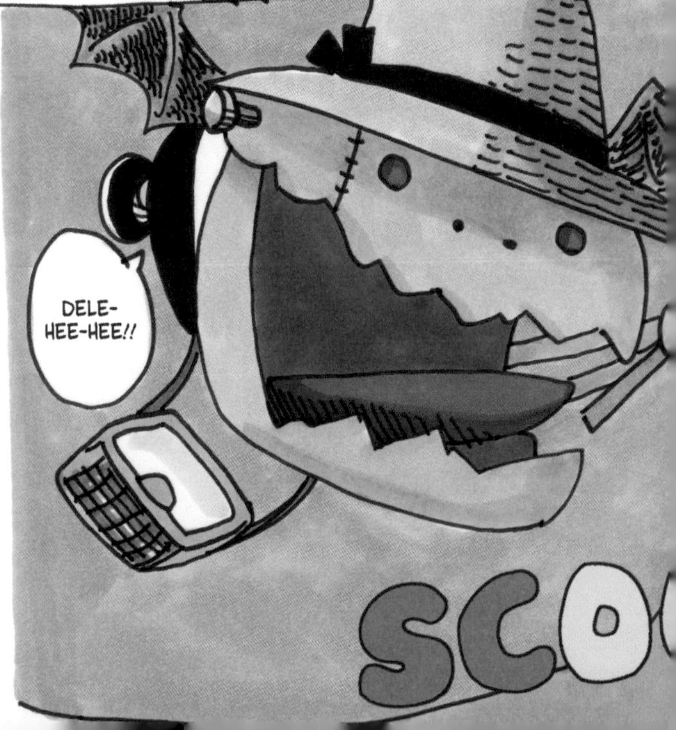
DELE-HEE-HEE!!
SCO

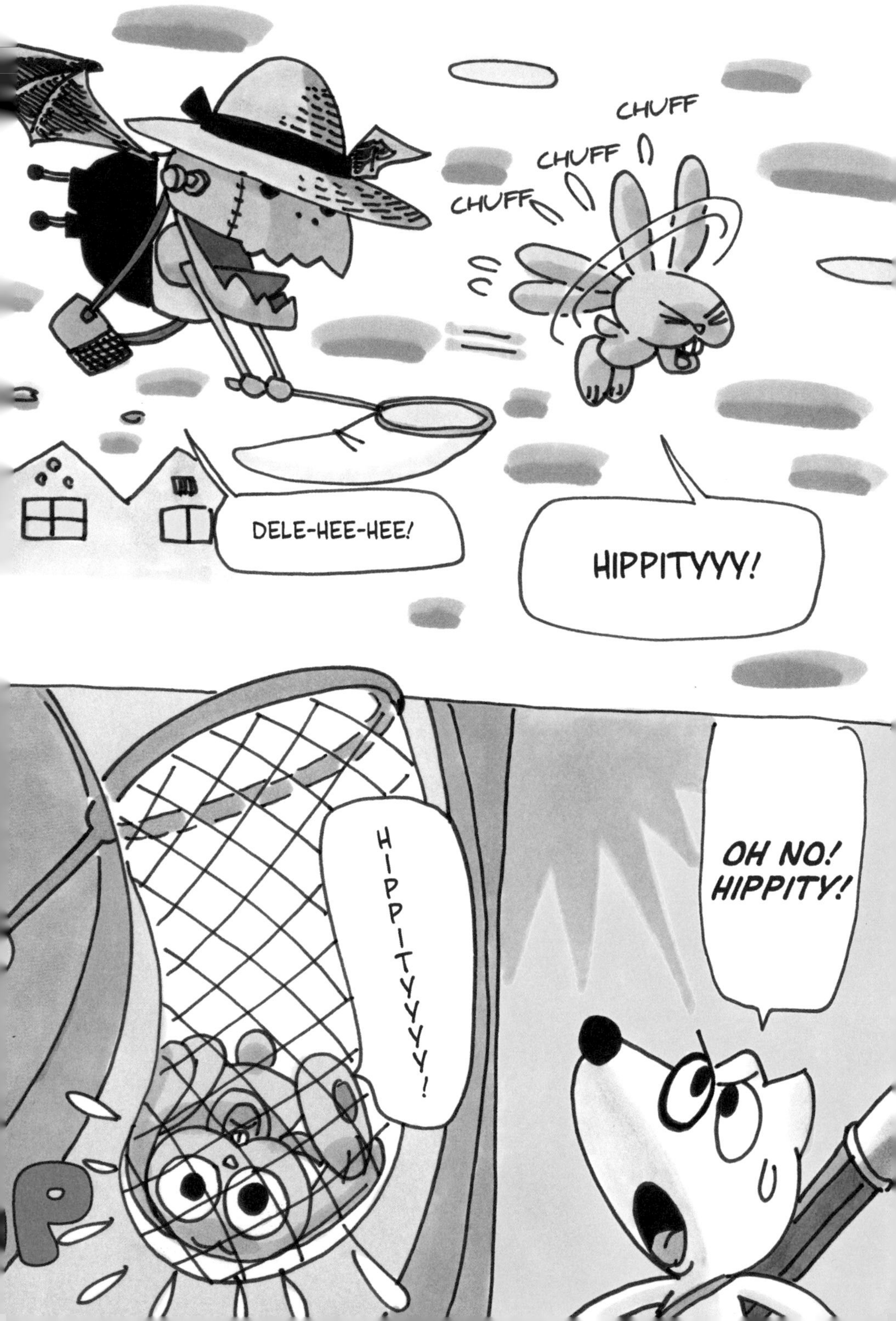
CHUFF
CHUFF
CHUFF
DELE-HEE-HEE!
HIPPITYYY!
HIPPITYYYY!
OH NO! HIPPITY!

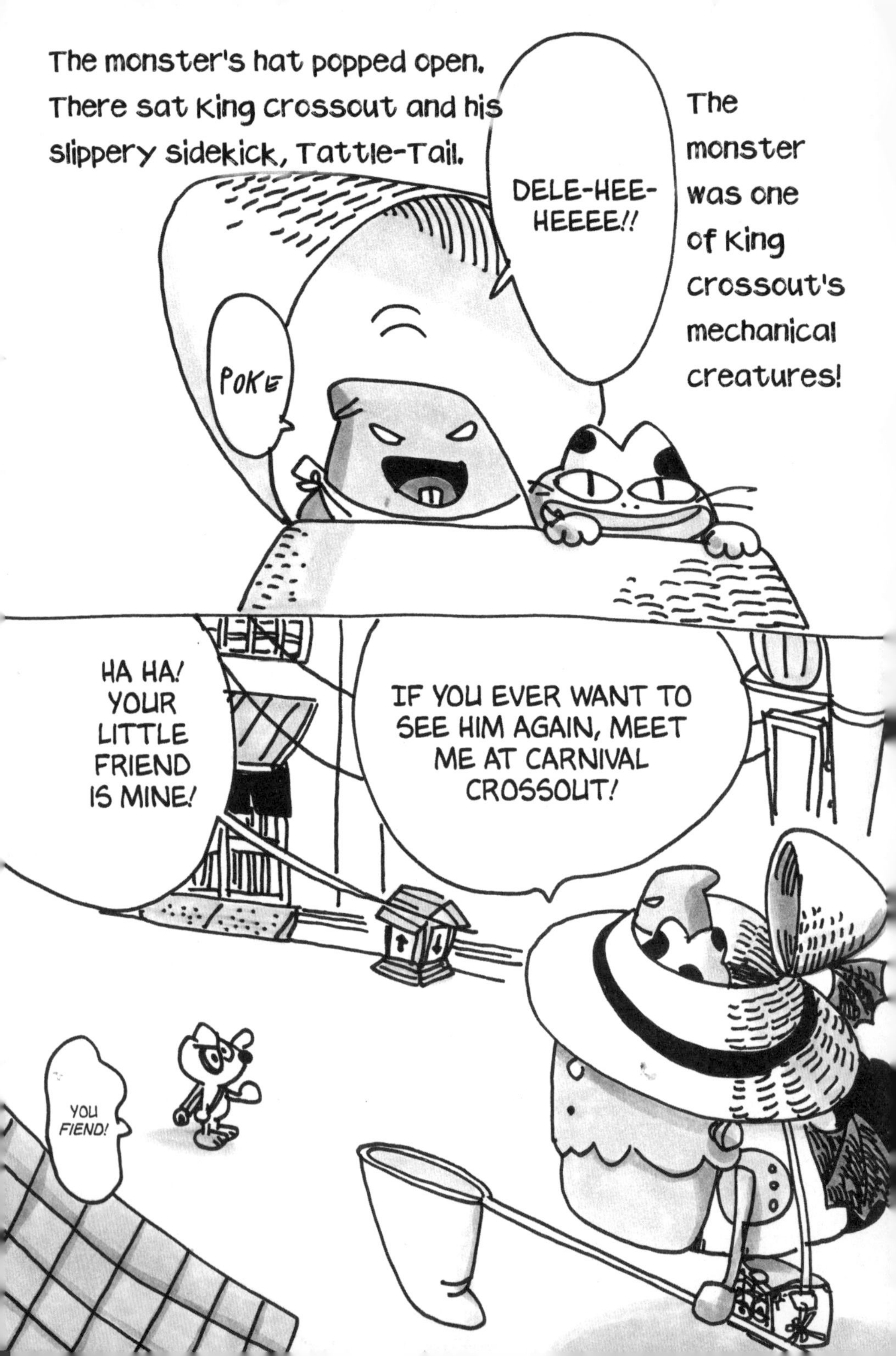
The monster's hat popped open. There sat King Crossout and his slippery sidekick, Tattle-Tail.
DELE-HEE-HEEEE!!
The monster was one of King Crossout's mechanical creatures!
POKE
HA HA! YOUR LITTLE FRIEND IS MINE!
IF YOU EVER WANT TO SEE HIM AGAIN, MEET ME AT CARNIVAL CROSSOUT!
YOU FIEND!

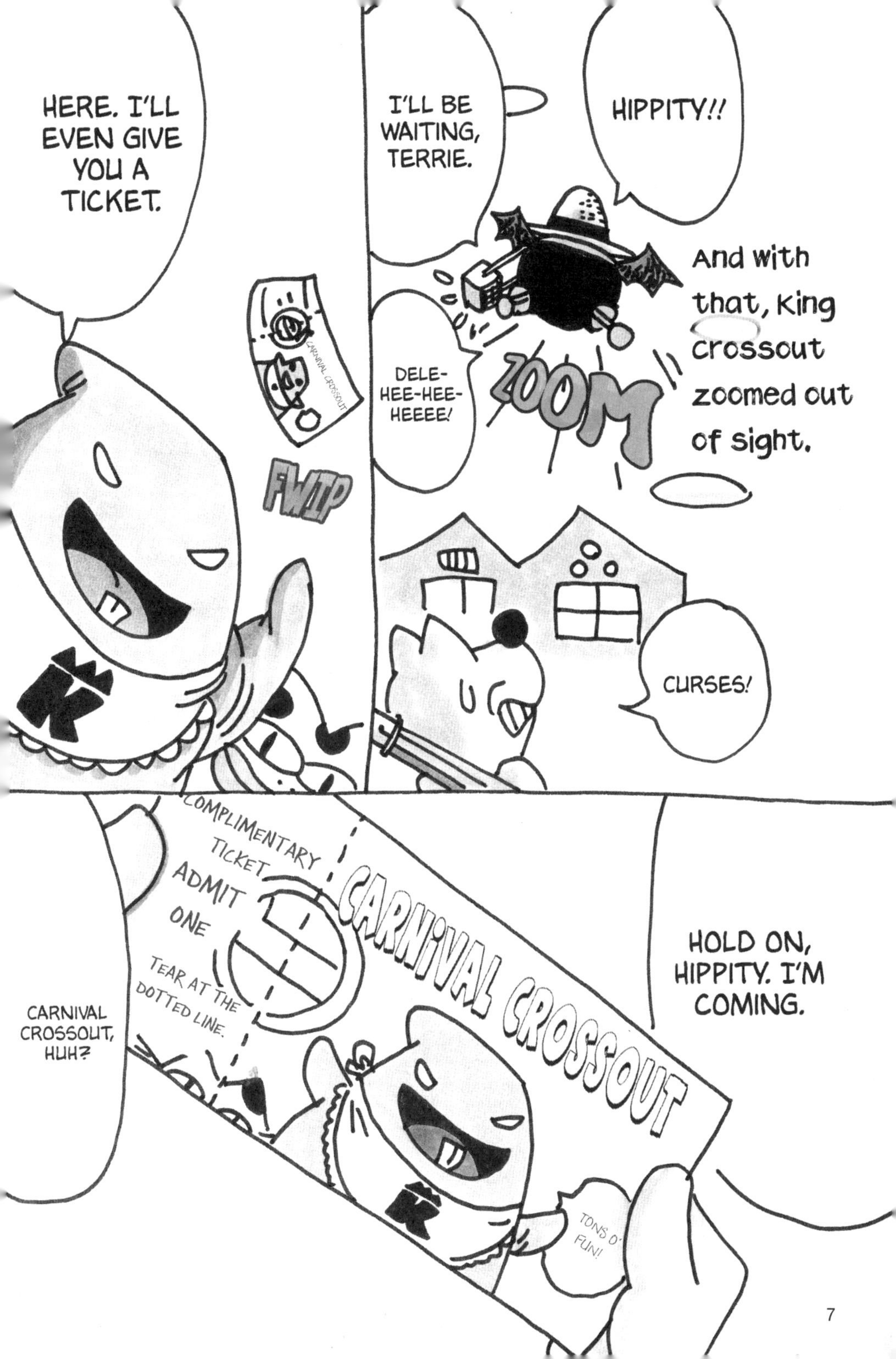
HERE. I'LL EVEN GIVE YOU A TICKET.
CARNIVAL CROSSOUT
FWIP
I'LL BE WAITING, TERRIE.
HIPPITY!!
DELE-HEE-HEE-HEEEE!
ZOOM
And with that, King crossout zoomed out of sight.
CURSES!
CARNIVAL CROSSOUT, HUH?
COMPLIMENTARY TICKET
ADMIT ONE
TEAR AT THE DOTTED LINE.
CARNIVAL CROSSOUT
TONS O' FUN!
HOLD ON, HIPPITY. I'M COMING.

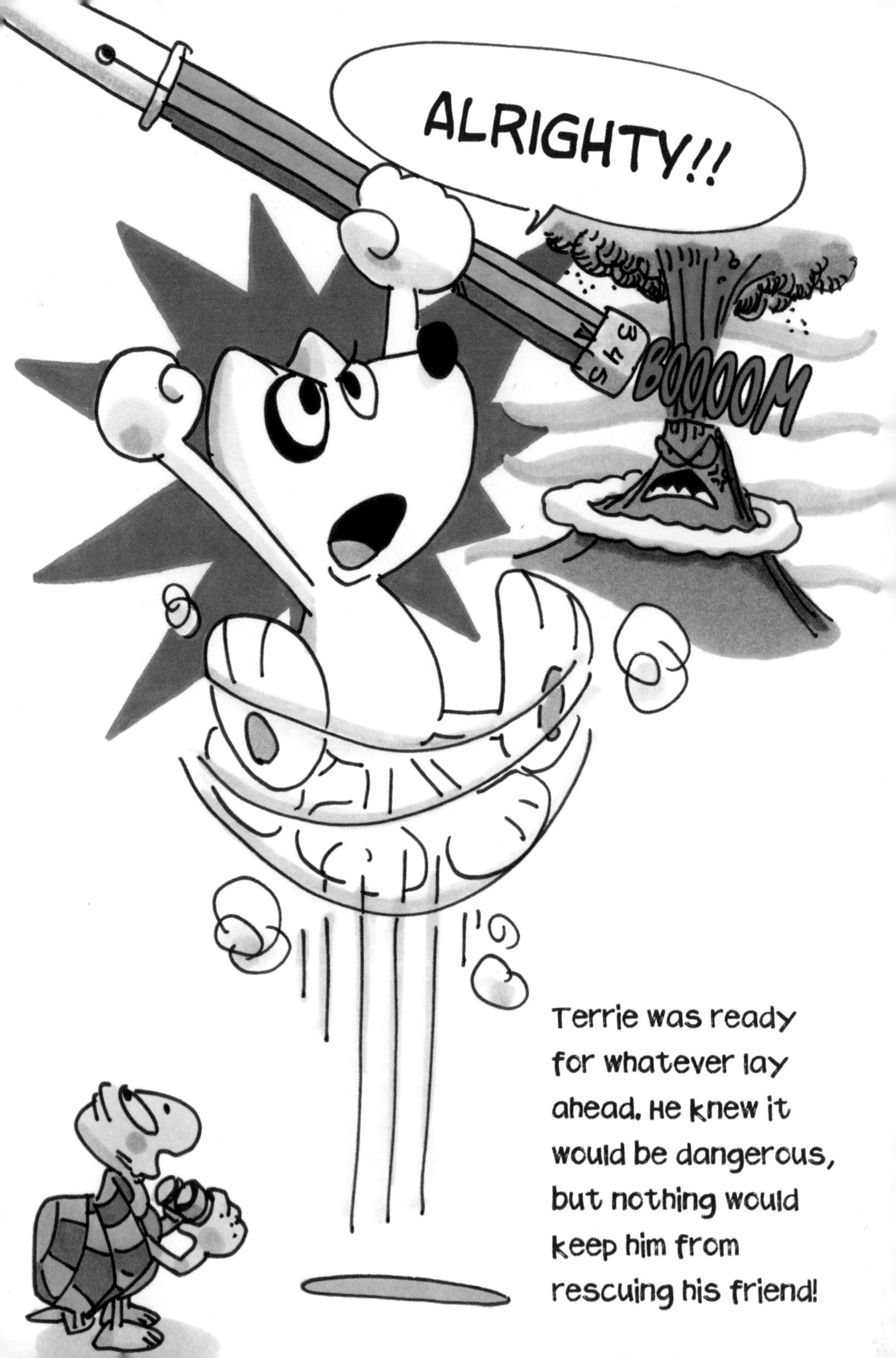
ALRIGHTY!!
3
4
5
BOOOOM

Terrie was ready for whatever lay ahead. He knew it would be dangerous, but nothing would keep him from rescuing his friend!

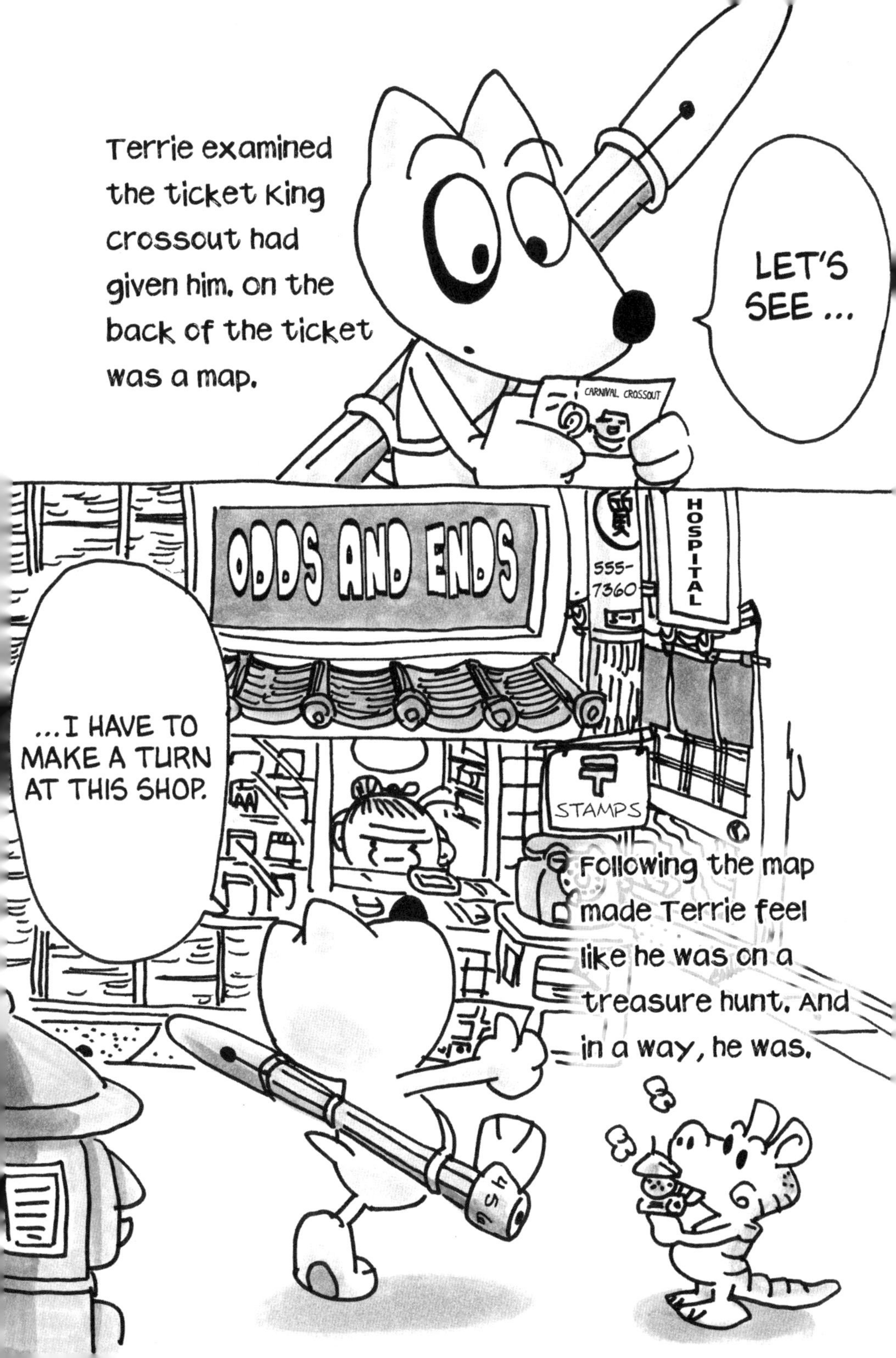
Terrie examined the ticket King Crossout had given him. On the back of the ticket was a map.
LET'S SEE ...
CARNIVAL CROSSOUT
ODDS AND ENDS
555-7360
HOSPITAL
...I HAVE TO MAKE A TURN AT THIS SHOP.
STAMPS
Following the map made Terrie feel like he was on a treasure hunt. And in a way, he was.

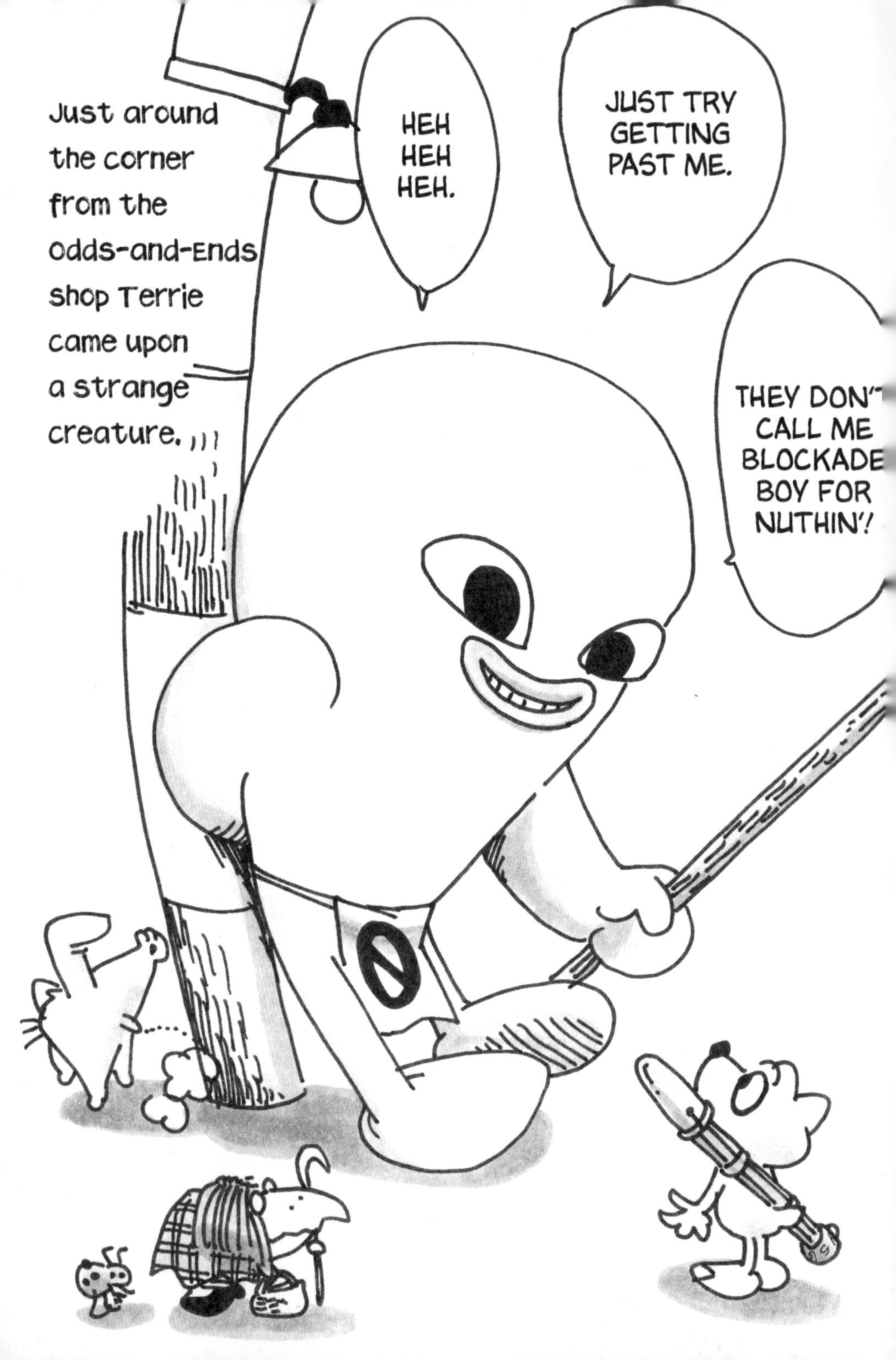
Just around the corner from the odds-and-ends shop Terrie came upon a strange creature.
HEH HEH HEH.
JUST TRY GETTING PAST ME.
THEY DON'T CALL ME BLOCKADE BOY FOR NUTHIN'!

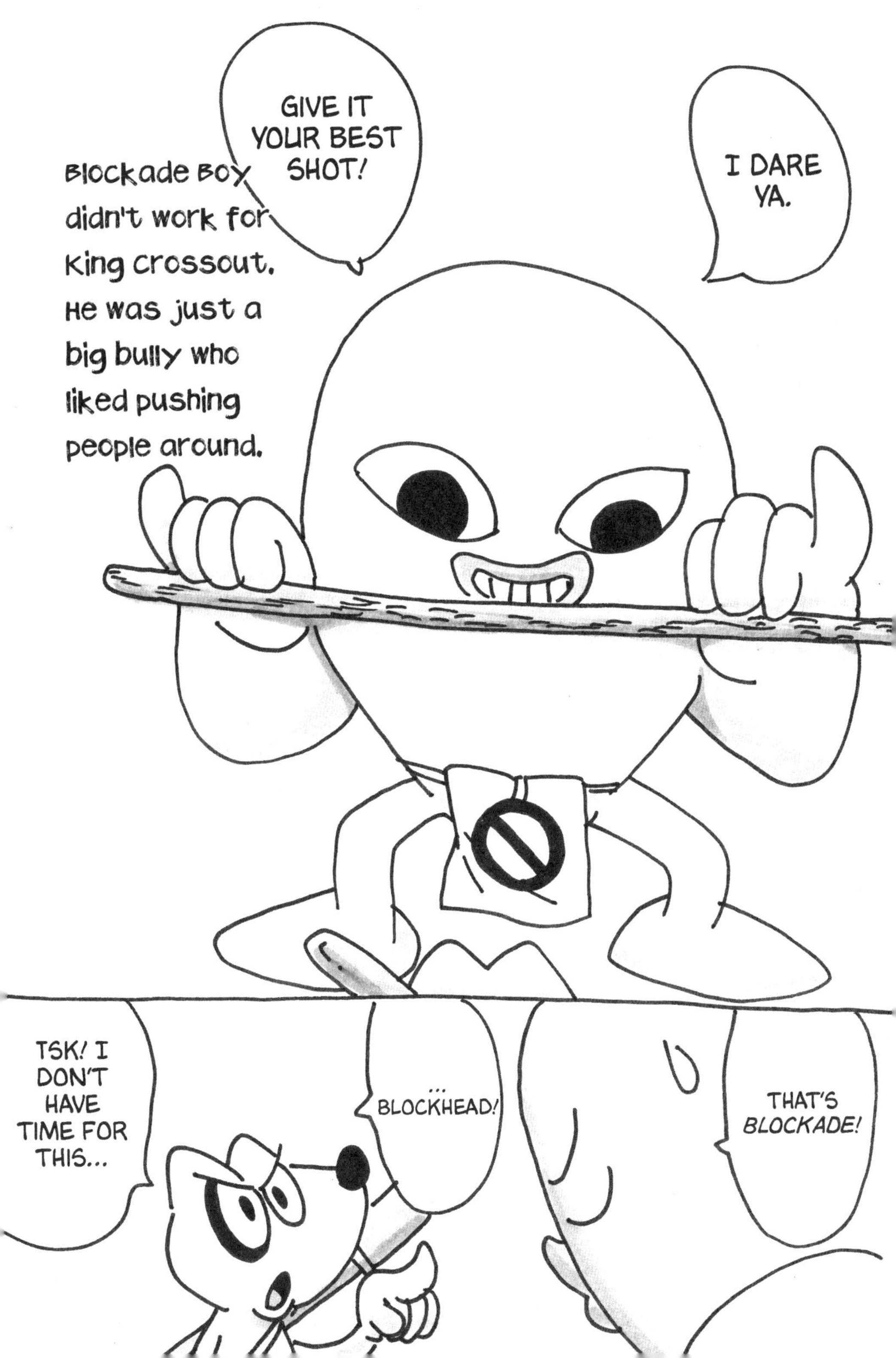
Blockade Boy didn't work for King Crossout. He was just a big bully who liked pushing people around.
GIVE IT YOUR BEST SHOT!
I DARE YA.
TSK! I DON'T HAVE TIME FOR THIS...
... BLOCKHEAD!
THAT'S BLOCKADE!

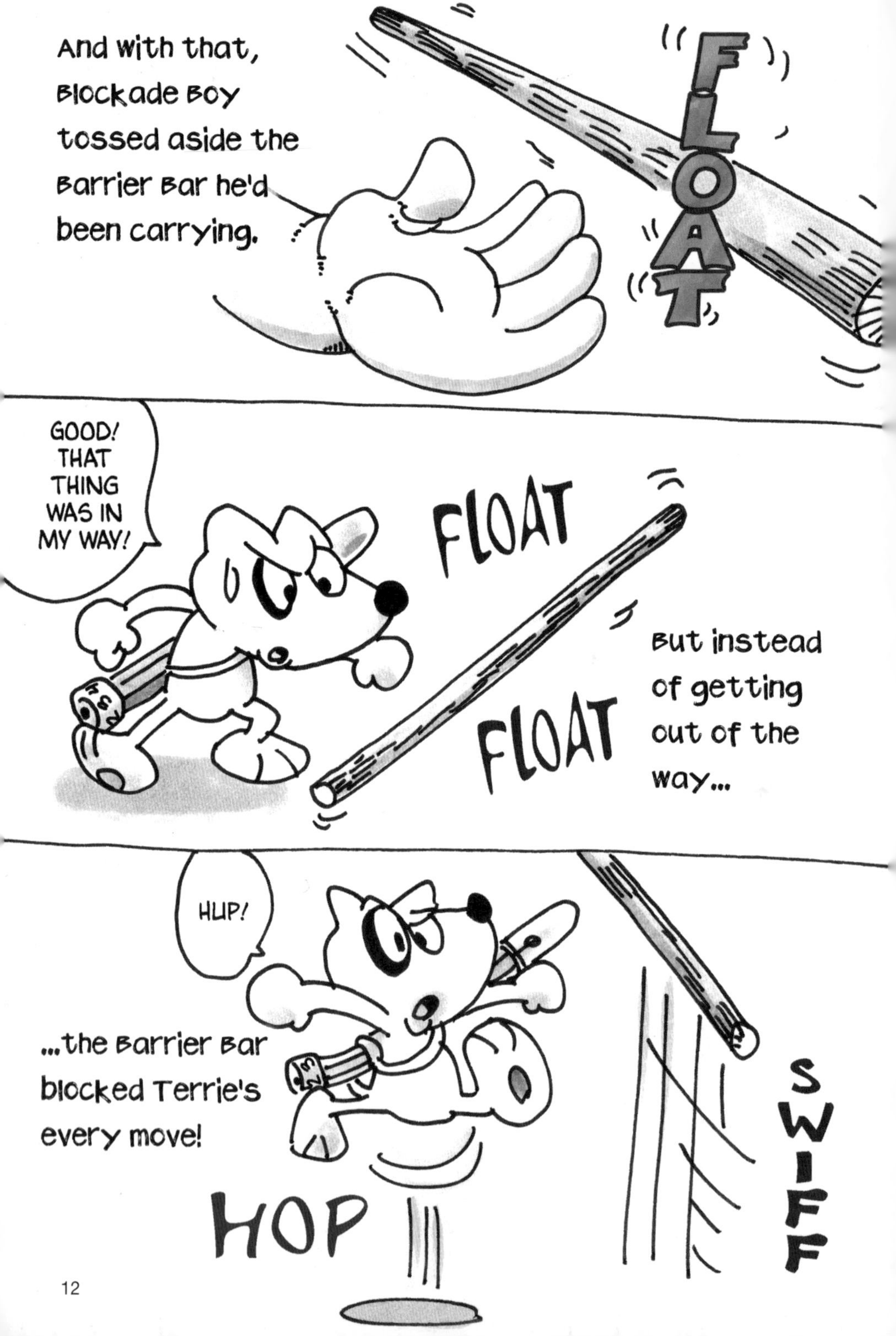
And with that, Blockade Boy tossed aside the Barrier Bar he'd been carrying.
FLOAT
GOOD! THAT THING WAS IN MY WAY!
FLOAT
FLOAT
But instead of getting out of the way...
HUP!
...the Barrier Bar blocked Terrie's every move!
HOP
SWIFF

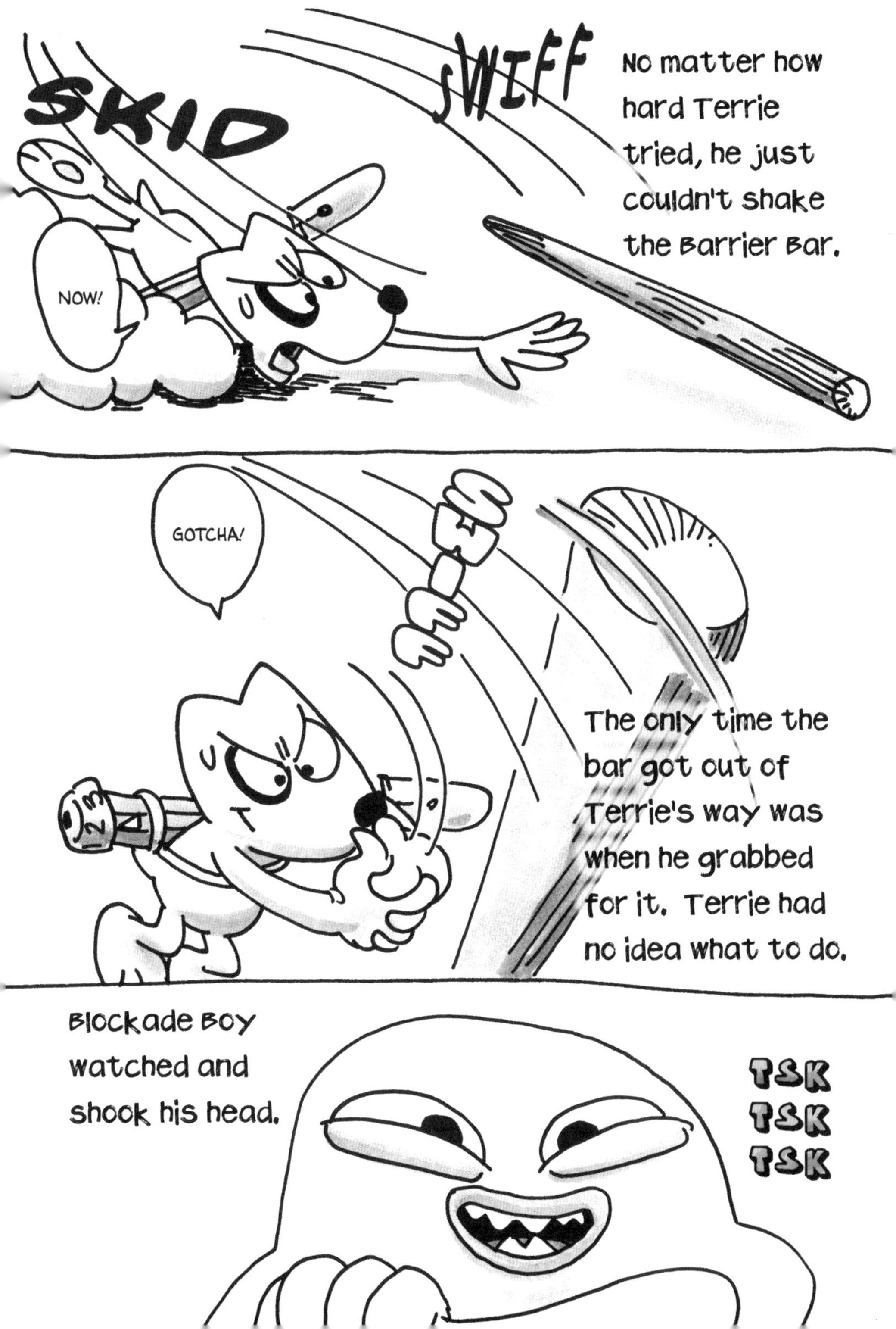
SKID
SWIFF
No matter how hard Terrie tried, he just couldn't shake the Barrier Bar.
NOW!
GOTCHA!
The only time the bar got out of Terrie's way was when he grabbed for it. Terrie had no idea what to do.
Blockade Boy watched and shook his head.
TSK
TSK
TSK

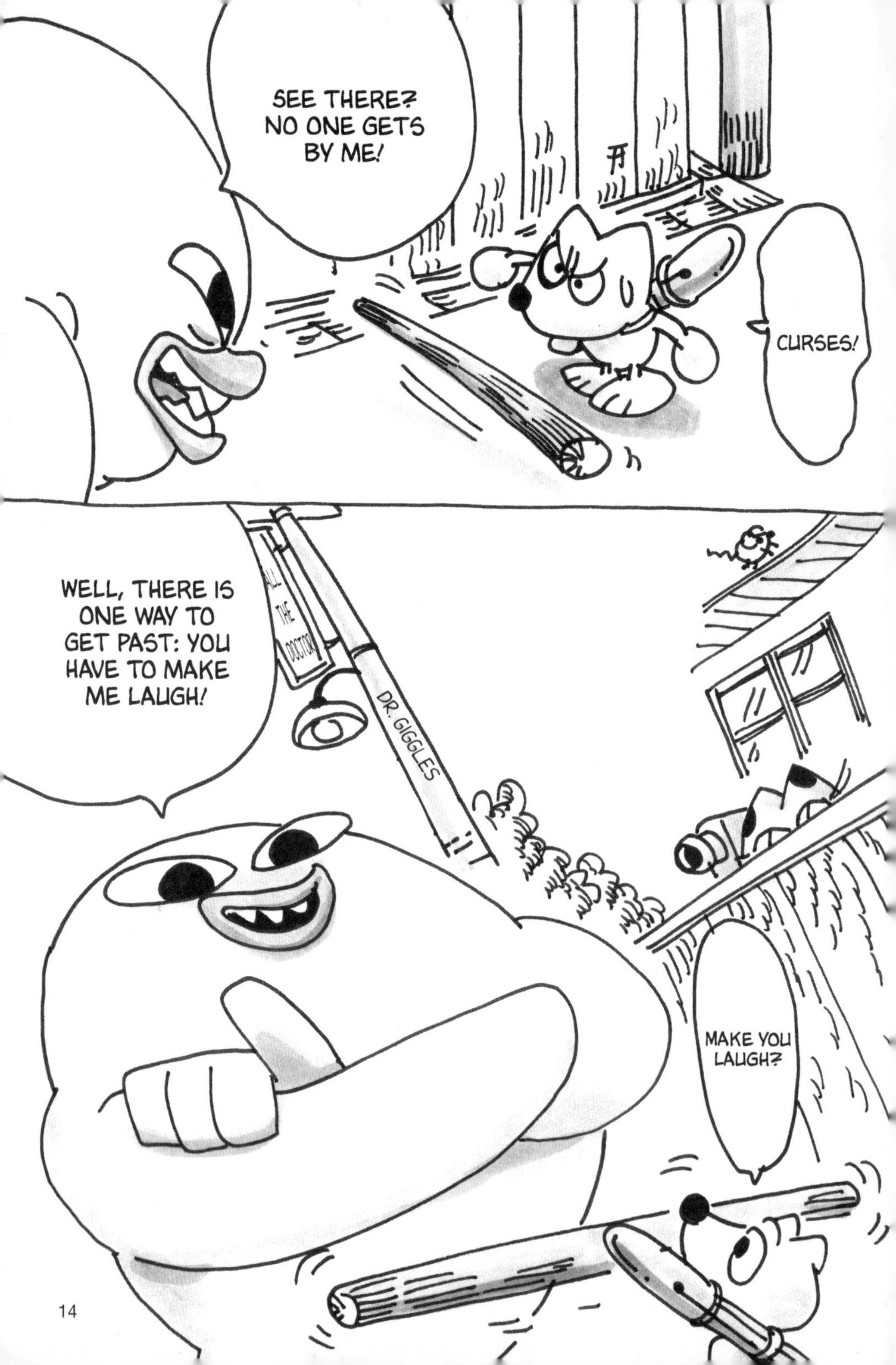
SEE THERE? NO ONE GETS BY ME!
CURSES!
WELL, THERE IS ONE WAY TO GET PAST: YOU HAVE TO MAKE ME LAUGH!
ALL THE DOCTOR
DR. GIGGLES
MAKE YOU LAUGH?

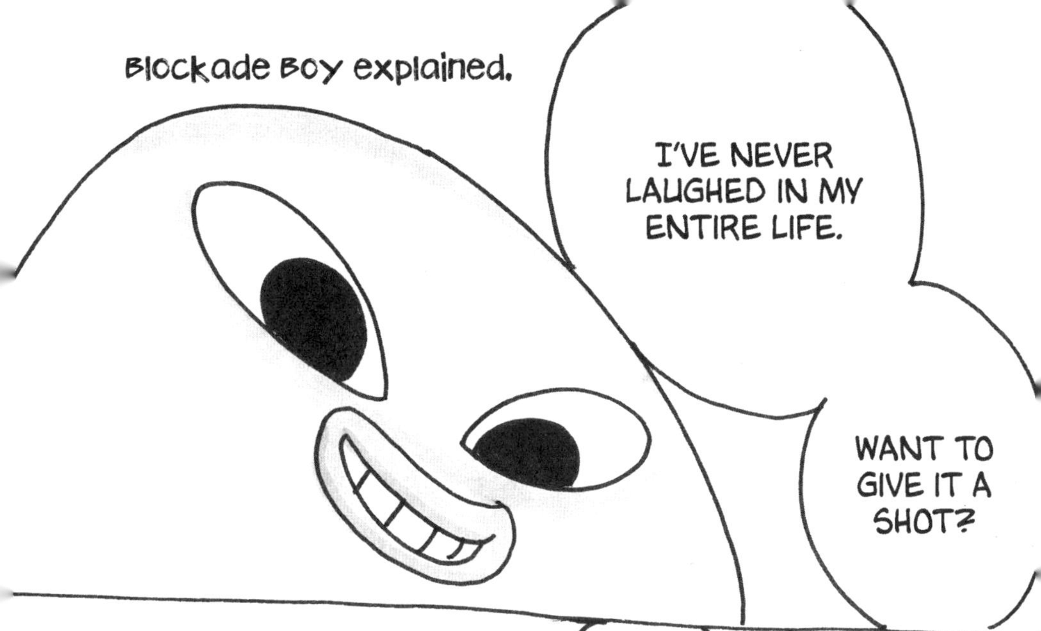
Blockade Boy explained.
I'VE NEVER LAUGHED IN MY ENTIRE LIFE.
WANT TO GIVE IT A SHOT?

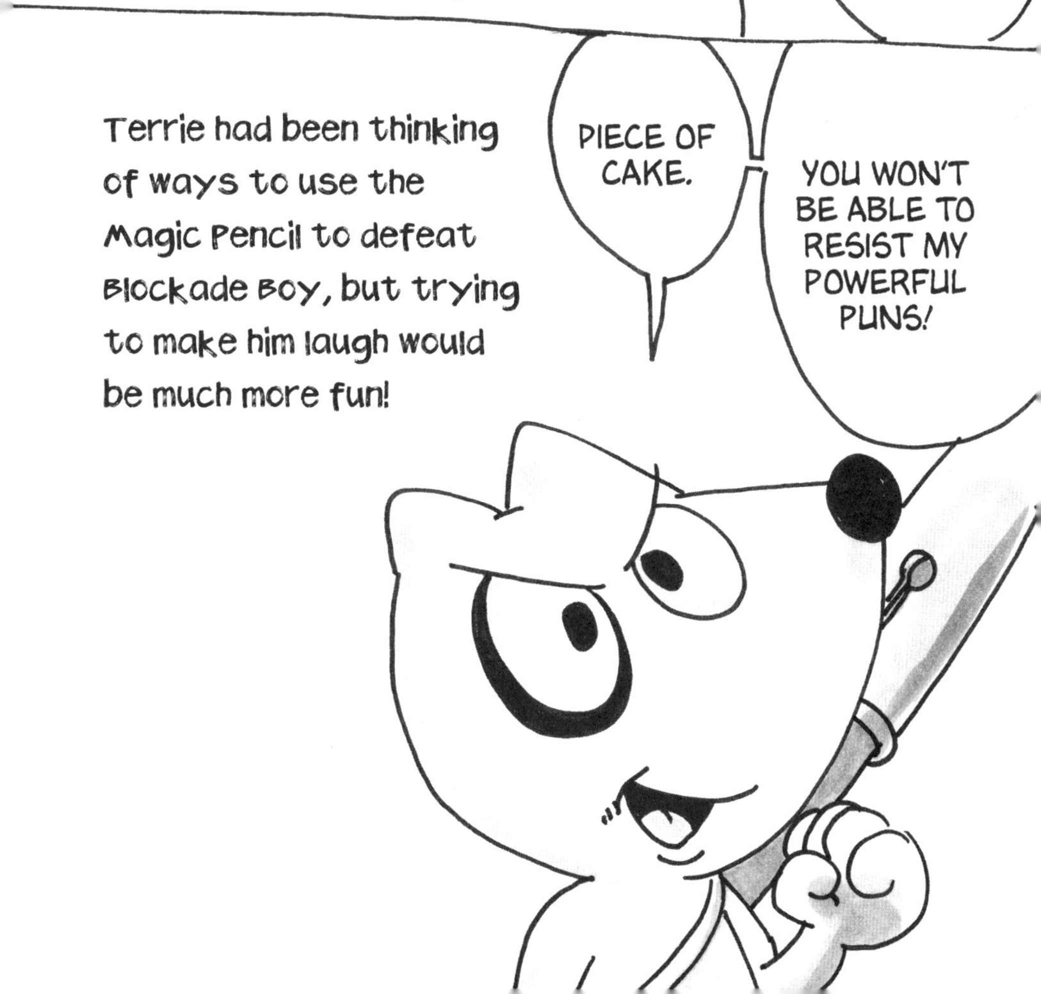
Terrie had been thinking of ways to use the Magic Pencil to defeat Blockade Boy, but trying to make him laugh would be much more fun!
PIECE OF CAKE.
YOU WON'T BE ABLE TO RESIST MY POWERFUL PUNS!

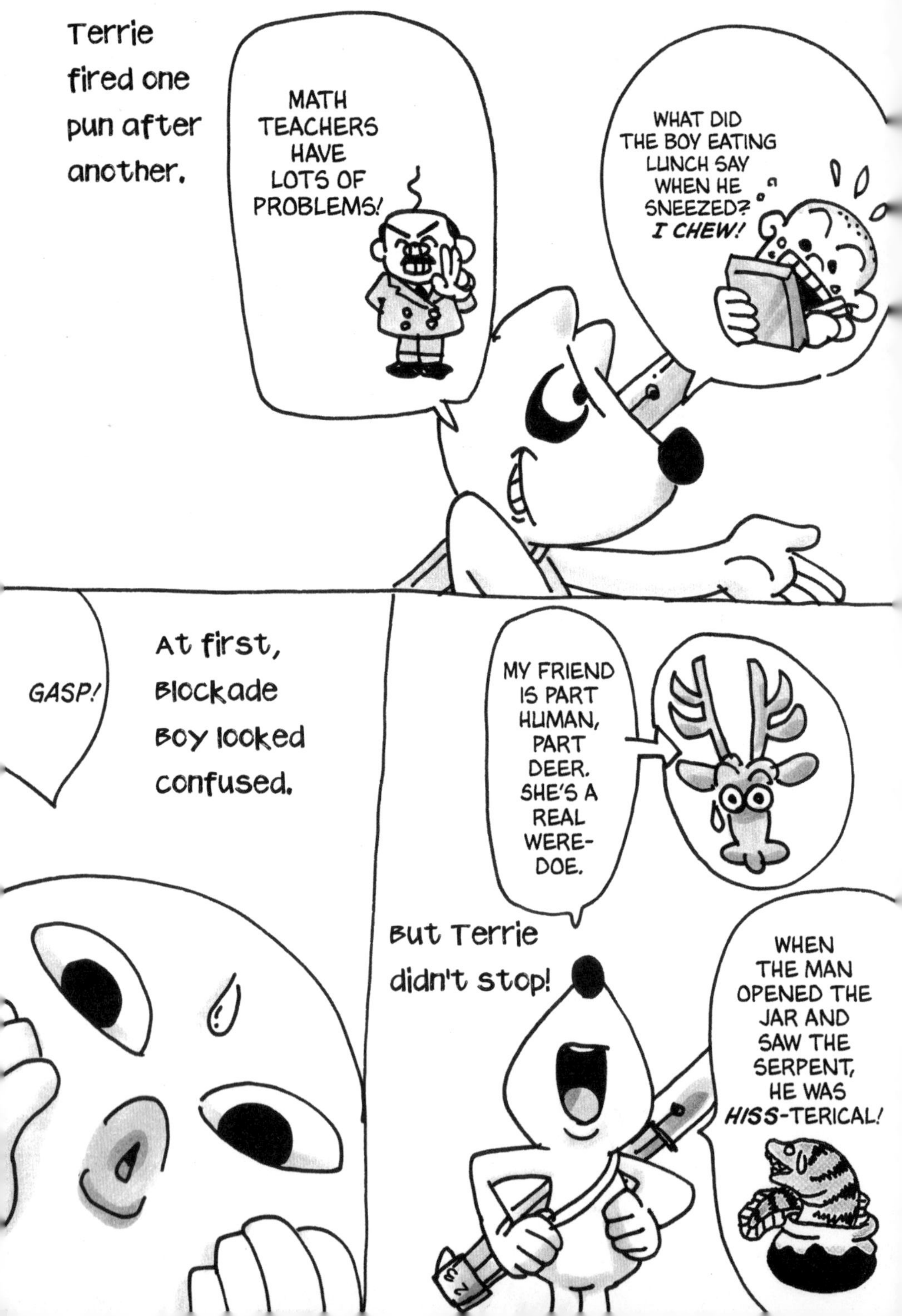
Terrie fired one pun after another.
MATH TEACHERS HAVE LOTS OF PROBLEMS!
WHAT DID THE BOY EATING LUNCH SAY WHEN HE SNEEZED? I CHEW!
GASP!
At first, Blockade Boy looked confused.
MY FRIEND IS PART HUMAN, PART DEER. SHE'S A REAL WERE-DOE.
But Terrie didn't stop!
WHEN THE MAN OPENED THE JAR AND SAW THE SERPENT, HE WAS HISS-TERICAL!

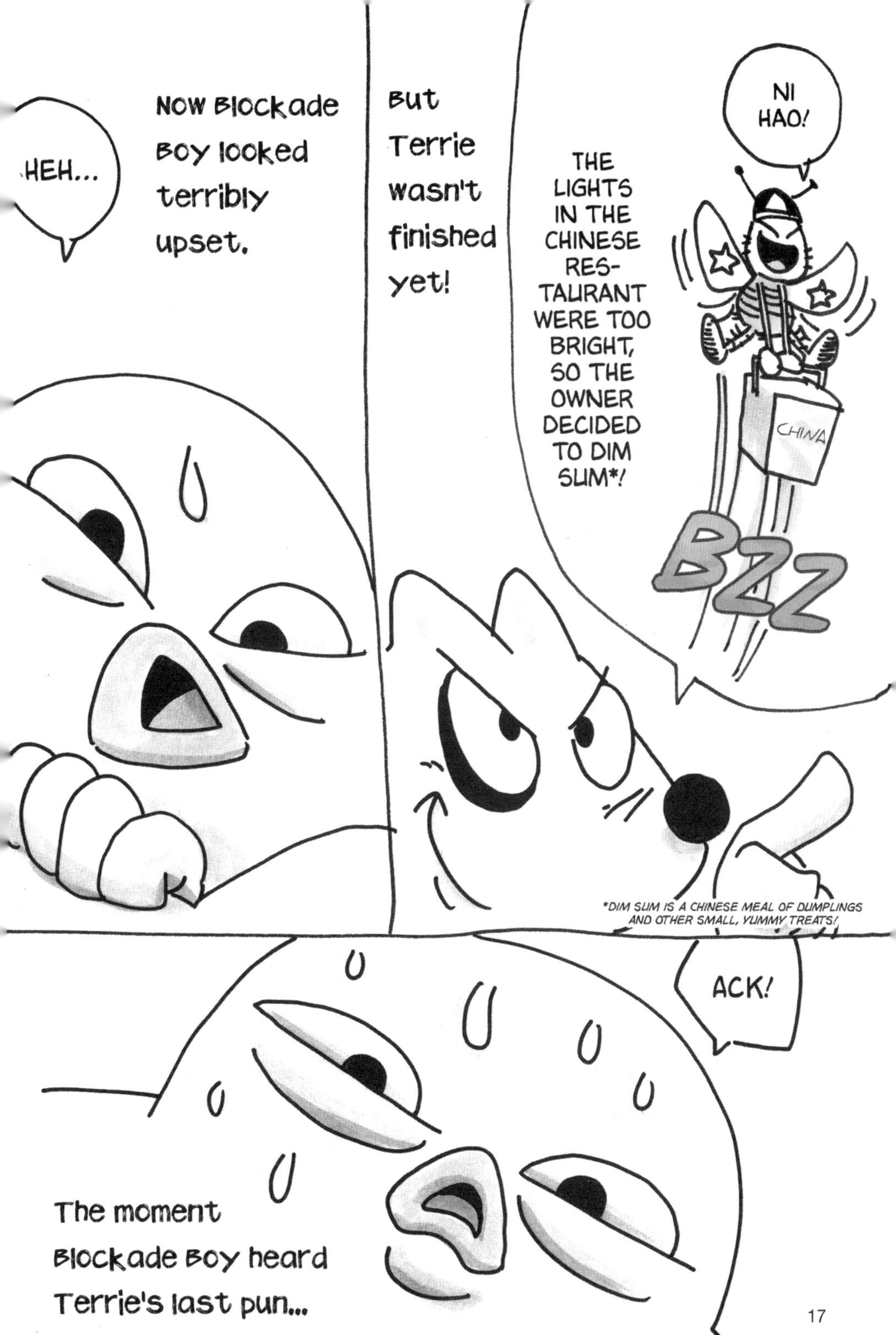
HEH...
Now Blockade Boy looked terribly upset.
But Terrie wasn't finished yet!
THE LIGHTS IN THE CHINESE RES-TAURANT WERE TOO BRIGHT, SO THE OWNER DECIDED TO DIM SUM*!
NI HAO!
CHINA
BZZ
*DIM SUM IS A CHINESE MEAL OF DUMPLINGS AND OTHER SMALL, YUMMY TREATS!
ACK!
The moment Blockade Boy heard Terrie's last pun...

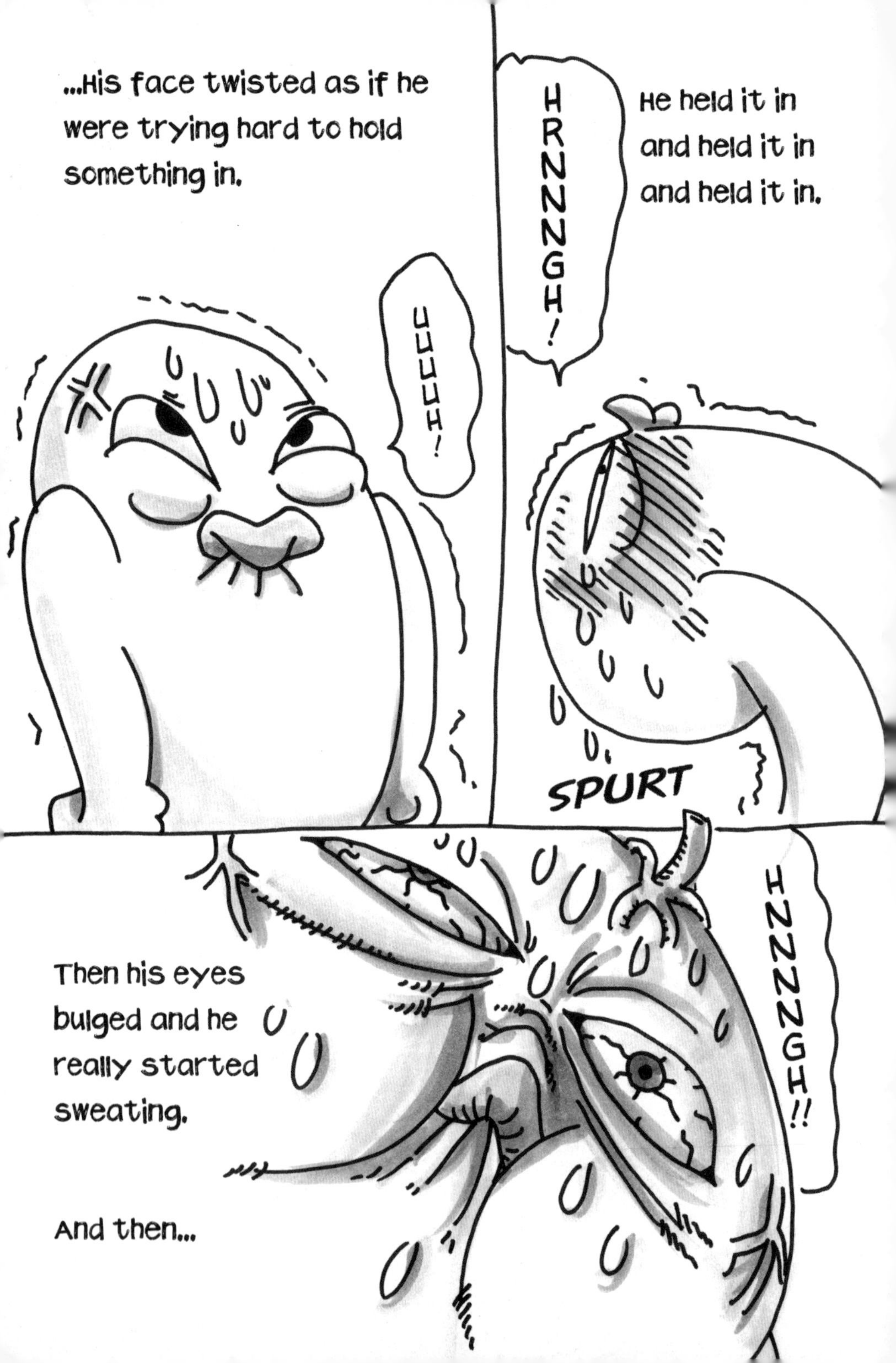

...His face twisted as if he were trying hard to hold something in.
UUUUH!
HRNNNNGH!
He held it in and held it in and held it in.
SPURT
Then his eyes bulged and he really started sweating.
HNNNNNGH!!
And then...

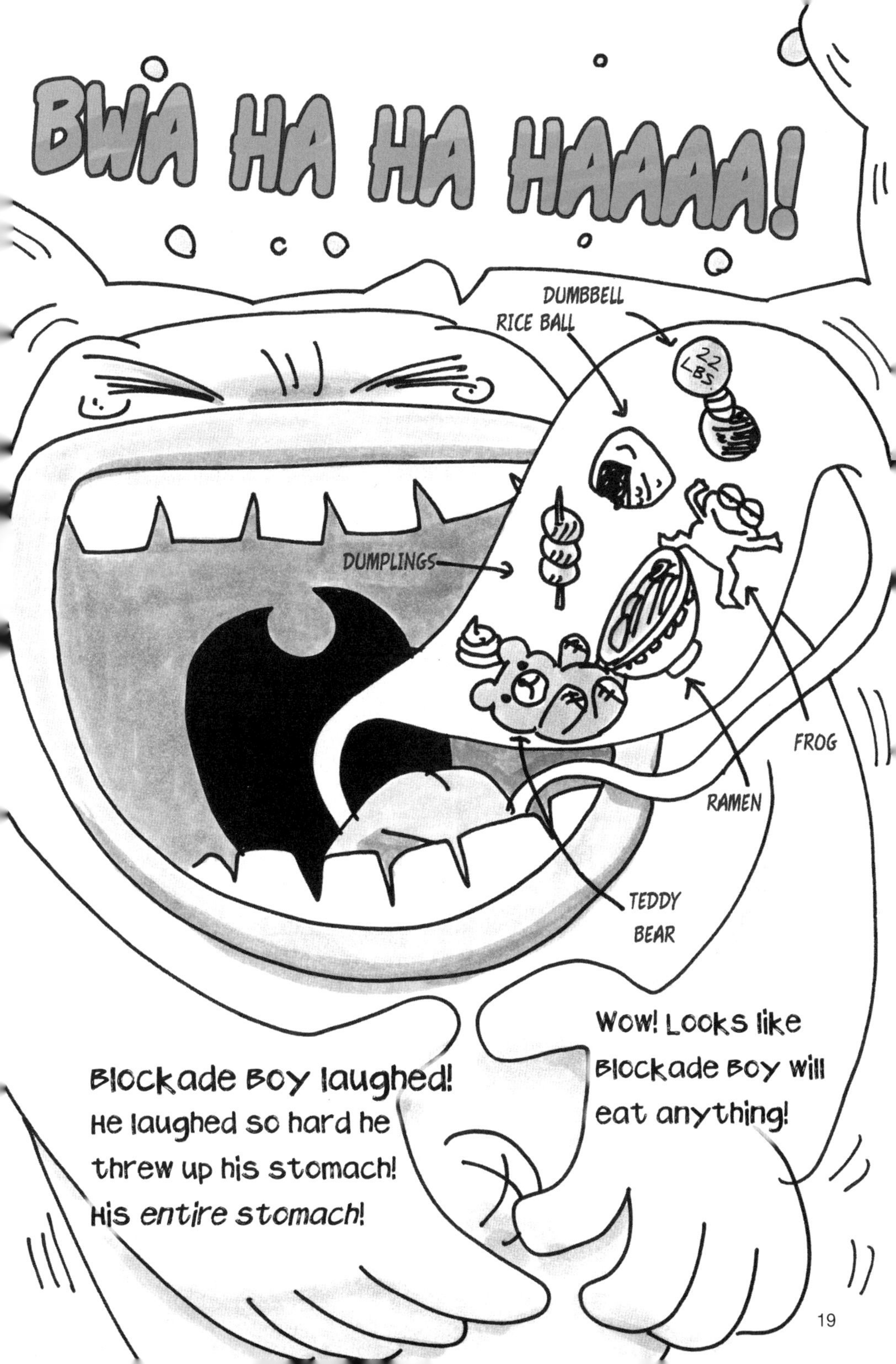
BWA HA HA HAAAA!
DUMBBELL
22 LBS.
RICE BALL
DUMPLINGS
FROG
RAMEN
TEDDY BEAR
Blockade Boy laughed! He laughed so hard he threw up his stomach! His *entire stomach*!
Wow! Looks like Blockade Boy will eat anything!

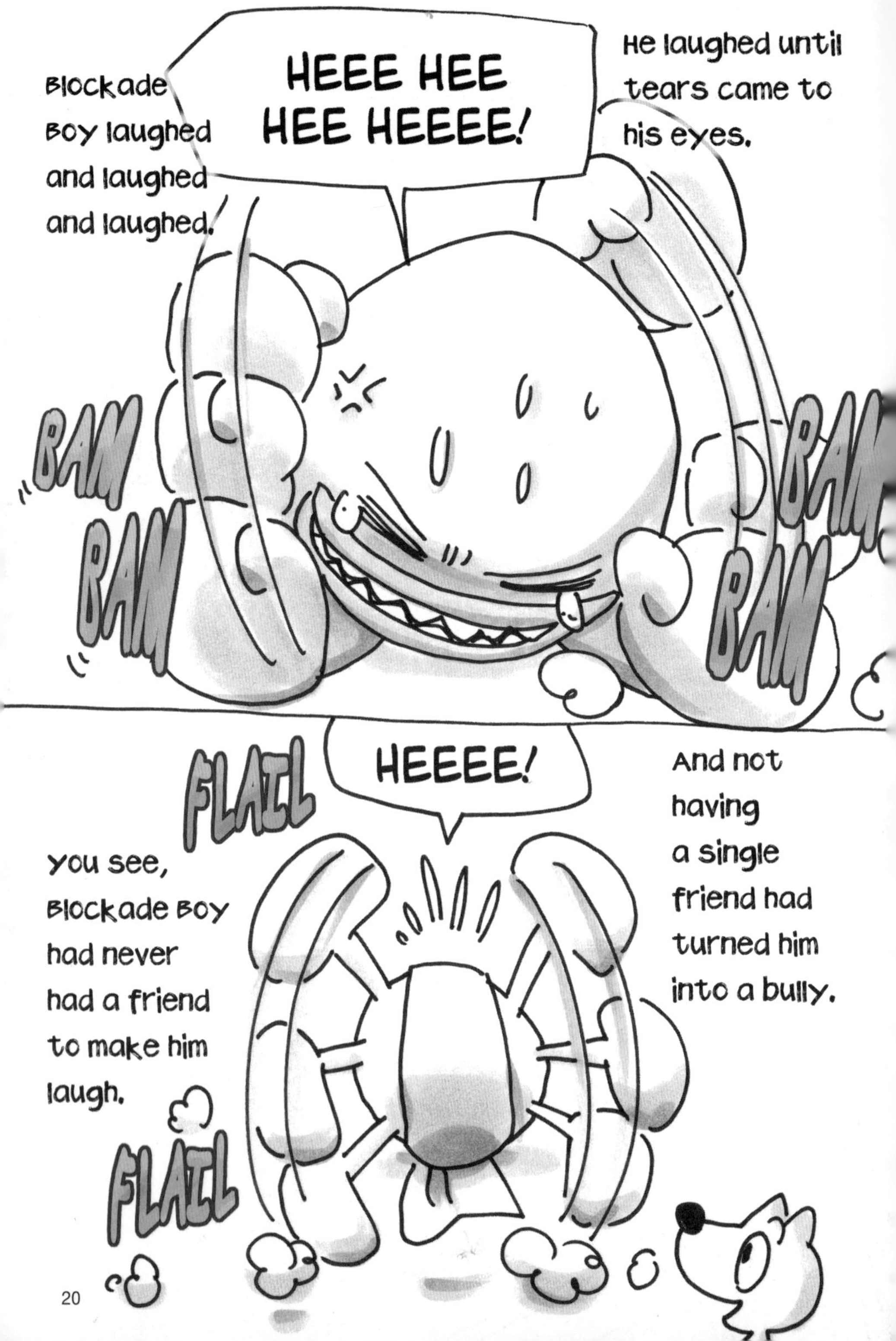
Blockade Boy laughed and laughed and laughed.
HEEE HEE HEE HEEEEE!
He laughed until tears came to his eyes.
BAM
BAM
BAM
BAM
FLAIL
HEEEEE!
you see, Blockade Boy had never had a friend to make him laugh.
And not having a single friend had turned him into a bully.
FLAIL

Seeing how much Blockade Boy enjoyed his puns, Terrie kept telling them. Blockade Boy carefully wrote them in a small notebook.

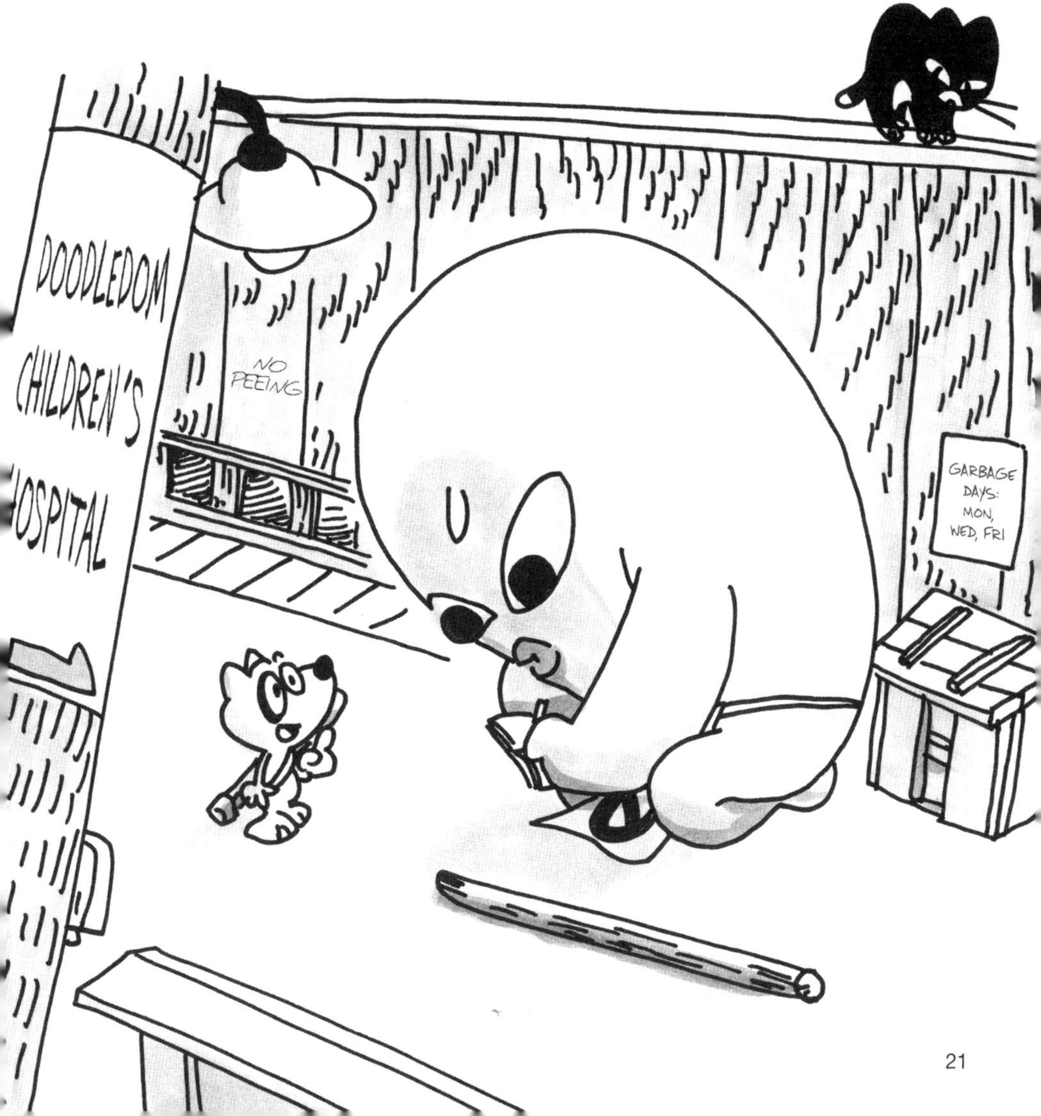
DOODLEDOM CHILDREN'S HOSPITAL
NO PEEING
GARBAGE DAYS: MON, WED, FRI

BLOCKADE BOY'S PUNNY NOTES

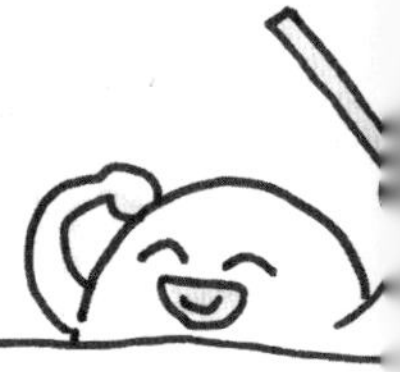

(1) CRIMINALS HAVE CROOKED THOUGHTS AND CAN'T THINK STRAIGHT.

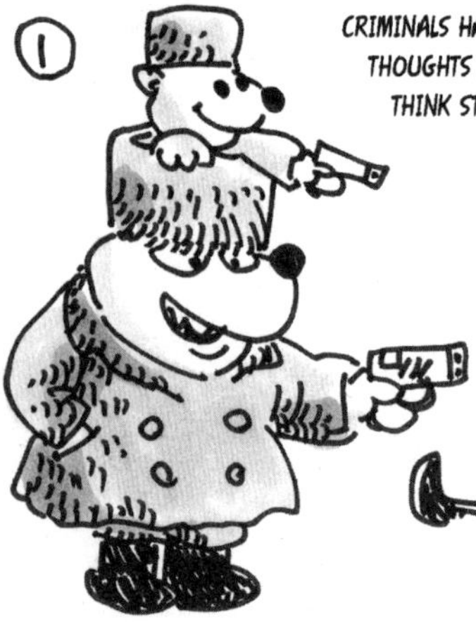

(2) SEALS ALWAYS HONK WHEN THEY DRIVE.

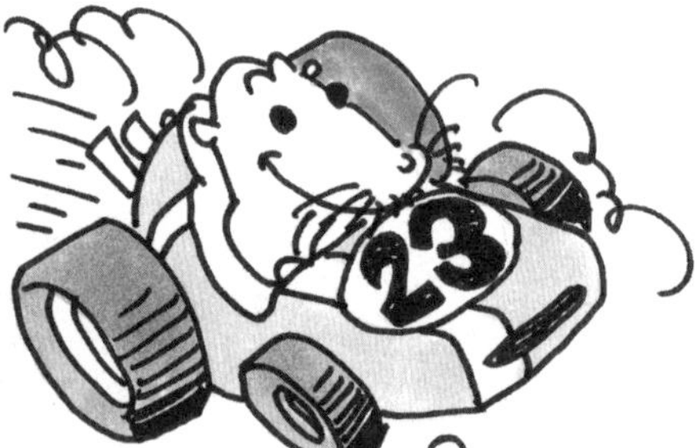

23

(3) MY NOSE KNOWS, YOU KNOW?

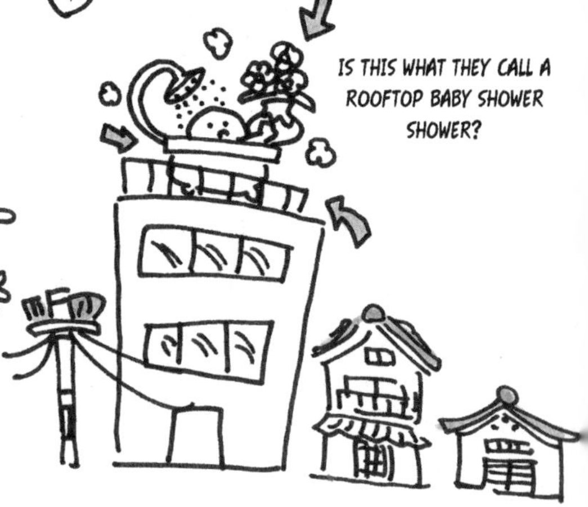

(4) IS THIS WHAT THEY CALL A ROOFTOP BABY SHOWER SHOWER?

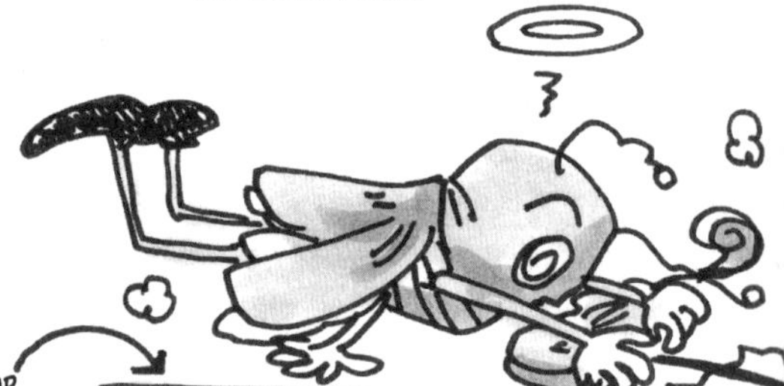

(5) THE GRASSHOPPER TRIED TO PLAY CLASSICAL MUSIC, BUT HE WAS NO BEE-TOVEN!

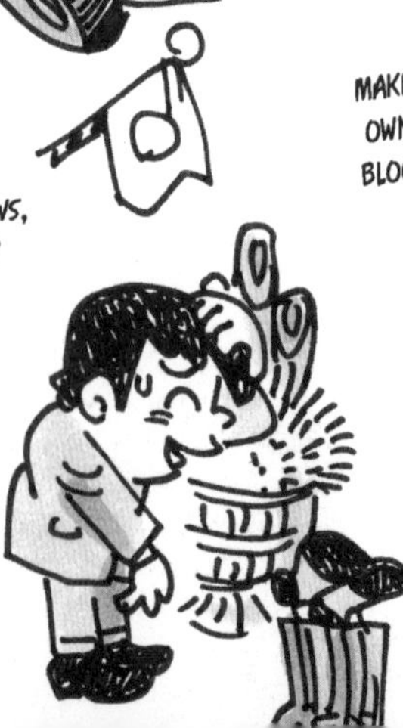

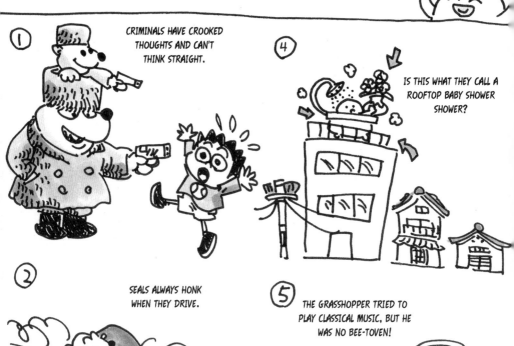

MAKE UP YOUR OWN PUN FOR BLOCKADE BOY!

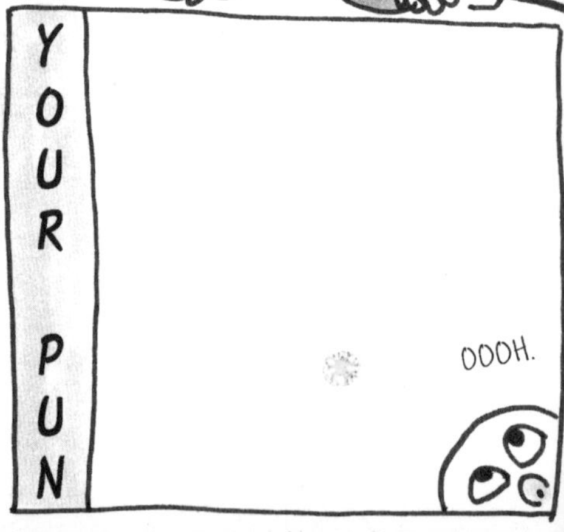

YOUR PUN
OOOH.

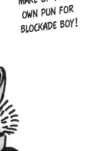

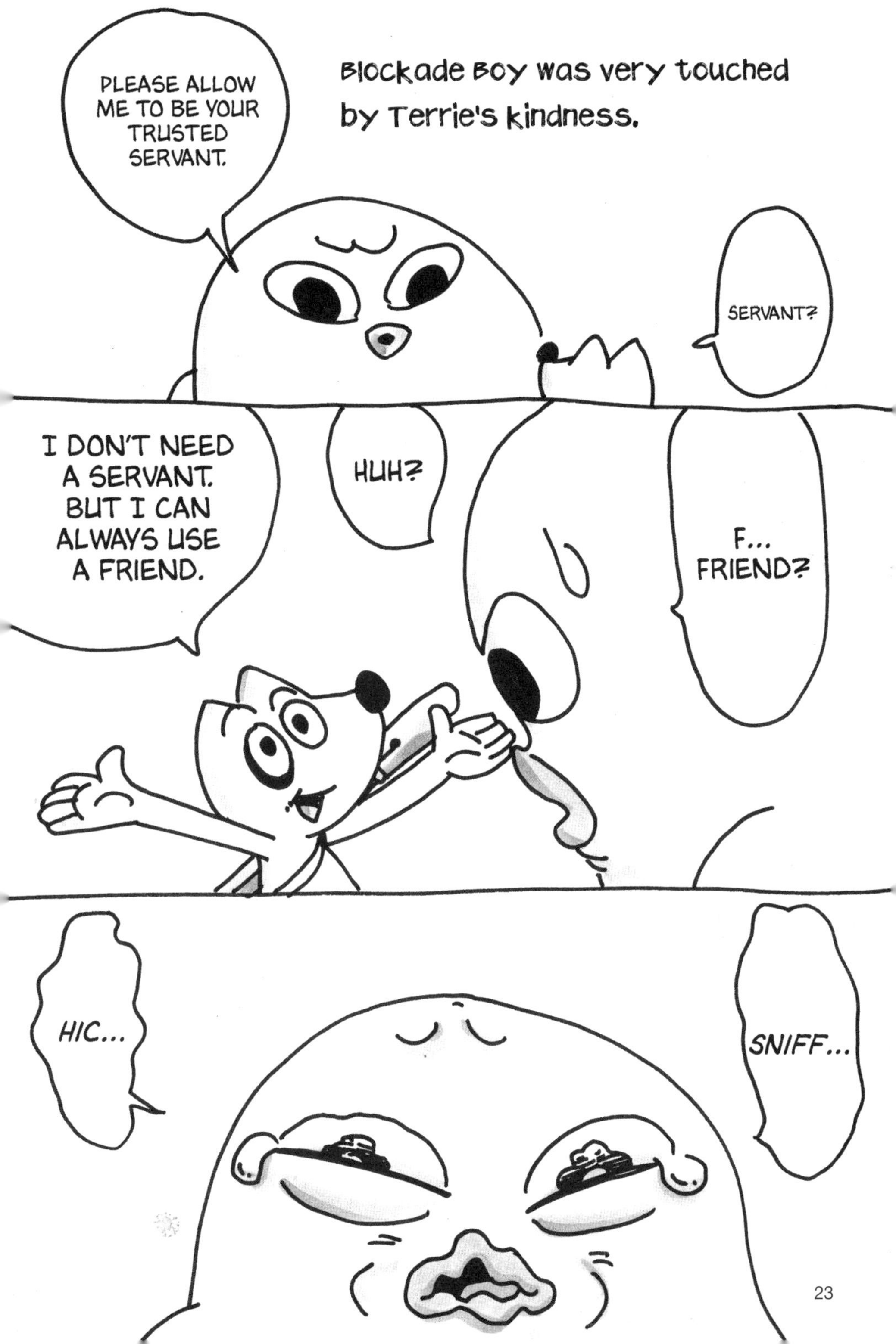
PLEASE ALLOW ME TO BE YOUR TRUSTED SERVANT.
Blockade Boy was very touched by Terrie's kindness.
SERVANT?
I DON'T NEED A SERVANT. BUT I CAN ALWAYS USE A FRIEND.
HUH?
F... FRIEND?
HIC...
SNIFF...

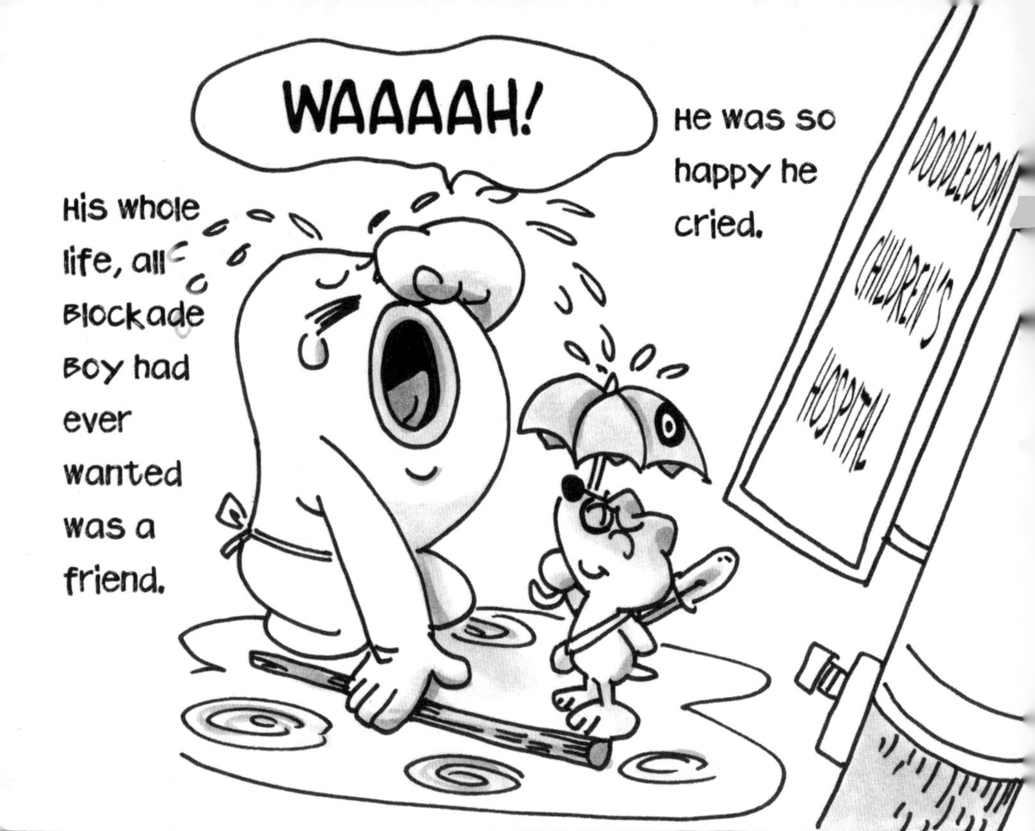
WAAAAH!
His whole life, all Blockade Boy had ever wanted was a friend.
He was so happy he cried.
DOODLEDOM CHILDREN'S HOSPITAL

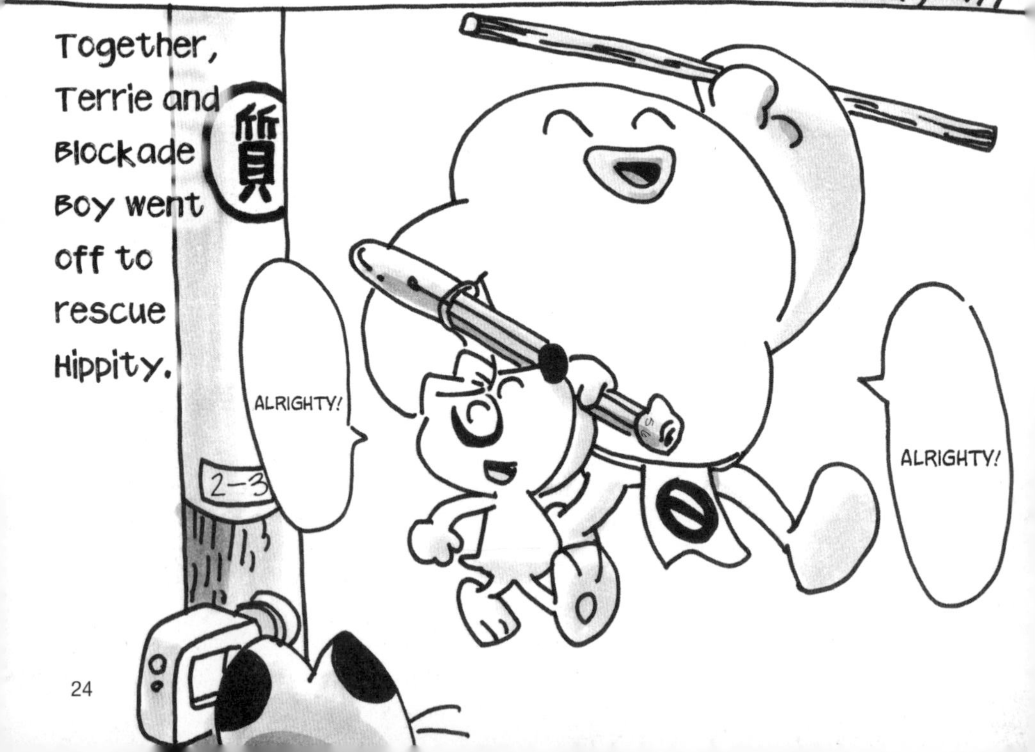
Together, Terrie and Blockade Boy went off to rescue Hippity.
質
ALRIGHTY!
ALRIGHTY!
2-3

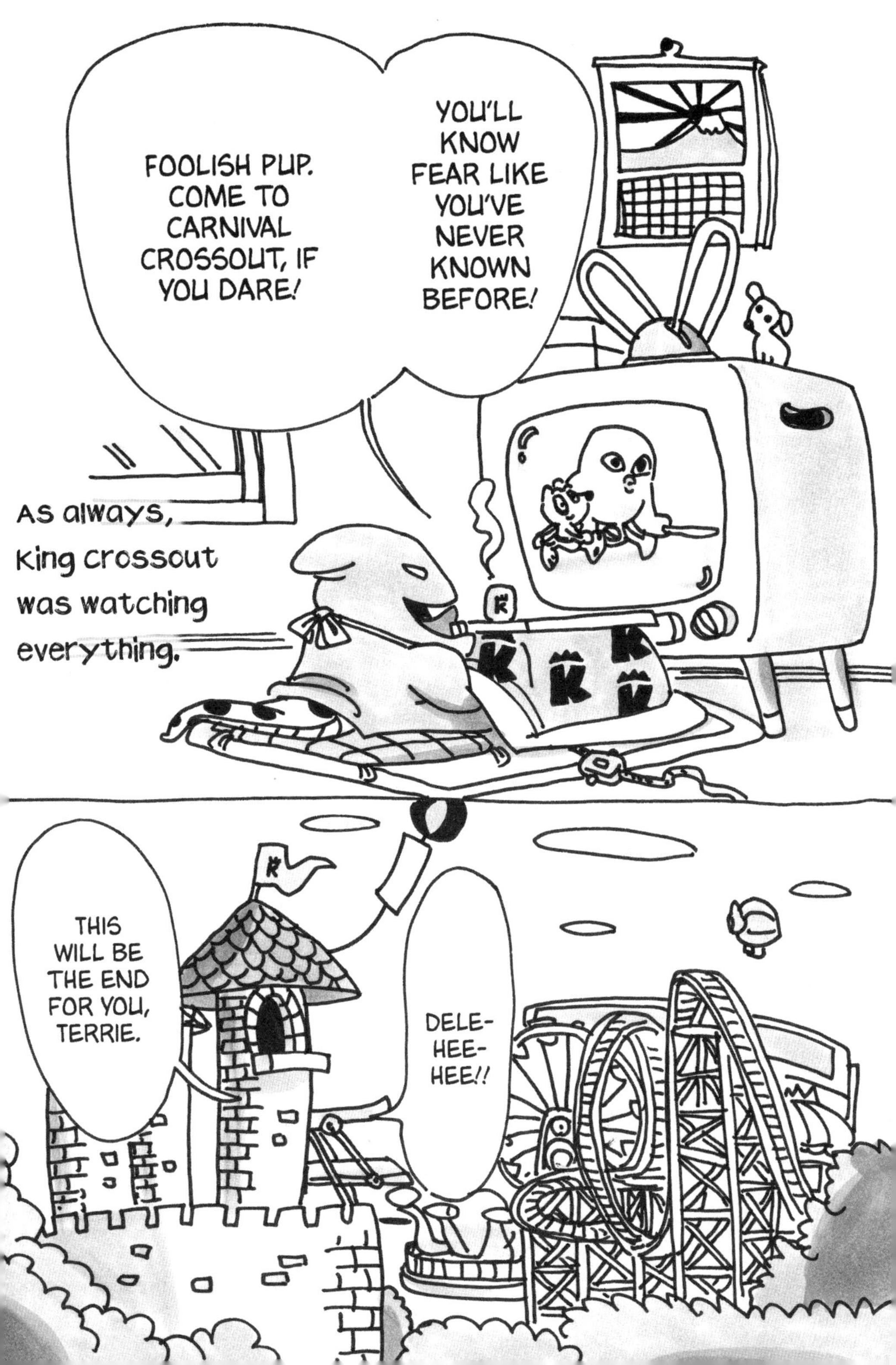
FOOLISH PUP. COME TO CARNIVAL CROSSOUT, IF YOU DARE!
YOU'LL KNOW FEAR LIKE YOU'VE NEVER KNOWN BEFORE!
As always, King Crossout was watching everything.
THIS WILL BE THE END FOR YOU, TERRIE.
DELE-HEE-HEE!!

Soon Terrie and Blockade Boy arrived at Carnival Crossout.

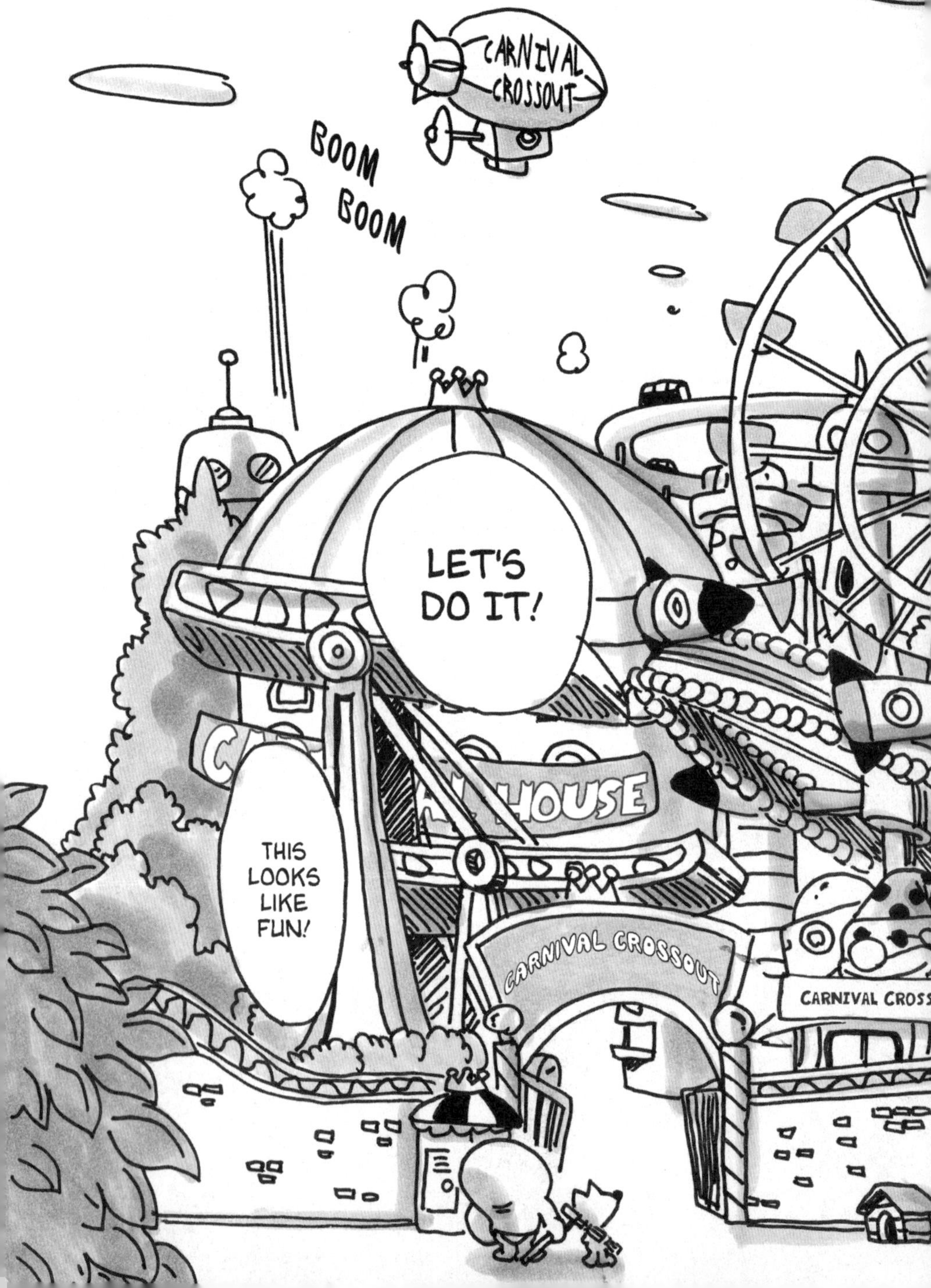
CARNIVAL CROSSOUT
BOOM BOOM
LET'S DO IT!
THIS LOOKS LIKE FUN!
HOUSE
CARNIVAL CROSSOUT

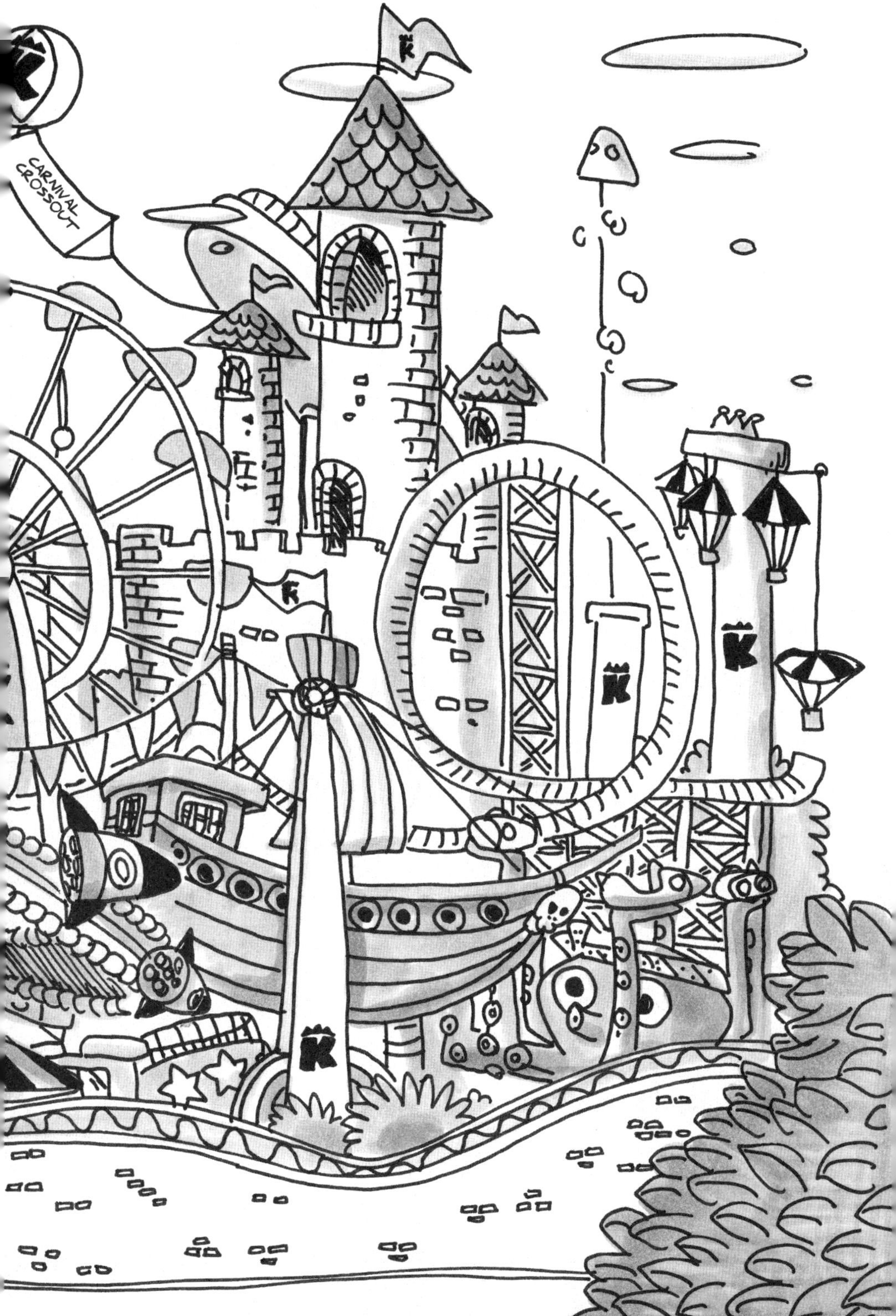
CARNIVAL CROSSOUT

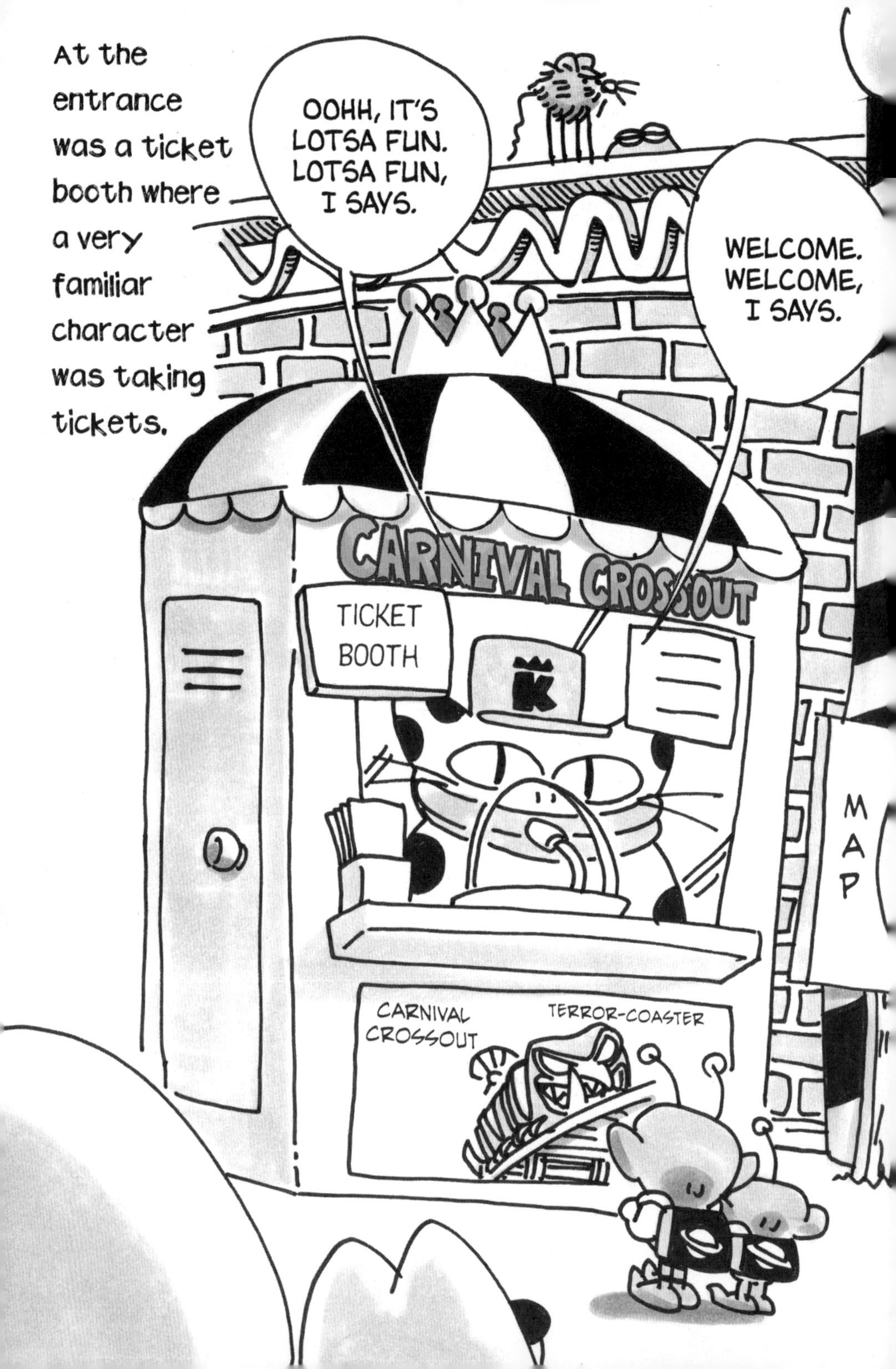
At the entrance was a ticket booth where a very familiar character was taking tickets.
OOHH, IT'S LOTSA FUN. LOTSA FUN, I SAYS.
WELCOME. WELCOME, I SAYS.
CARNIVAL CROSSOUT
TICKET BOOTH
K
MAP
CARNIVAL CROSSOUT
TERROR-COASTER

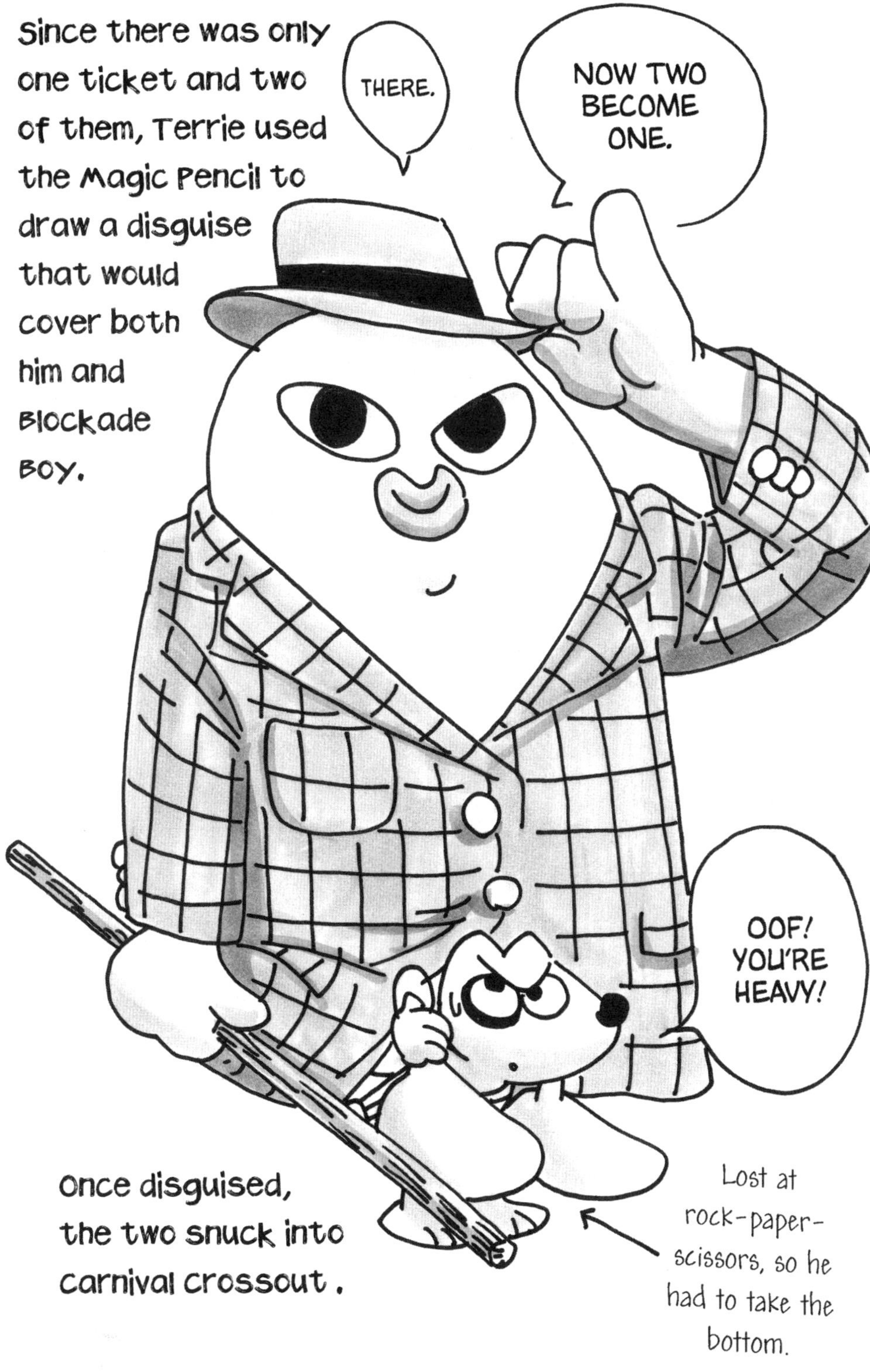
Since there was only one ticket and two of them, Terrie used the Magic Pencil to draw a disguise that would cover both him and Blockade Boy.
THERE.
NOW TWO BECOME ONE.
OOF! YOU'RE HEAVY!
Once disguised, the two snuck into Carnival Crossout.
Lost at rock-paper-scissors, so he had to take the bottom.

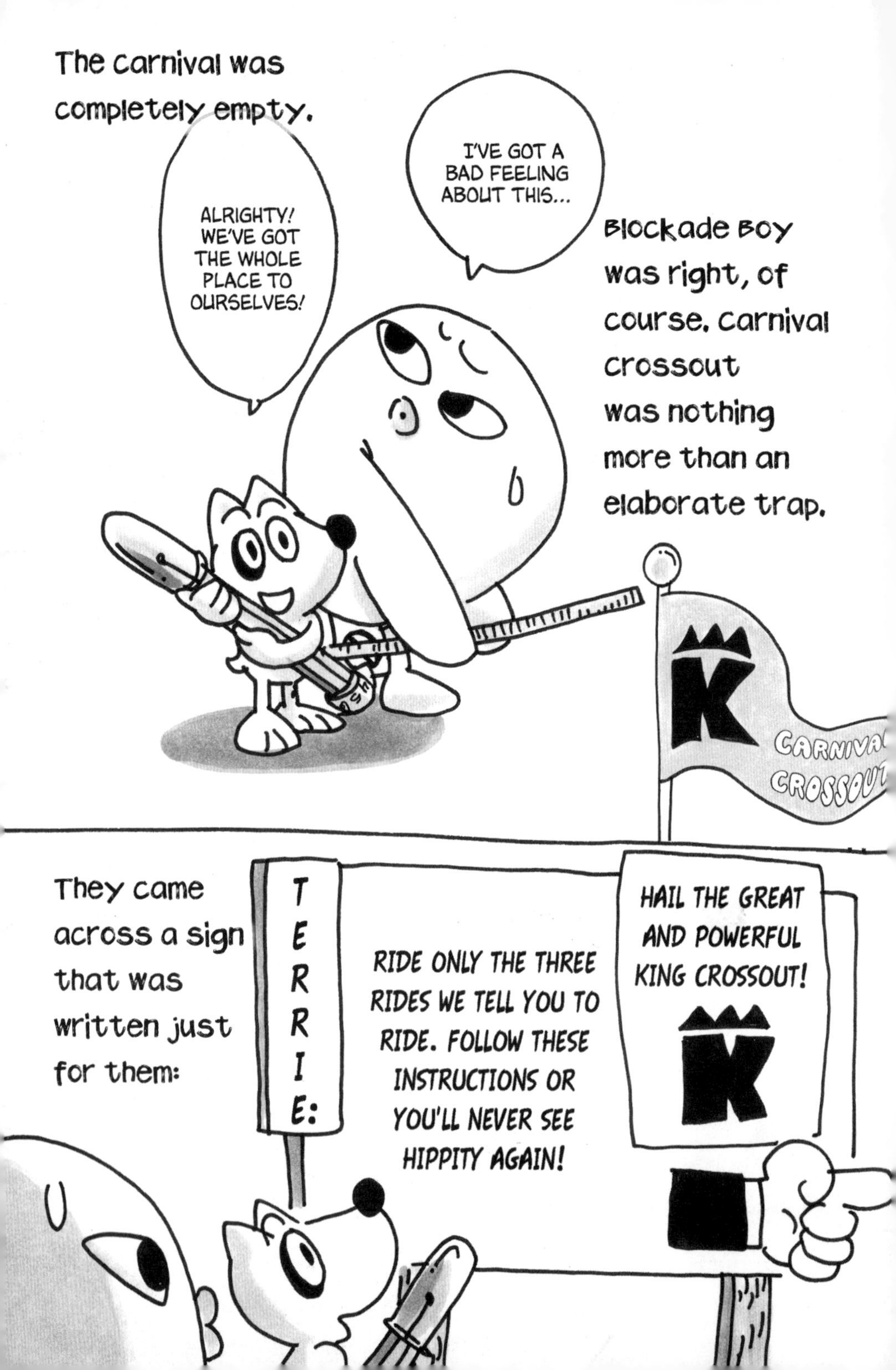
The carnival was completely empty.
ALRIGHTY! WE'VE GOT THE WHOLE PLACE TO OURSELVES!
I'VE GOT A BAD FEELING ABOUT THIS...
Blockade Boy was right, of course. Carnival Crossout was nothing more than an elaborate trap.
CARNIVAL CROSSOUT
They came across a sign that was written just for them:
TERRIE:
RIDE ONLY THE THREE RIDES WE TELL YOU TO RIDE. FOLLOW THESE INSTRUCTIONS OR YOU'LL NEVER SEE HIPPITY AGAIN!
HAIL THE GREAT AND POWERFUL KING CROSSOUT!

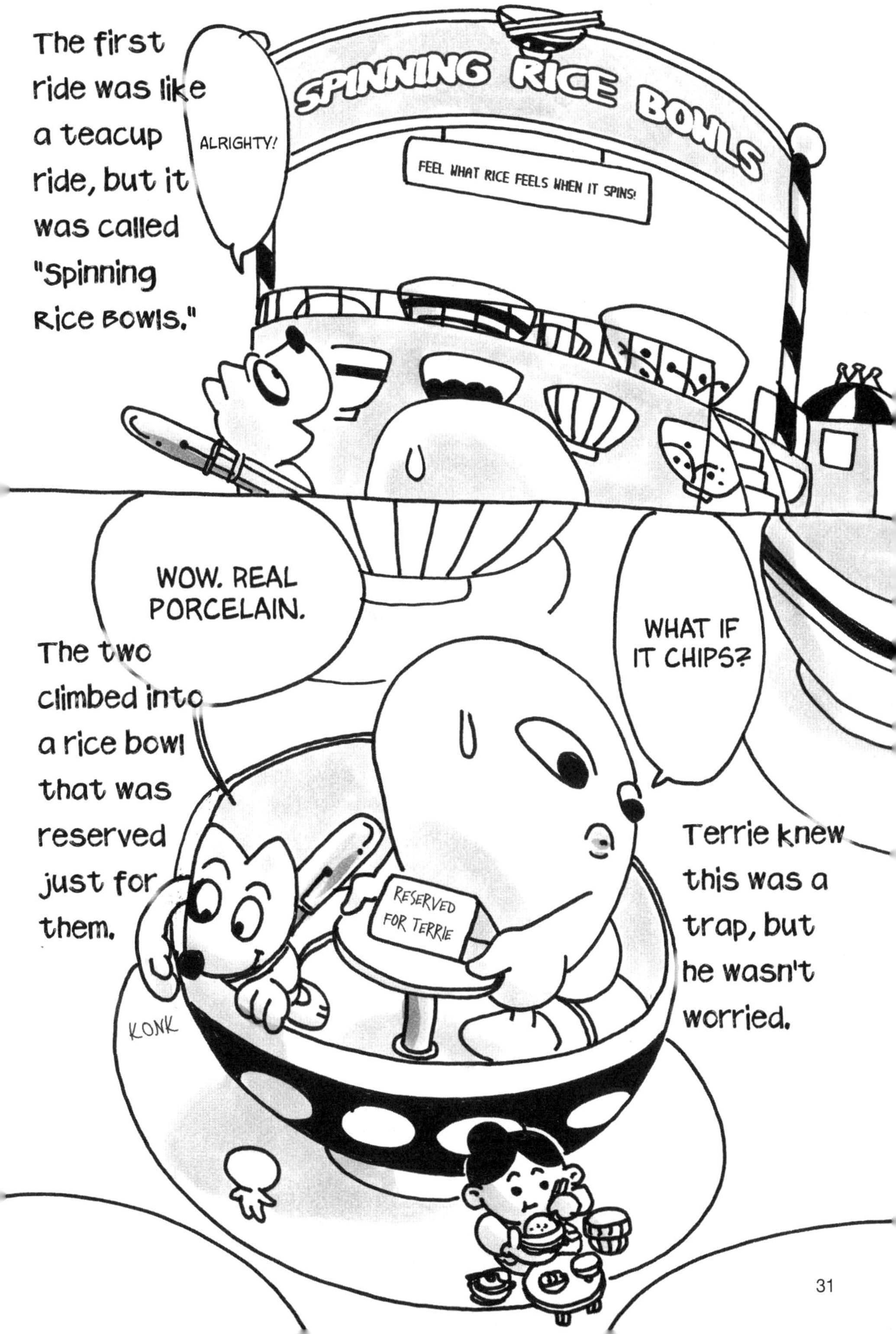
The first ride was like a teacup ride, but it was called "Spinning Rice Bowls."
ALRIGHTY!
SPINNING RICE BOWLS
FEEL WHAT RICE FEELS WHEN IT SPINS!
WOW. REAL PORCELAIN.
The two climbed into a rice bowl that was reserved just for them.
WHAT IF IT CHIPS?
RESERVED FOR TERRIE
Terrie knew this was a trap, but he wasn't worried.
KONK

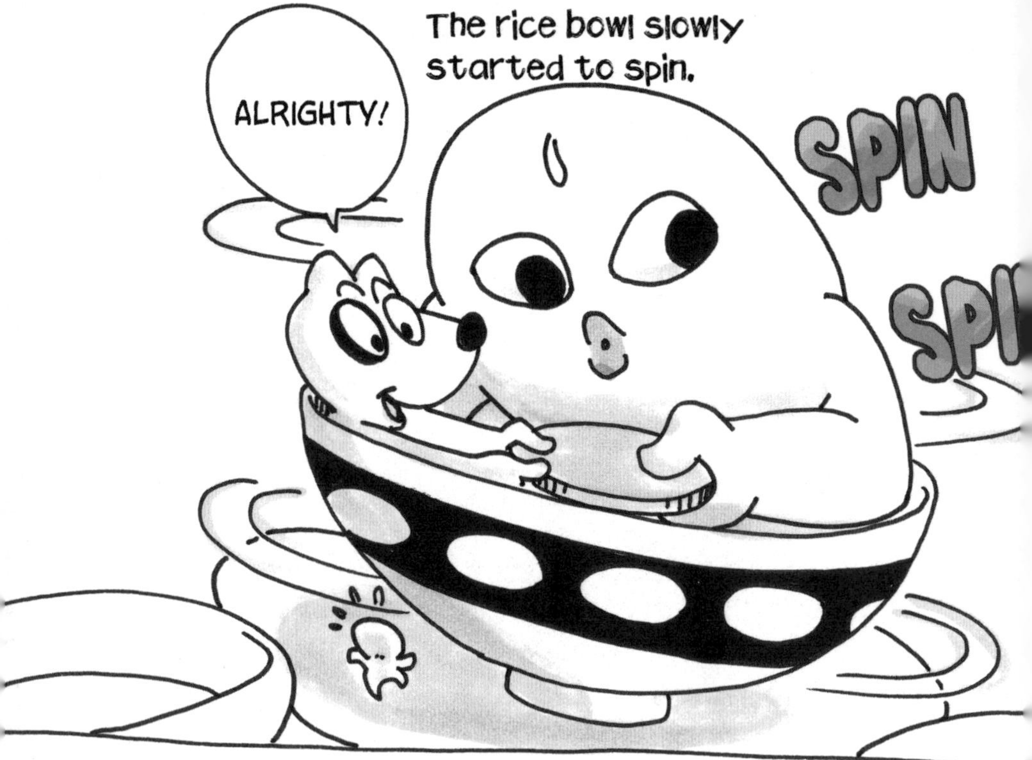
ALRIGHTY!
The rice bowl slowly started to spin.
SPIN
SPI

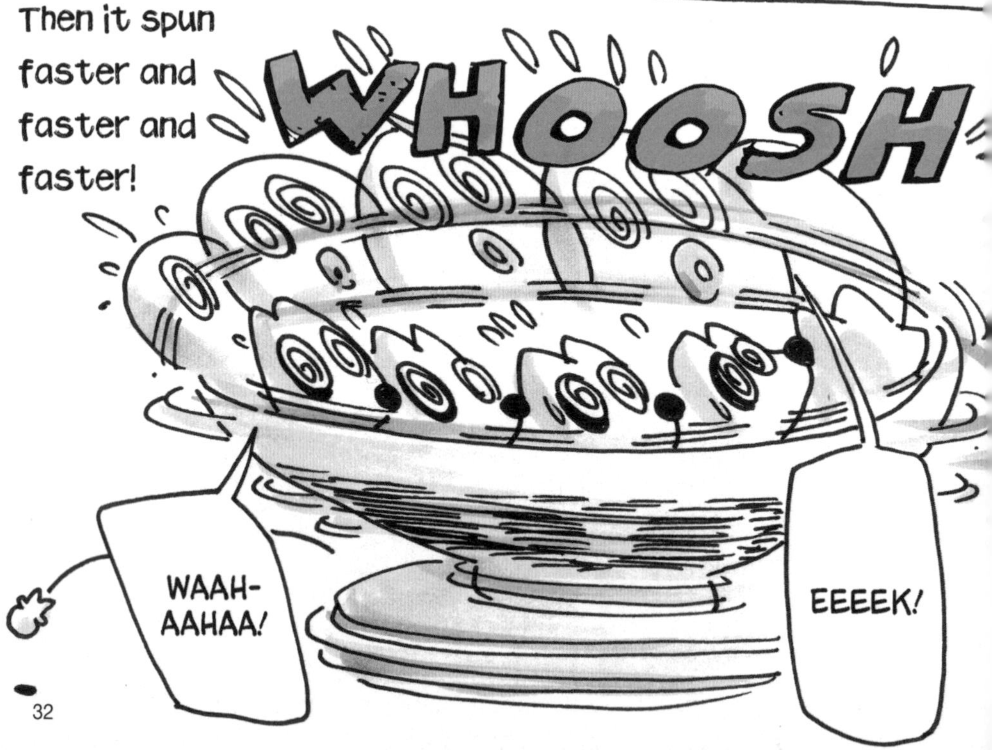
Then it spun faster and faster and faster!
WHOOSH
WAAH-AAHAA!
EEEEK!

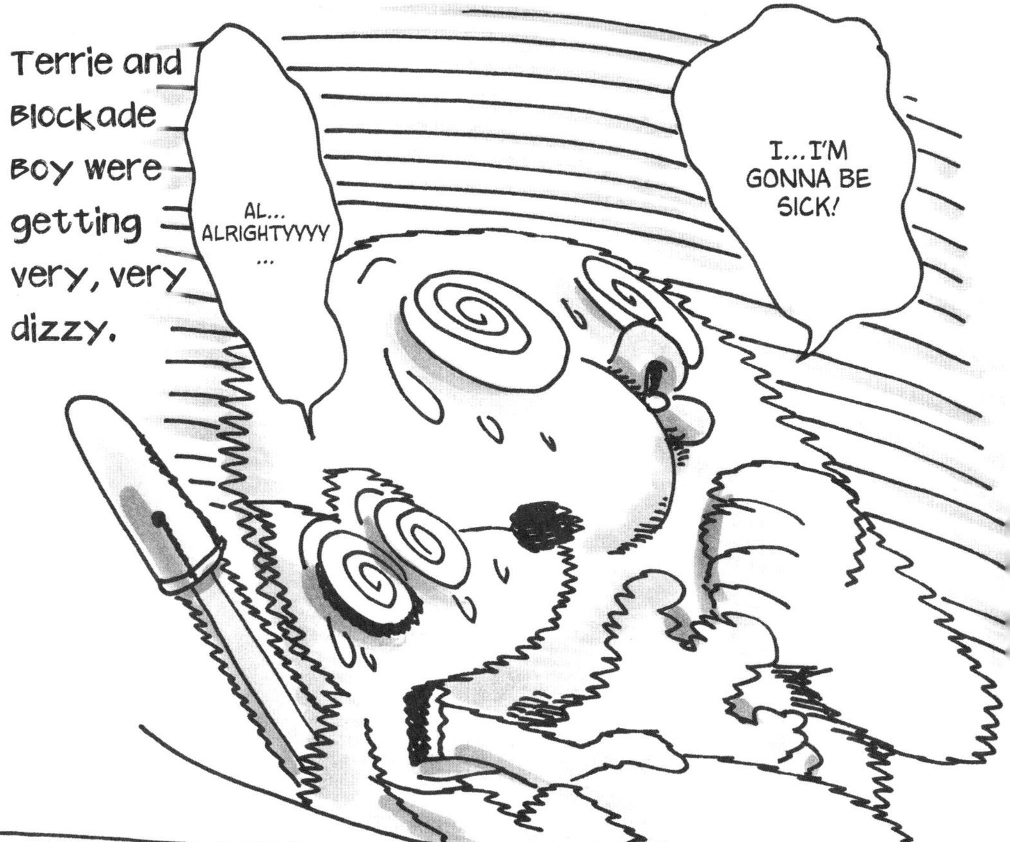
Terrie and Blockade Boy were getting very, very dizzy.
AL... ALRIGHTYYYY ...
I... I'M GONNA BE SICK!

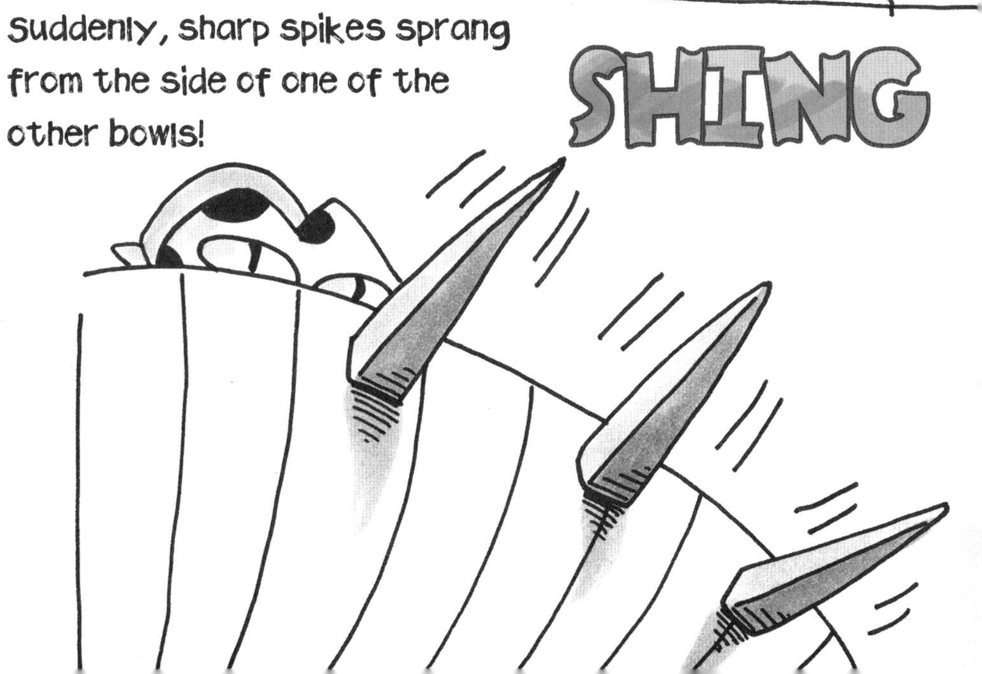
Suddenly, sharp spikes sprang from the side of one of the other bowls!
SHING

Tattle Tail aimed the spiked bowl directly at Terrie and Blockade Boy. If just one spike touched the spinning bowl, Terrie and Blockade Boy would go flying!

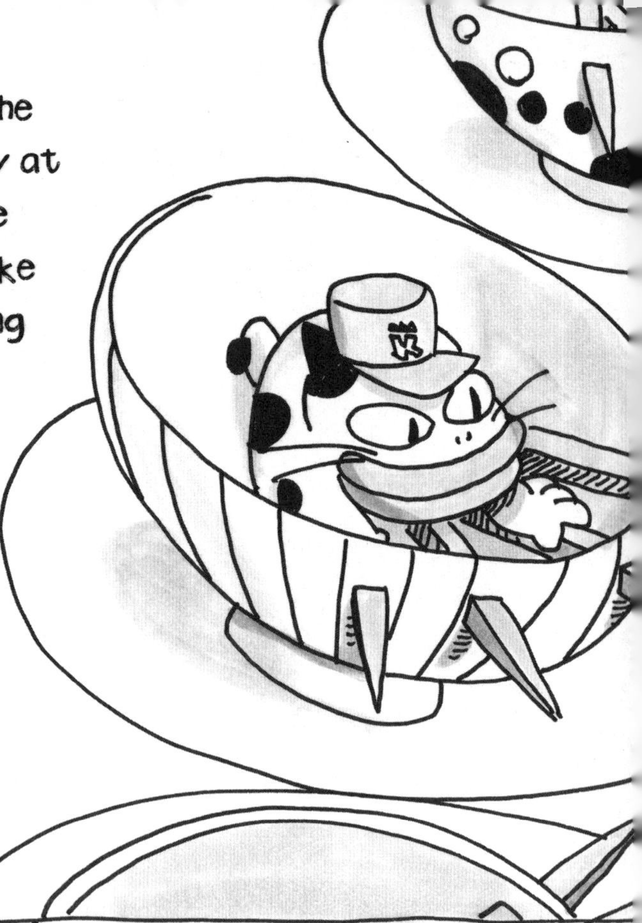

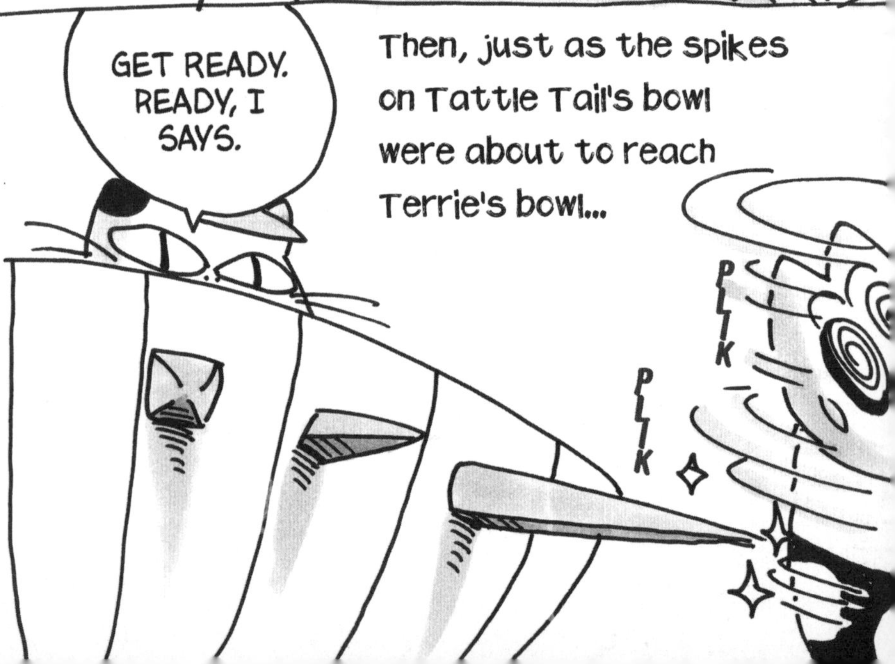
GET READY. READY, I SAYS.
PLIK
PLIK

Then, just as the spikes on Tattle Tail's bowl were about to reach Terrie's bowl...

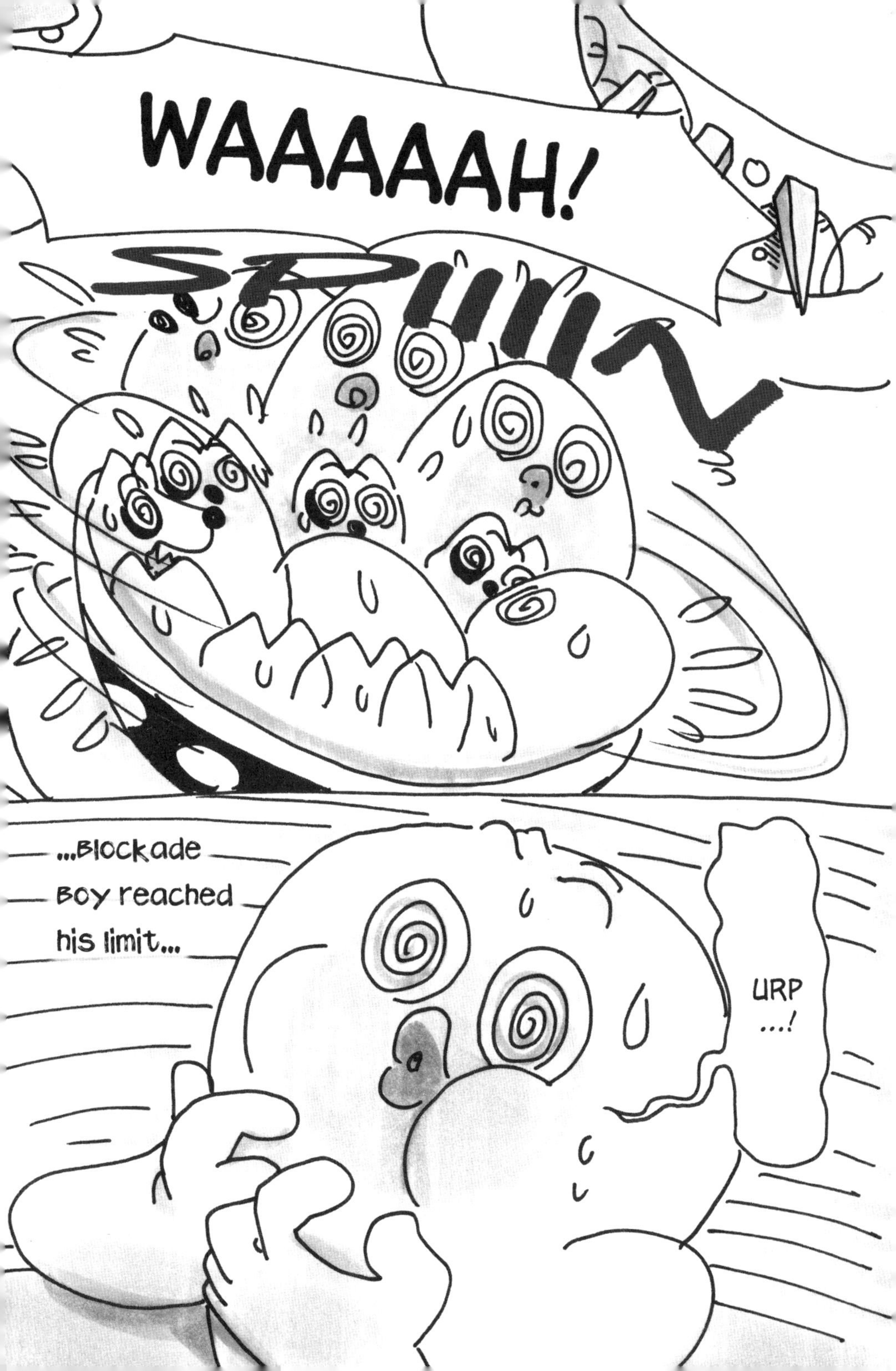
WAAAAAH!
...Blockade Boy reached his limit...
URP ...!

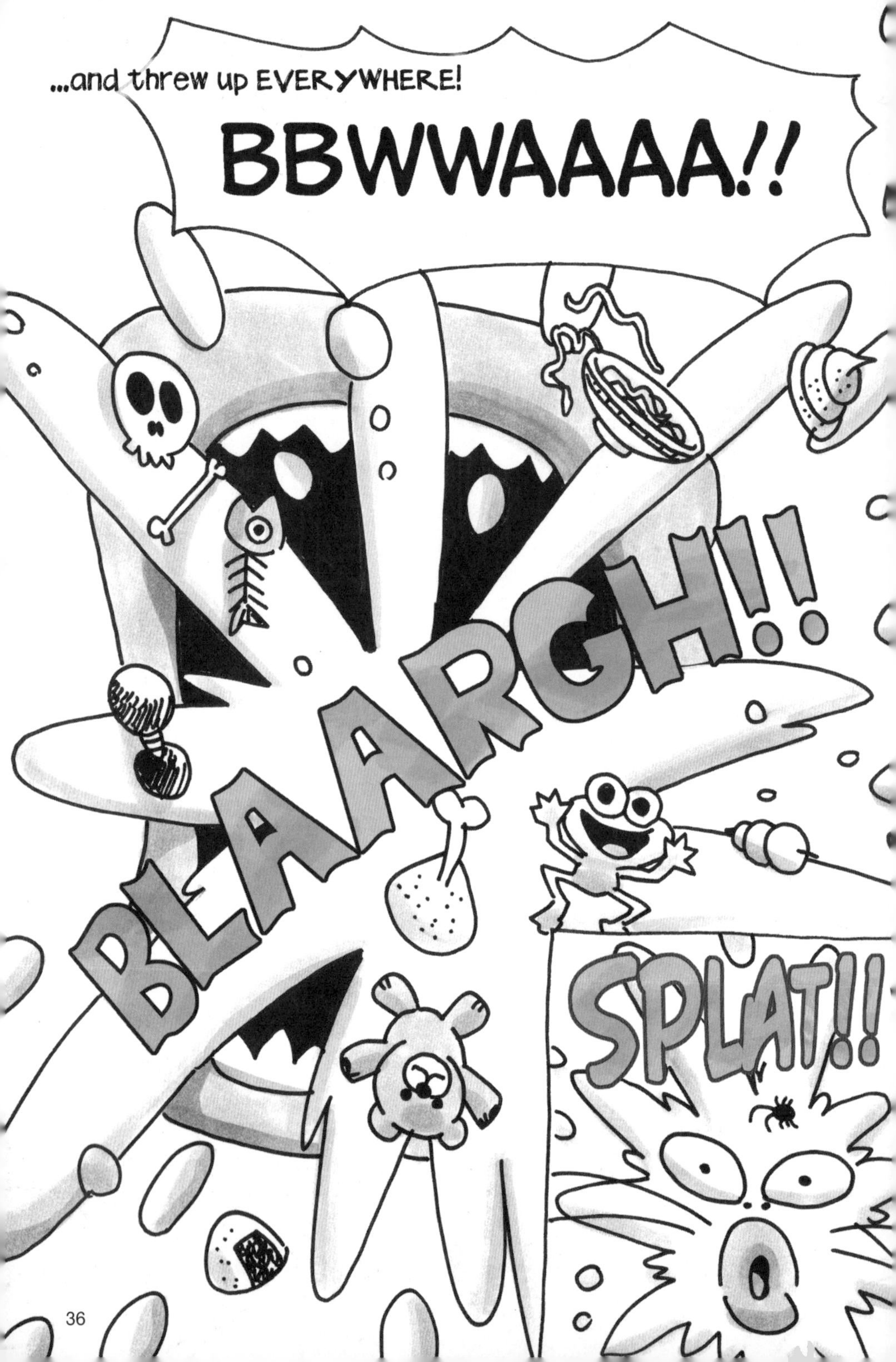
...and threw up EVERYWHERE!
BBWWAAAAA!!
BLAARGH!!
SPLAT!!

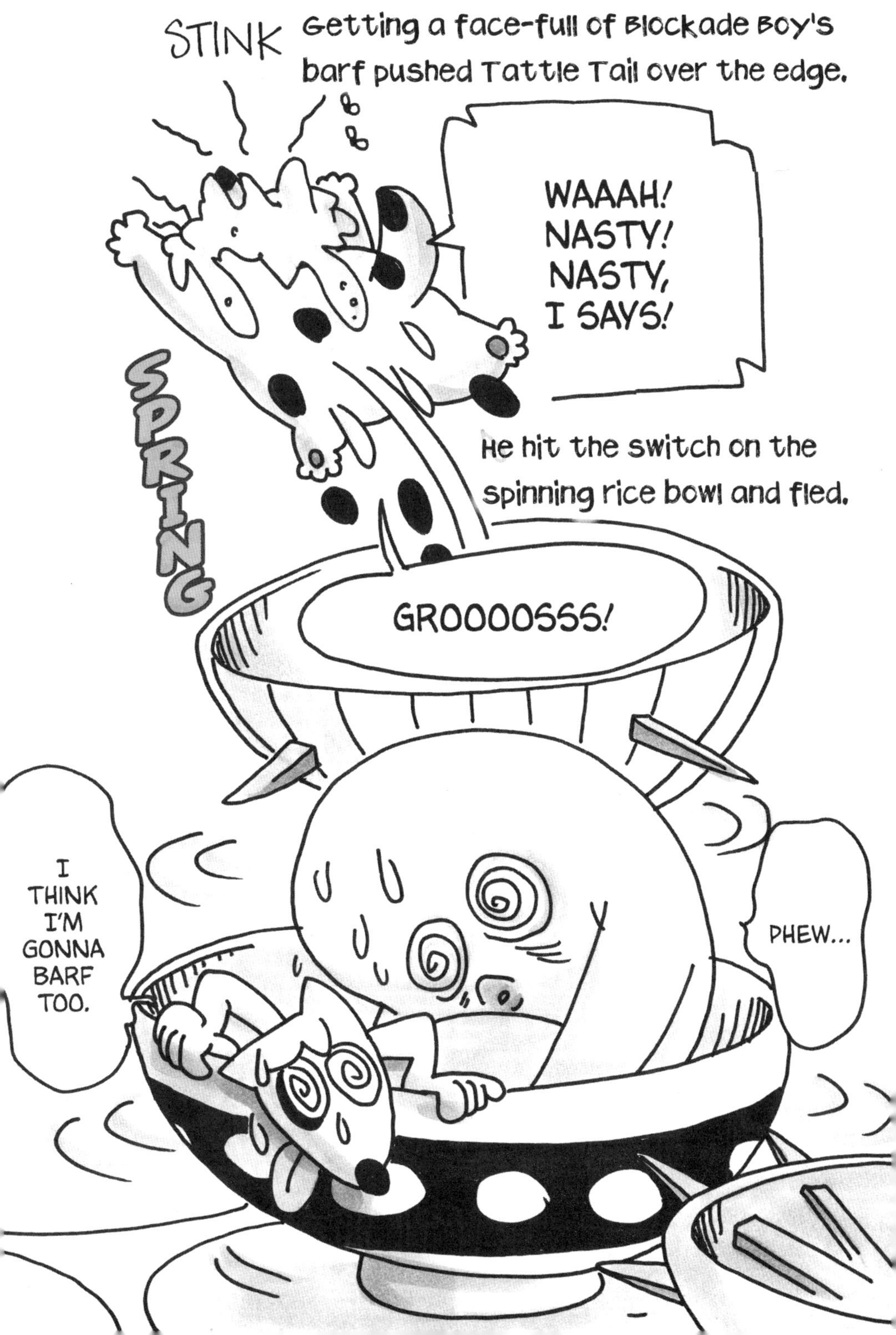
STINK
Getting a face-full of Blockade Boy's barf pushed Tattle Tail over the edge.
WAAAH! NASTY! NASTY, I SAYS!
SPRING
He hit the switch on the spinning rice bowl and fled.
GROOOOSSS!
I THINK I'M GONNA BARF TOO.
PHEW...

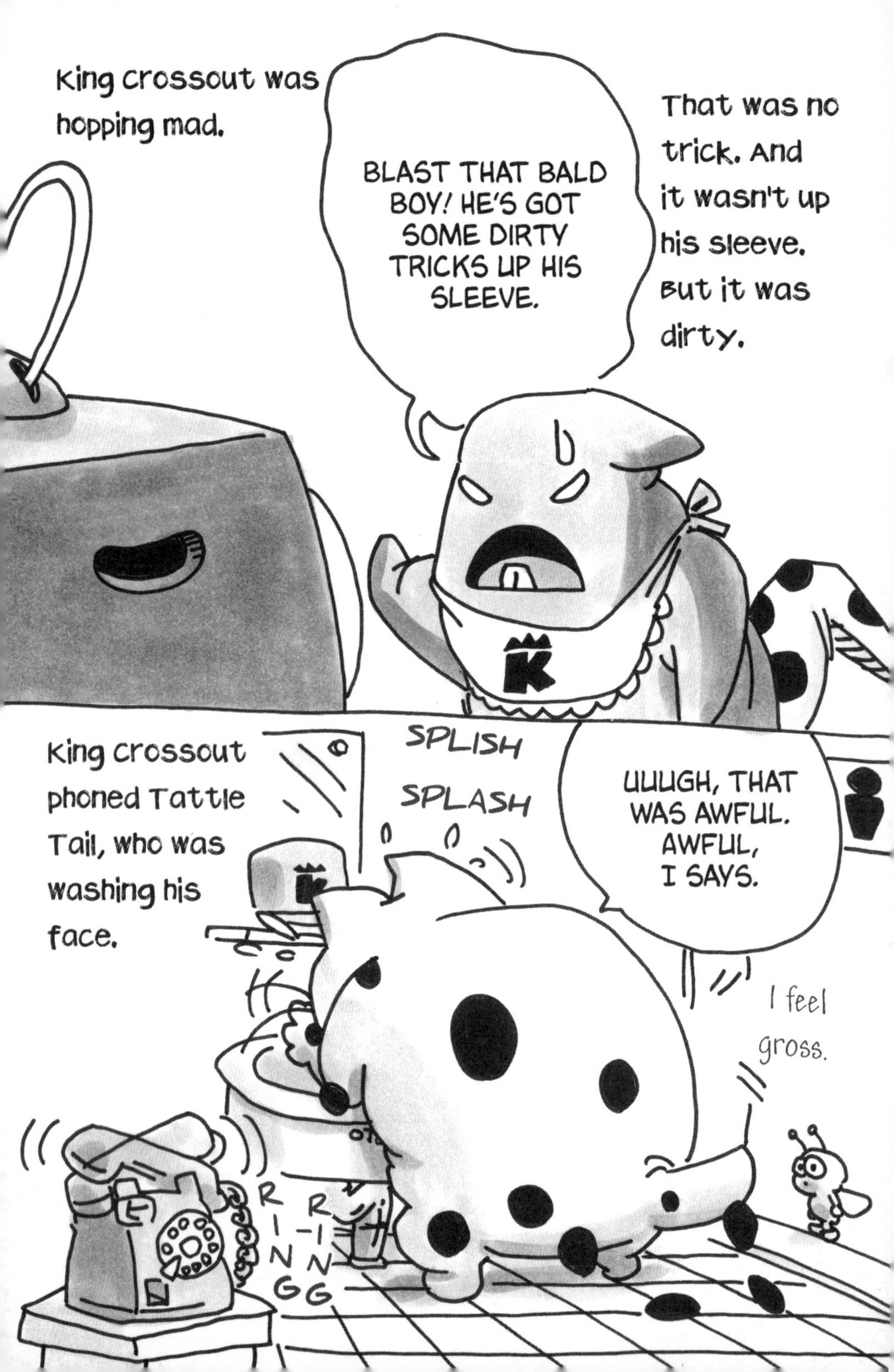
King crossout was hopping mad.
BLAST THAT BALD BOY! HE'S GOT SOME DIRTY TRICKS UP HIS SLEEVE.
That was no trick. And it wasn't up his sleeve. But it was dirty.
King crossout phoned Tattle Tail, who was washing his face.
SPLISH
SPLASH
UUUGH, THAT WAS AWFUL. AWFUL, I SAYS.
I feel gross.
RING
RING

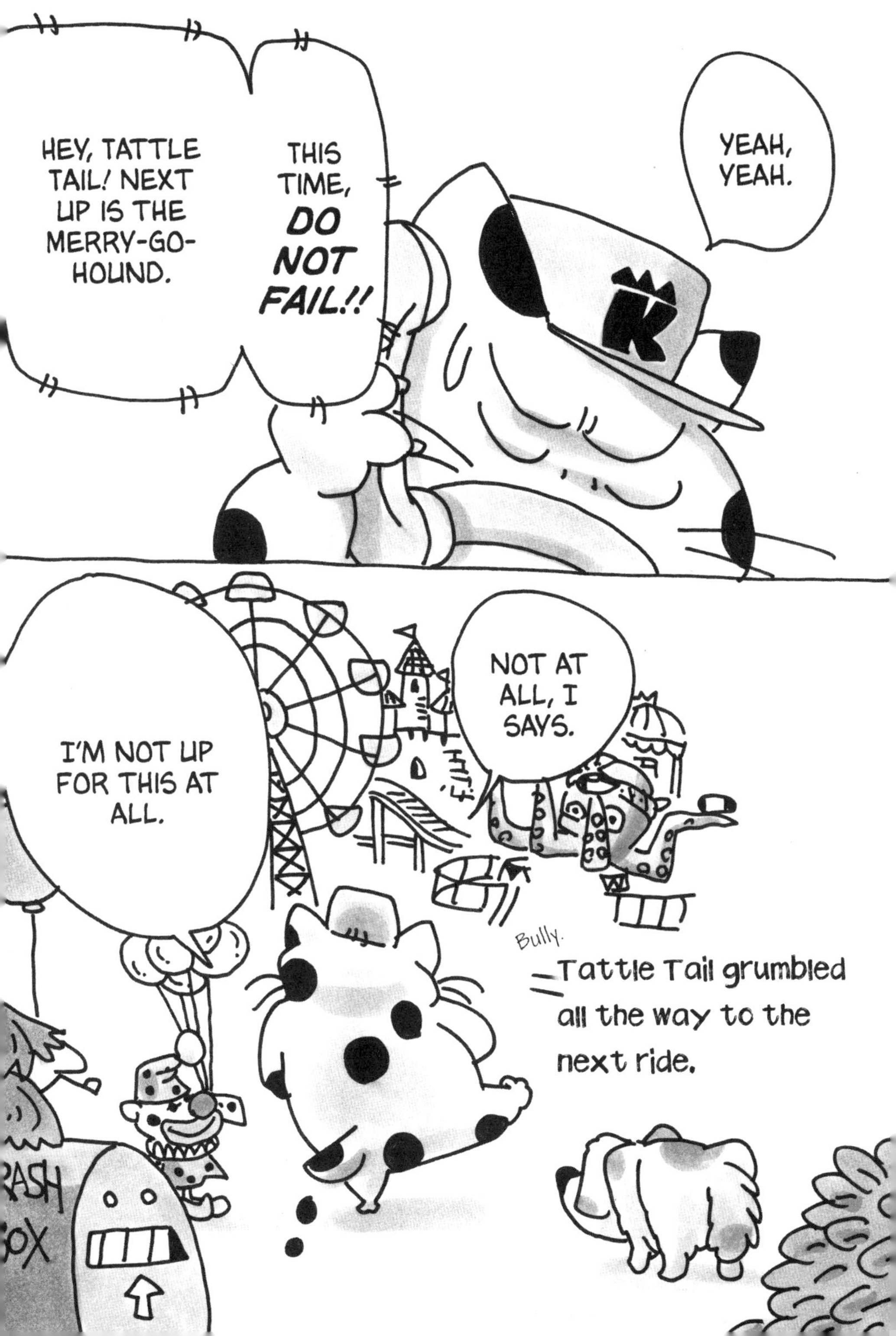
HEY, TATTLE TAIL! NEXT UP IS THE MERRY-GO-HOUND.
THIS TIME, **DO NOT FAIL!!**
YEAH, YEAH.
I'M NOT UP FOR THIS AT ALL.
NOT AT ALL, I SAYS.
Bully.
Tattle Tail grumbled all the way to the next ride.
TRASH BOX

By the time Tattle Tail arrived, Terrie and Blockade Boy were already on the merry-go-round waiting for it to start. But, this was no ordinary merry-go-round.

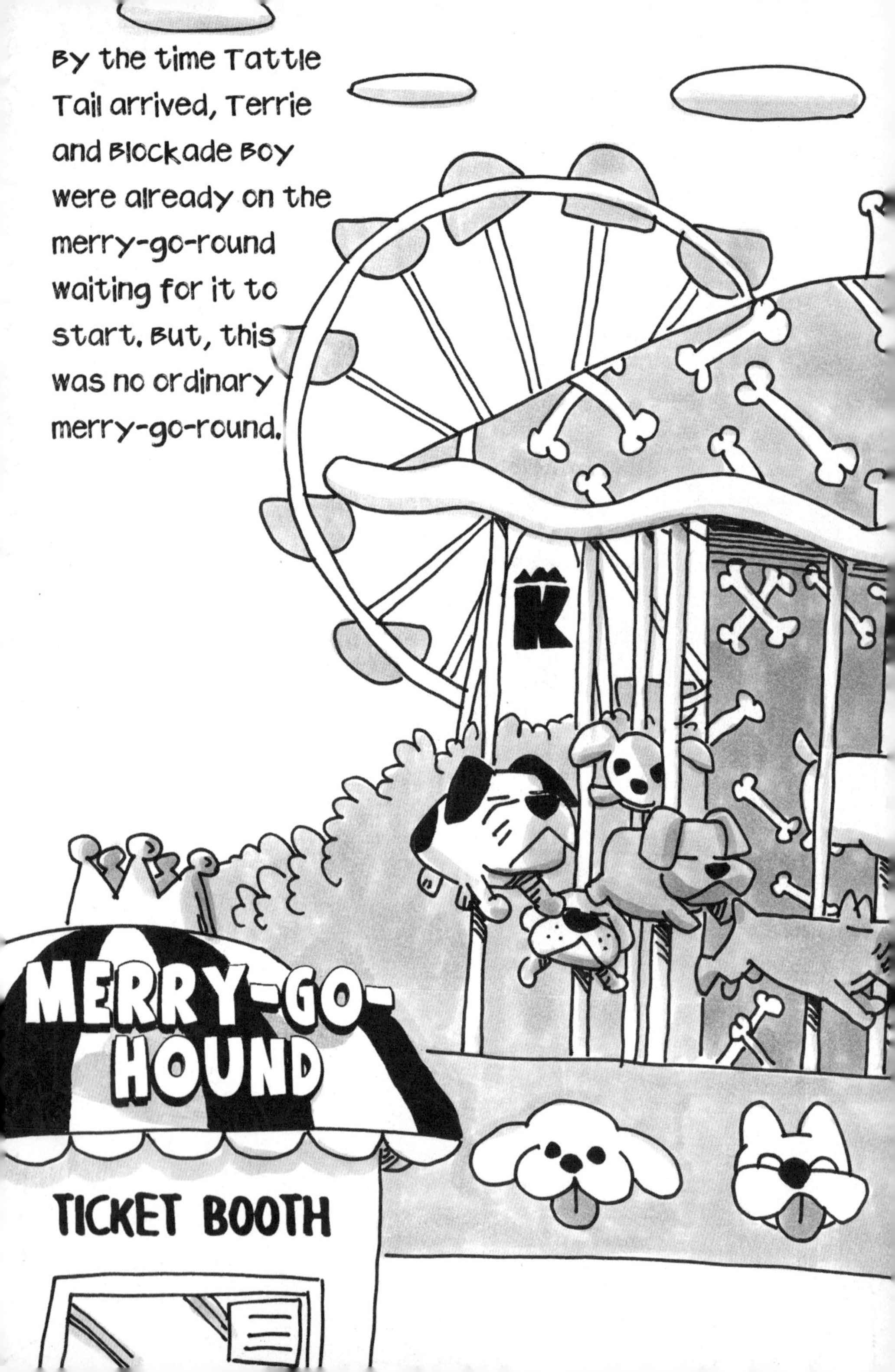
MERRY-GO-HOUND
TICKET BOOTH

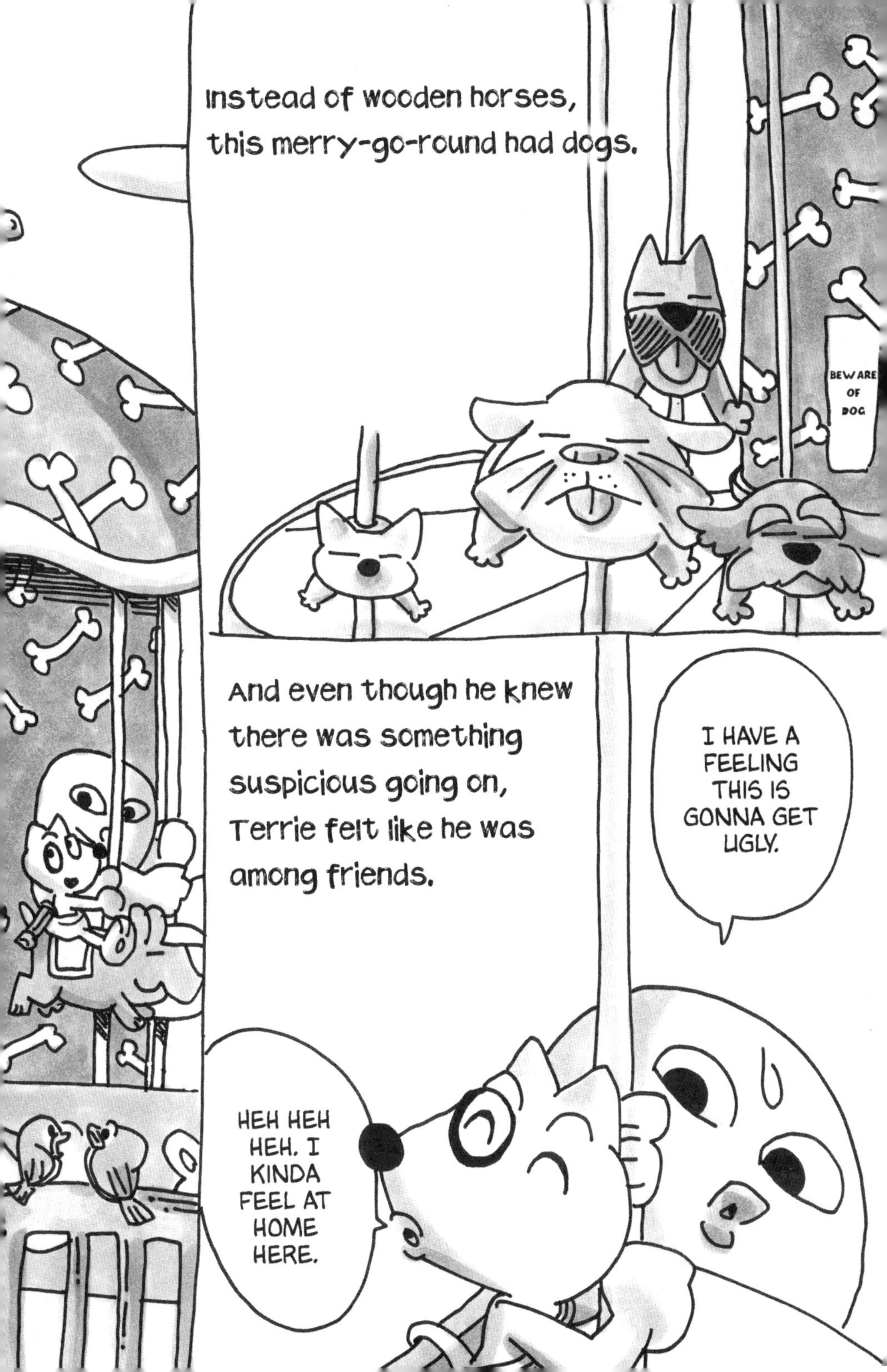
Instead of wooden horses, this merry-go-round had dogs.
BEWARE OF DOG
And even though he knew there was something suspicious going on, Terrie felt like he was among friends.
I HAVE A FEELING THIS IS GONNA GET UGLY.
HEH HEH HEH. I KINDA FEEL AT HOME HERE.

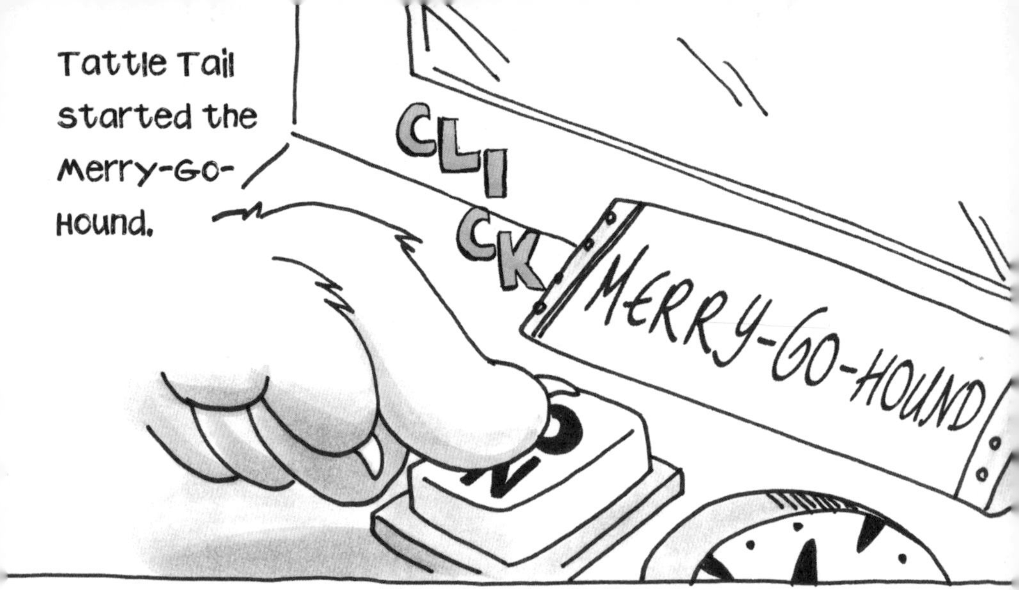
Tattle Tail started the Merry-Go-Hound.
CLICK
MERRY-GO-HOUND
ON

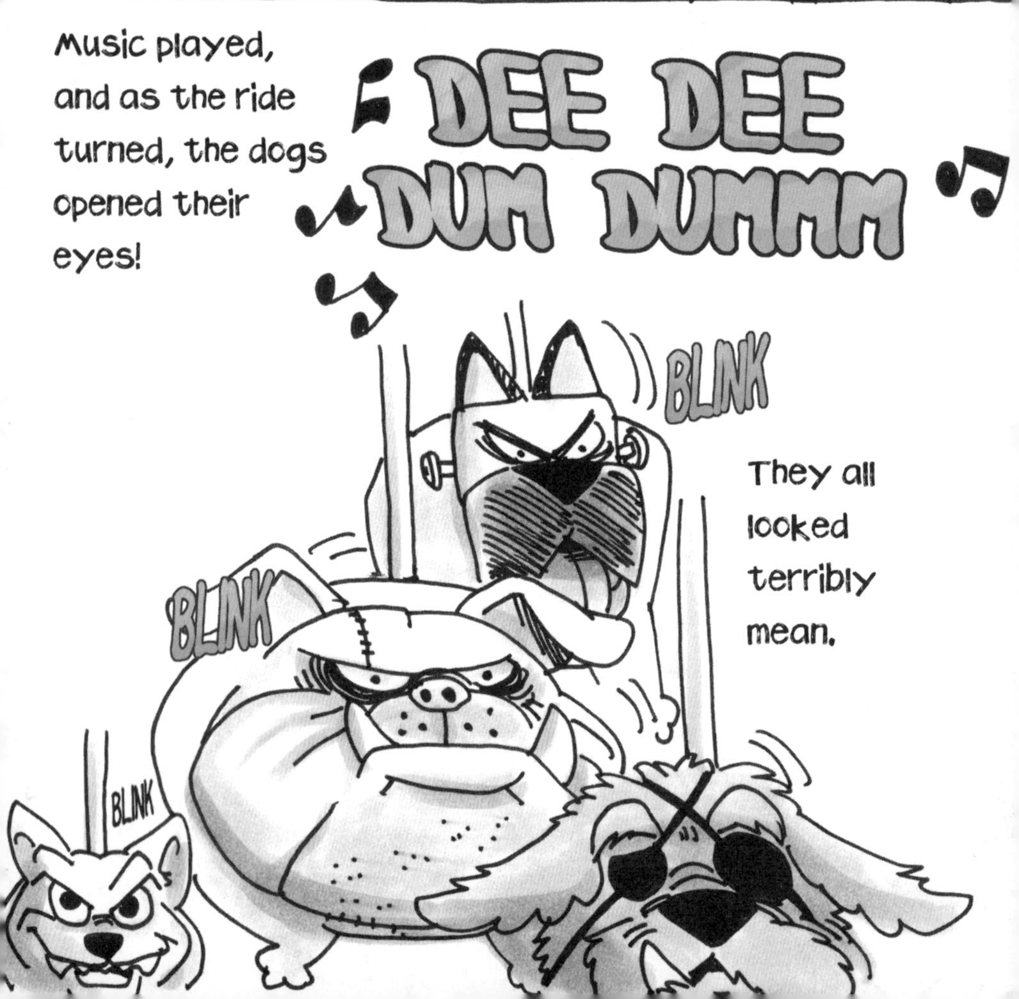
Music played, and as the ride turned, the dogs opened their eyes!
DEE DEE DUM DUMMM
BLINK
They all looked terribly mean.
BLINK
BLINK

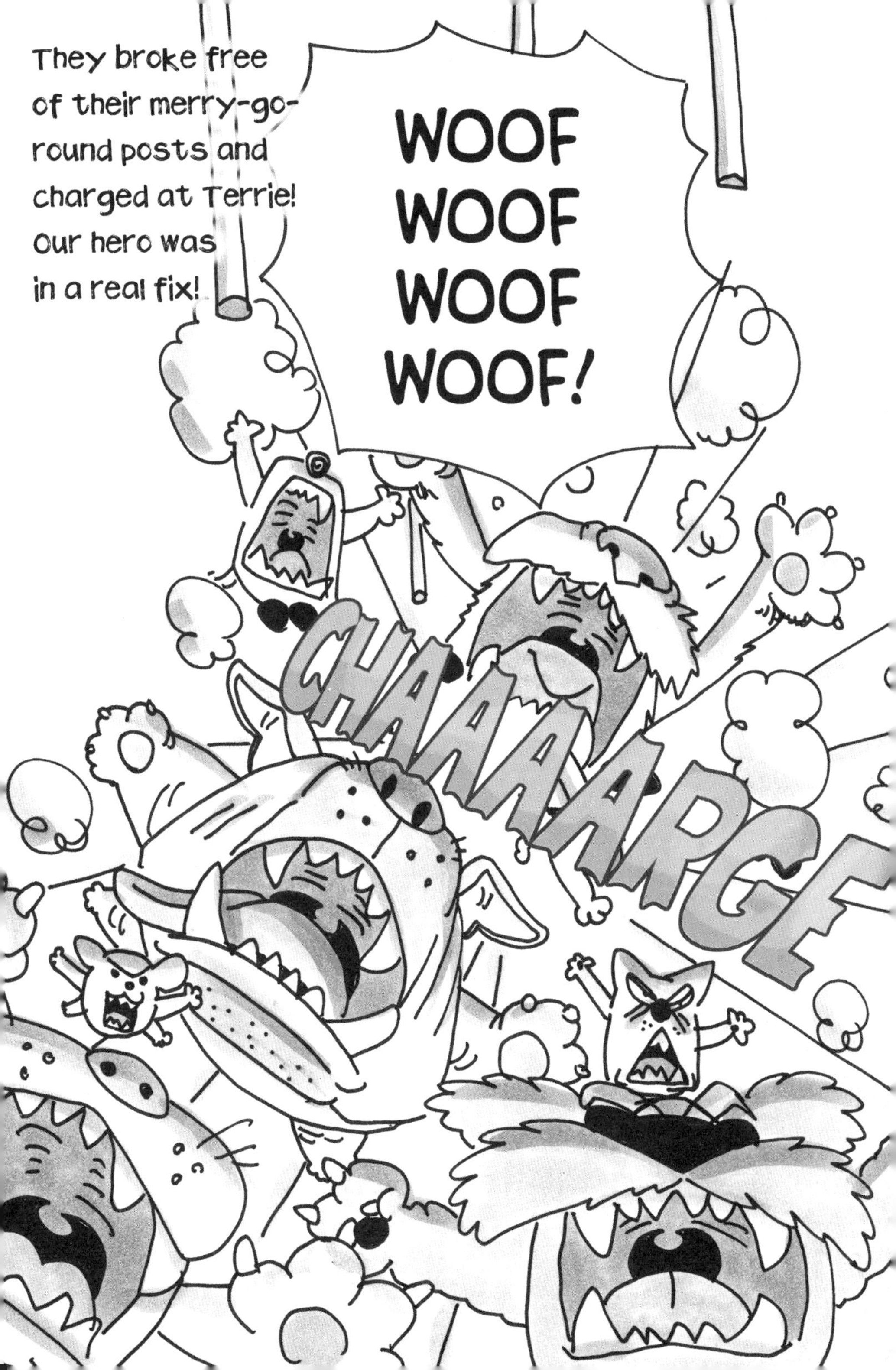
They broke free of their merry-go-round posts and charged at Terrie! Our hero was in a real fix!
WOOF WOOF WOOF WOOF!
CHAAAAARGE

or so it seemed.

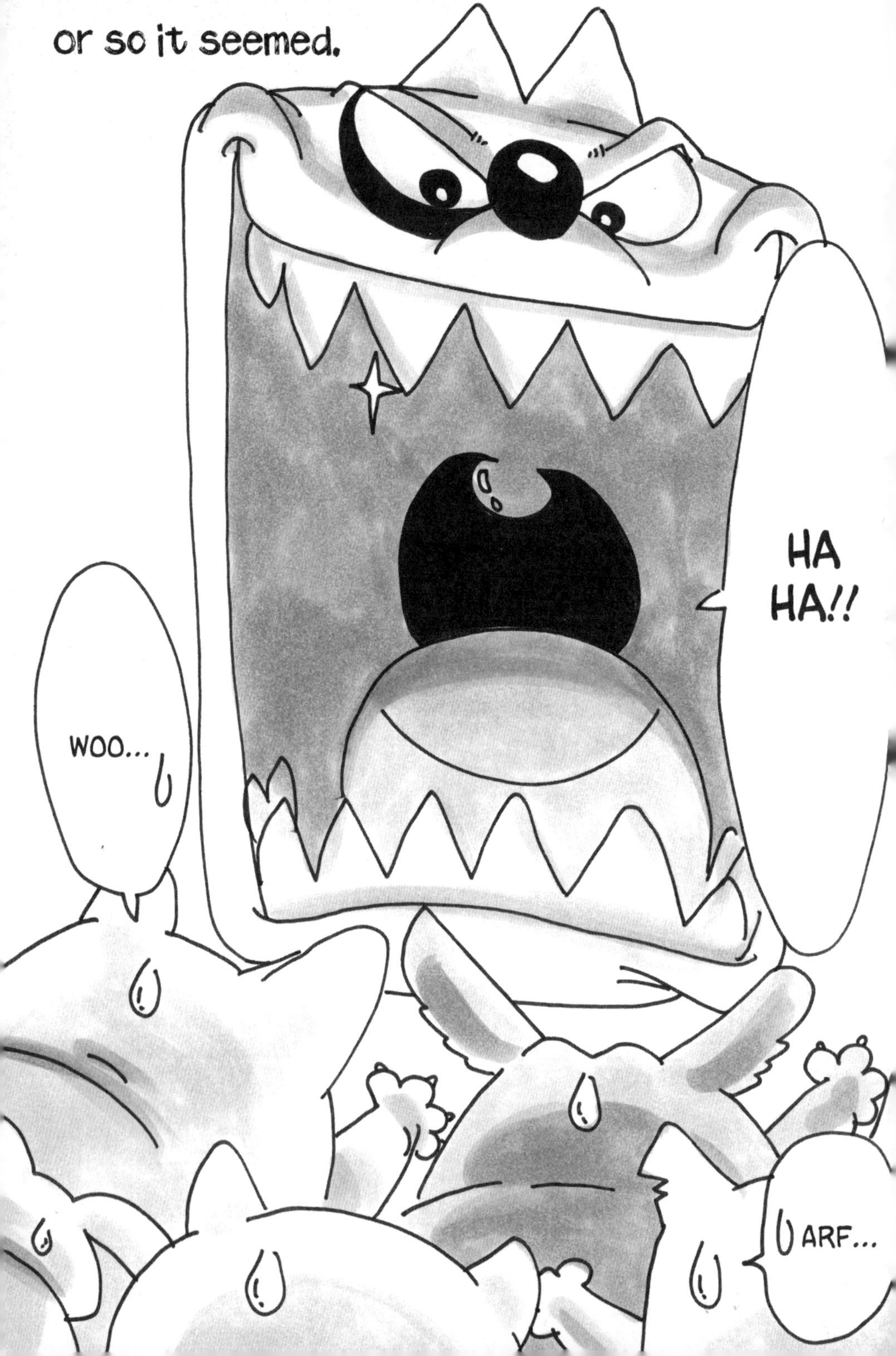
WOO...
HA HA!!
ARF...

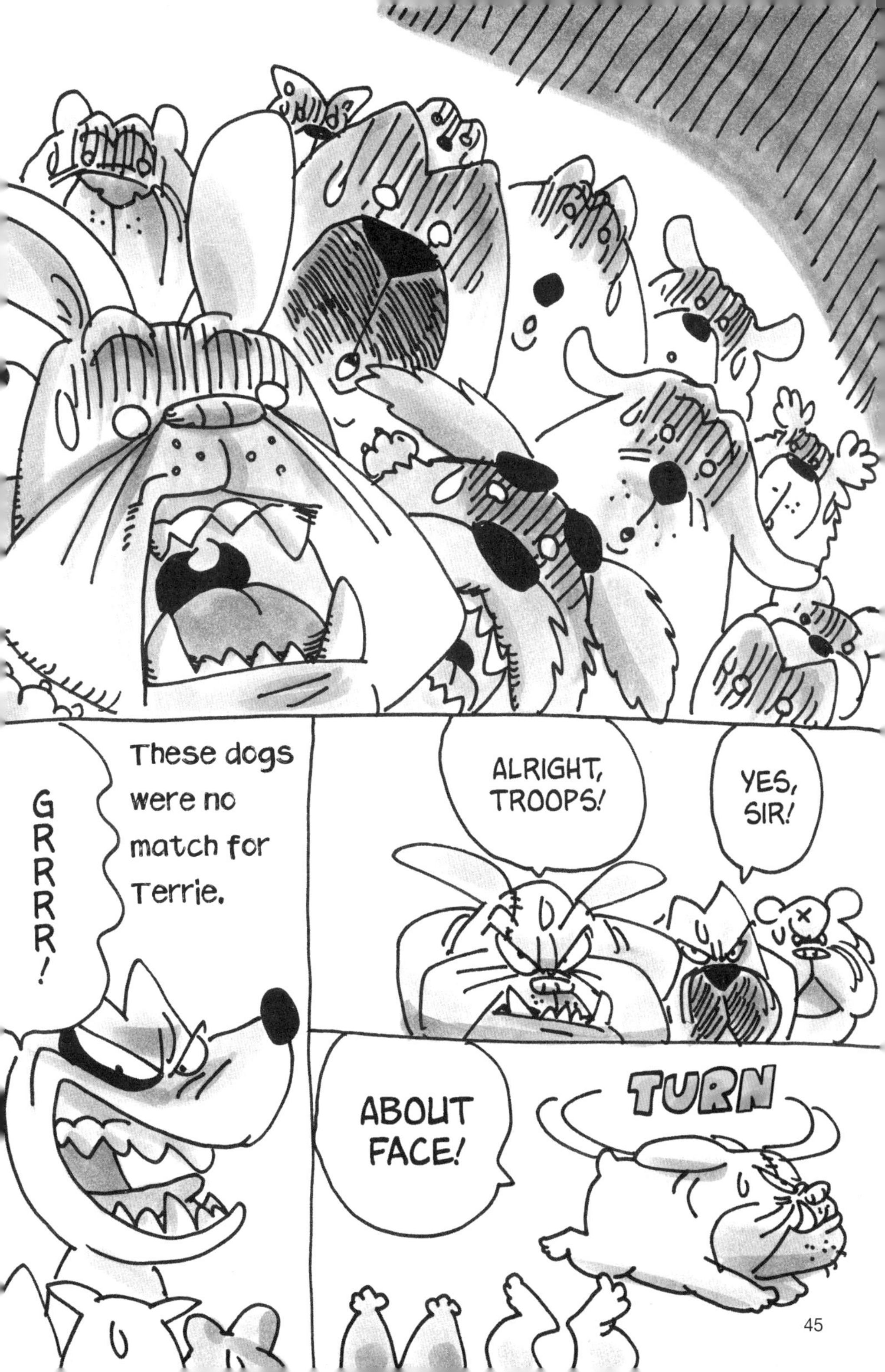

These dogs were no match for Terrie.
GRRRR!
ALRIGHT, TROOPS!
YES, SIR!
ABOUT FACE!
TURN

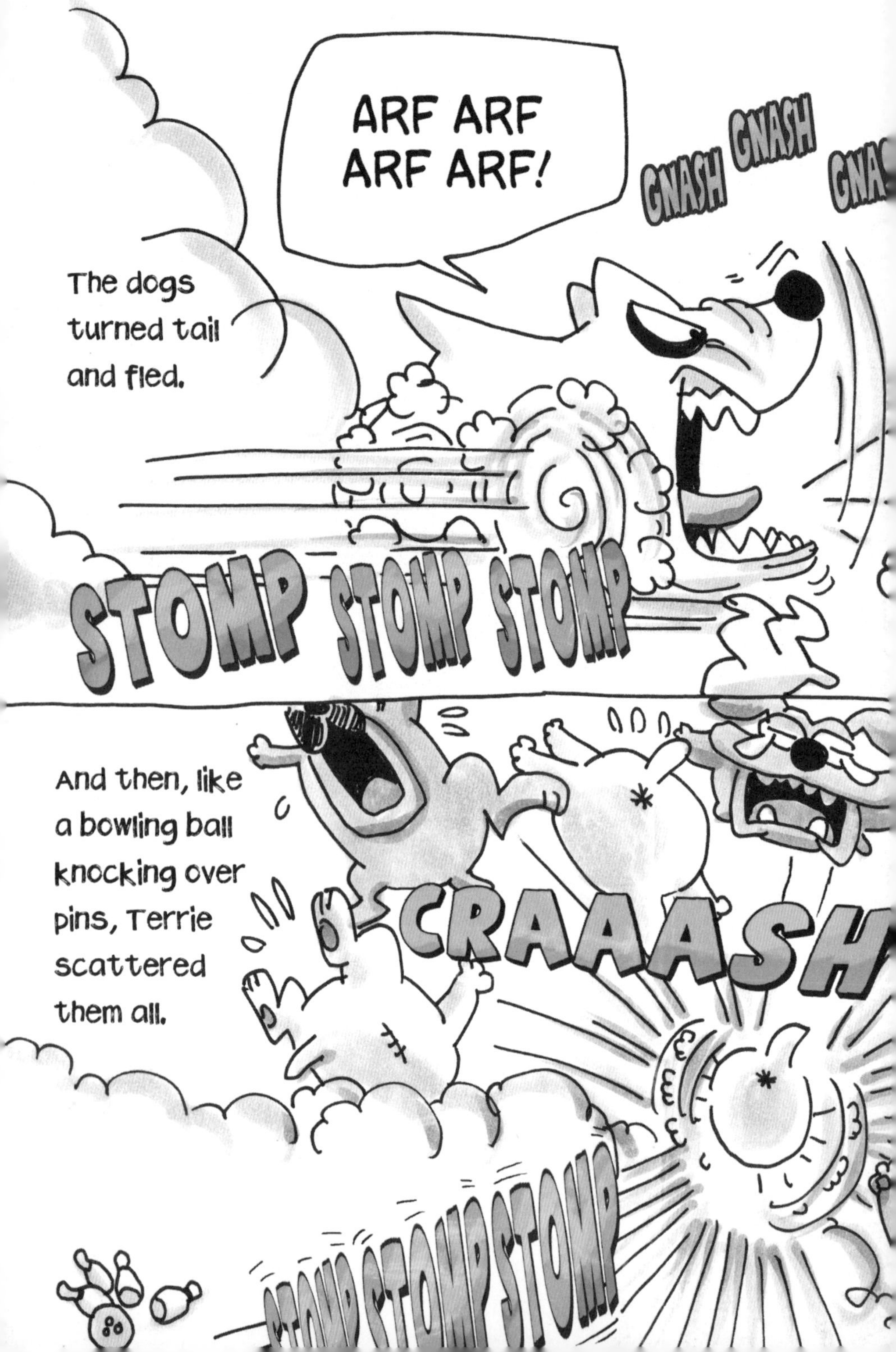
The dogs turned tail and fled.
ARF ARF ARF ARF!
GNASH GNASH
STOMP STOMP STOMP
And then, like a bowling ball knocking over pins, Terrie scattered them all.
CRAAASH
STOMP STOMP

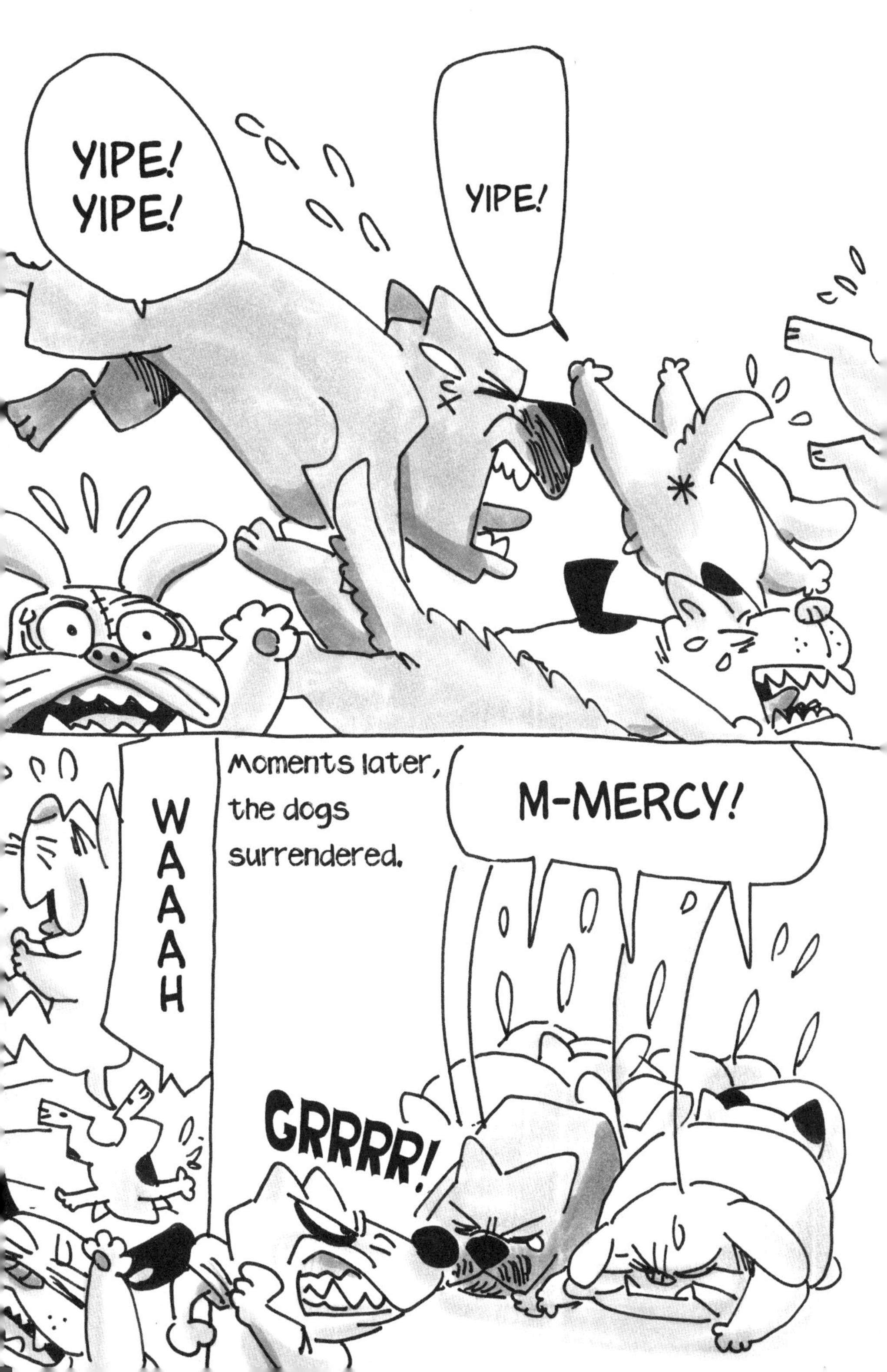
YIPE! YIPE!
YIPE!
WAAAH
Moments later, the dogs surrendered.
M-MERCY!
GRRRRR!

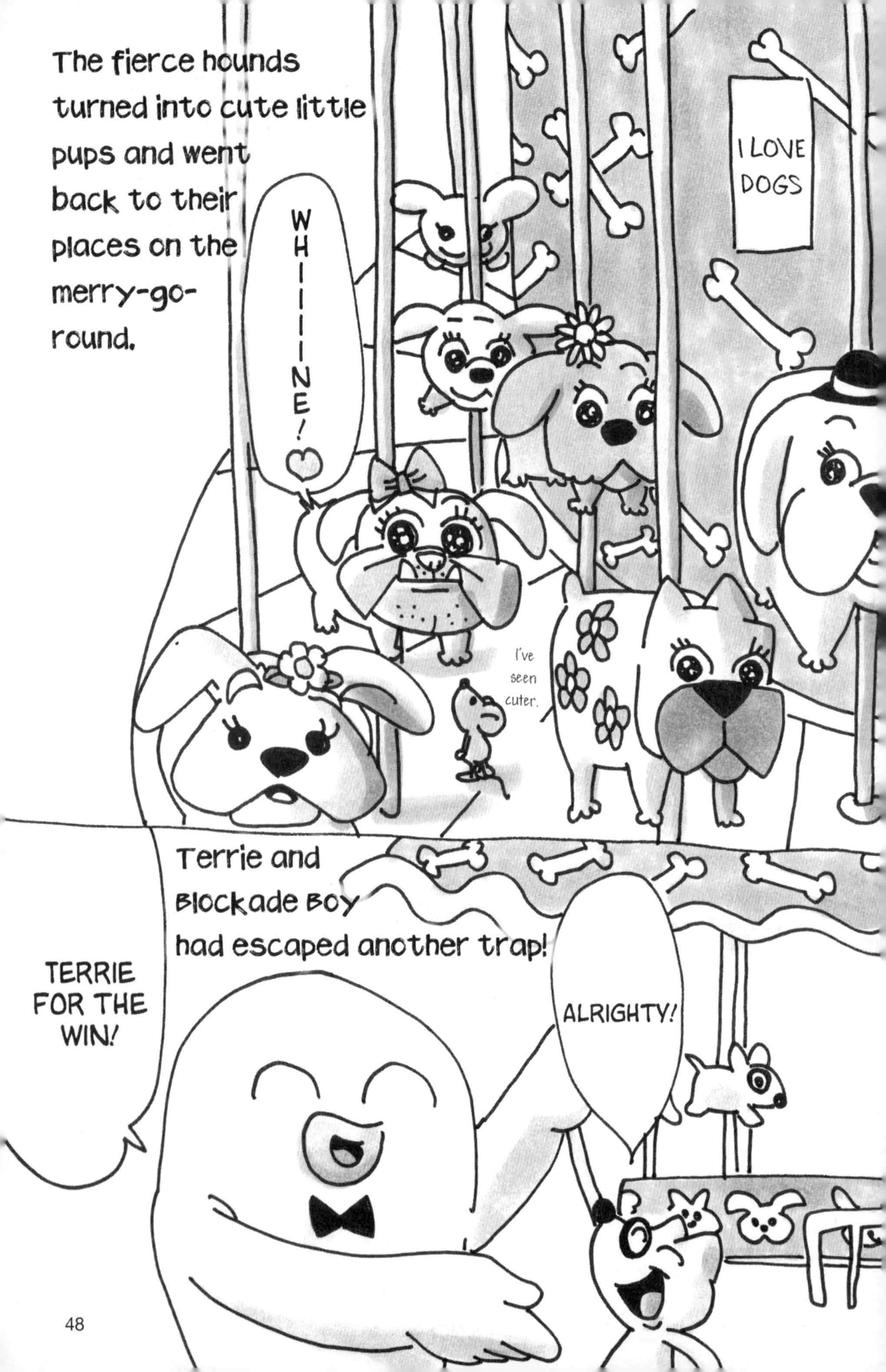
The fierce hounds turned into cute little pups and went back to their places on the merry-go-round.
WHIIIINE! ♥
I LOVE DOGS
I've seen cuter.
Terrie and Blockade Boy had escaped another trap!
TERRIE FOR THE WIN!
ALRIGHTY!

TERRIE'S BREED

EVER WONDER WHAT KIND OF DOG TERRIE IS? HE'S A PIT BULL TERRIER. THEIR BODIES MAY BE SMALL, BUT THEY'RE THE STRONGEST DOGS AROUND! THEY HAVE THE COURAGE AND GUTS TO FACE ANY FOE.

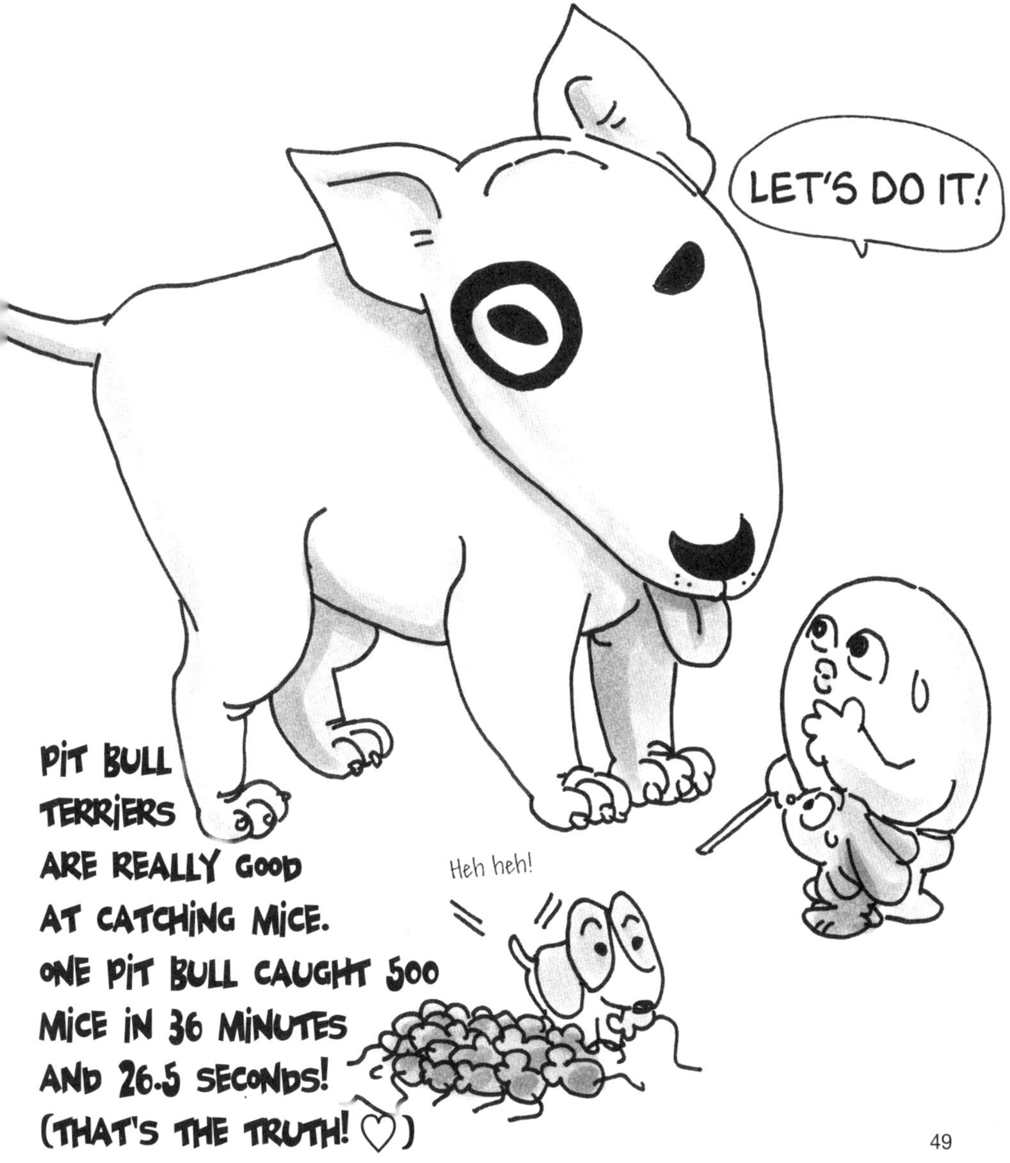
LET'S DO IT!
Heh heh!

PIT BULL TERRIERS ARE REALLY GOOD AT CATCHING MICE. ONE PIT BULL CAUGHT 500 MICE IN 36 MINUTES AND 26.5 SECONDS! (THAT'S THE TRUTH! ♡)

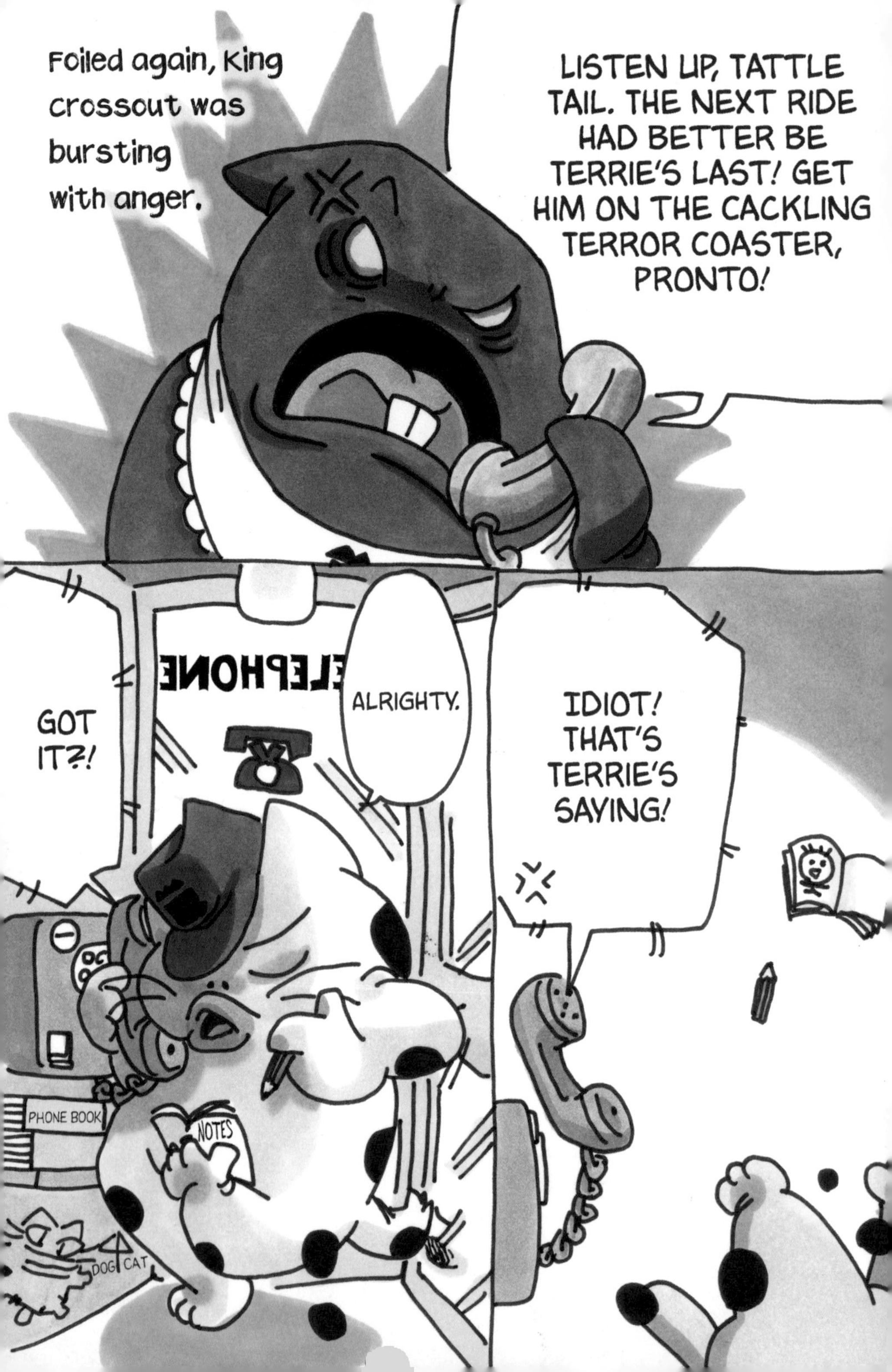
Foiled again, King crossout was bursting with anger.
LISTEN UP, TATTLE TAIL. THE NEXT RIDE HAD BETTER BE TERRIE'S LAST! GET HIM ON THE CACKLING TERROR COASTER, PRONTO!
GOT IT?!
ELEPHONE
ALRIGHTY.
PHONE BOOK
NOTES
DOG CAT
IDIOT! THAT'S TERRIE'S SAYING!

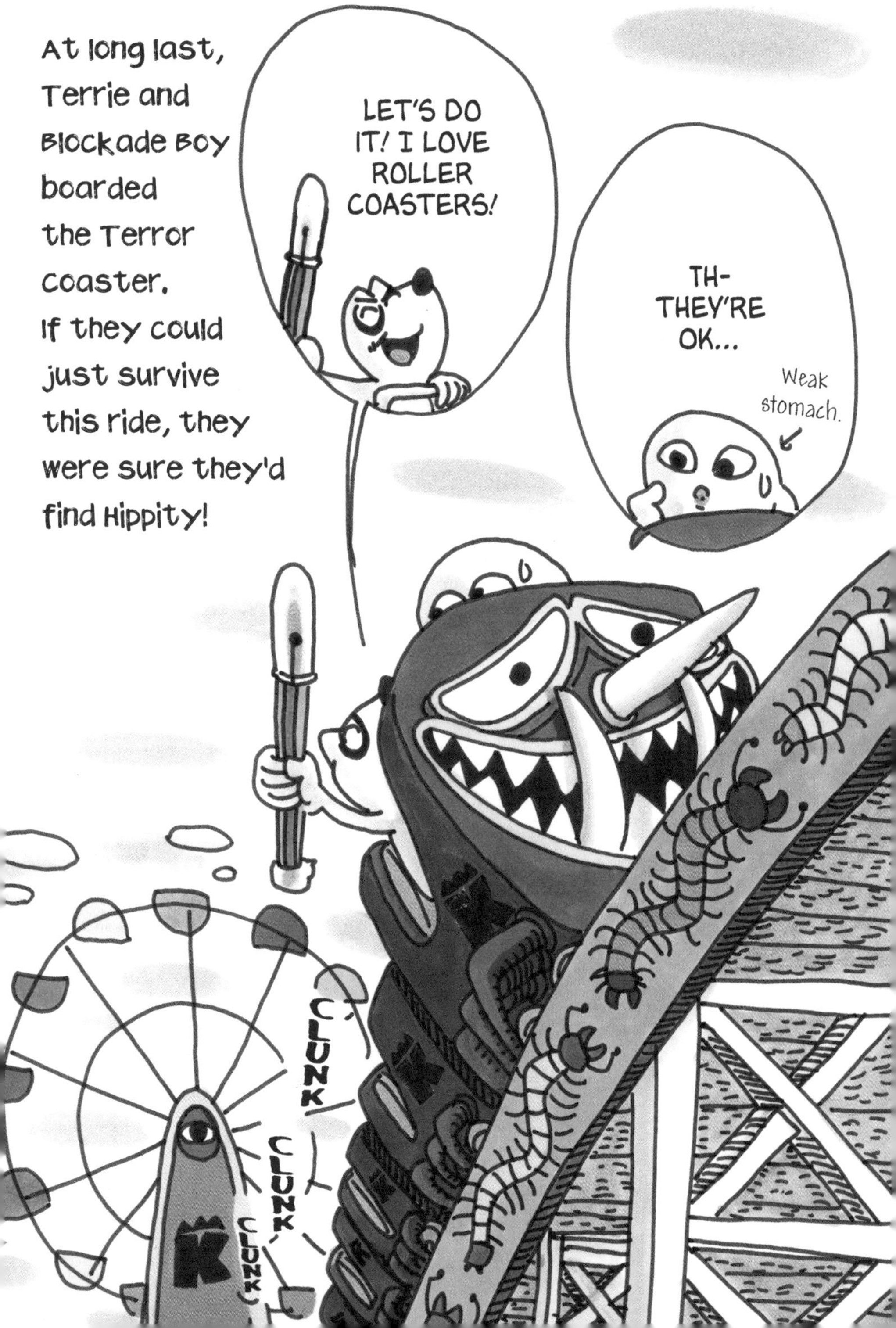
At long last, Terrie and Blockade Boy boarded the Terror coaster. If they could just survive this ride, they were sure they'd find Hippity!
LET'S DO IT! I LOVE ROLLER COASTERS!
TH- THEY'RE OK...
Weak stomach.
CLUNK
CLUNK
CLUNK

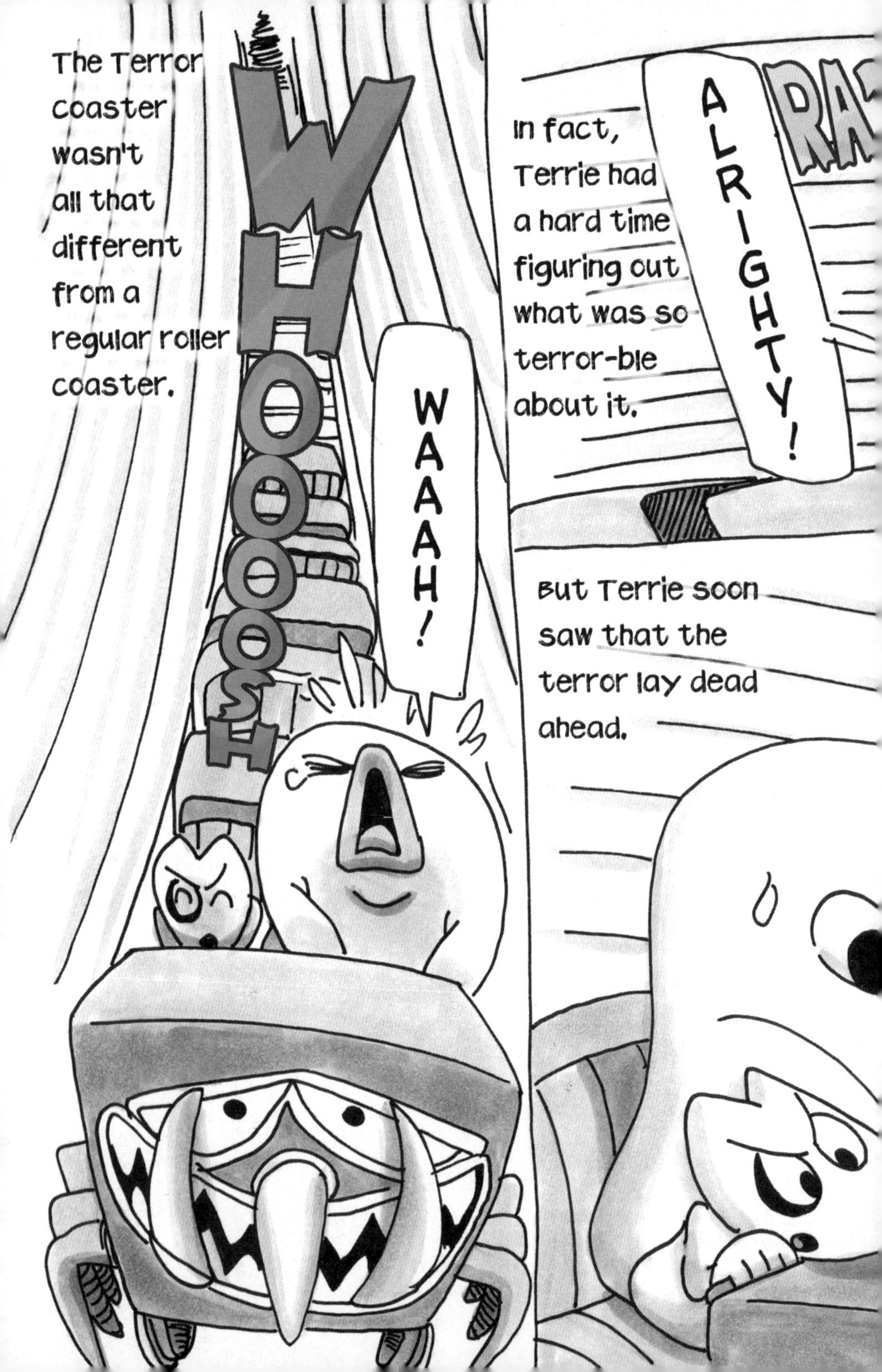
The Terror coaster wasn't all that different from a regular roller coaster.
WHOOOOOSH
WAAAAH!
In fact, Terrie had a hard time figuring out what was so terror-ble about it.
ALRIGHTY!
But Terrie soon saw that the terror lay dead ahead.

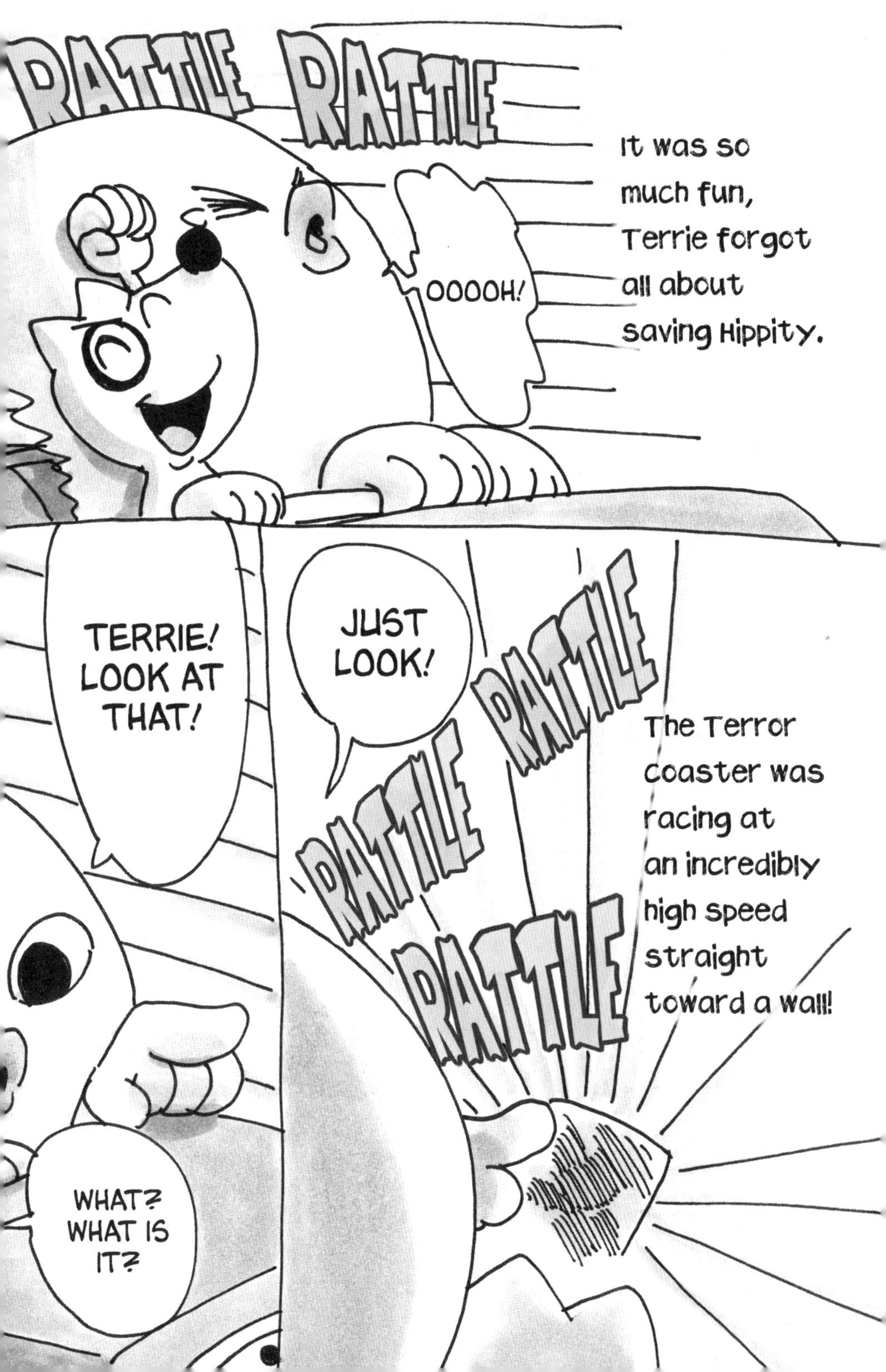
RATTLE RATTLE
OOOOH!
It was so much fun, Terrie forgot all about saving Hippity.
TERRIE! LOOK AT THAT!
WHAT? WHAT IS IT?
JUST LOOK!
RATTLE RATTLE
RATTLE
The Terror coaster was racing at an incredibly high speed straight toward a wall!

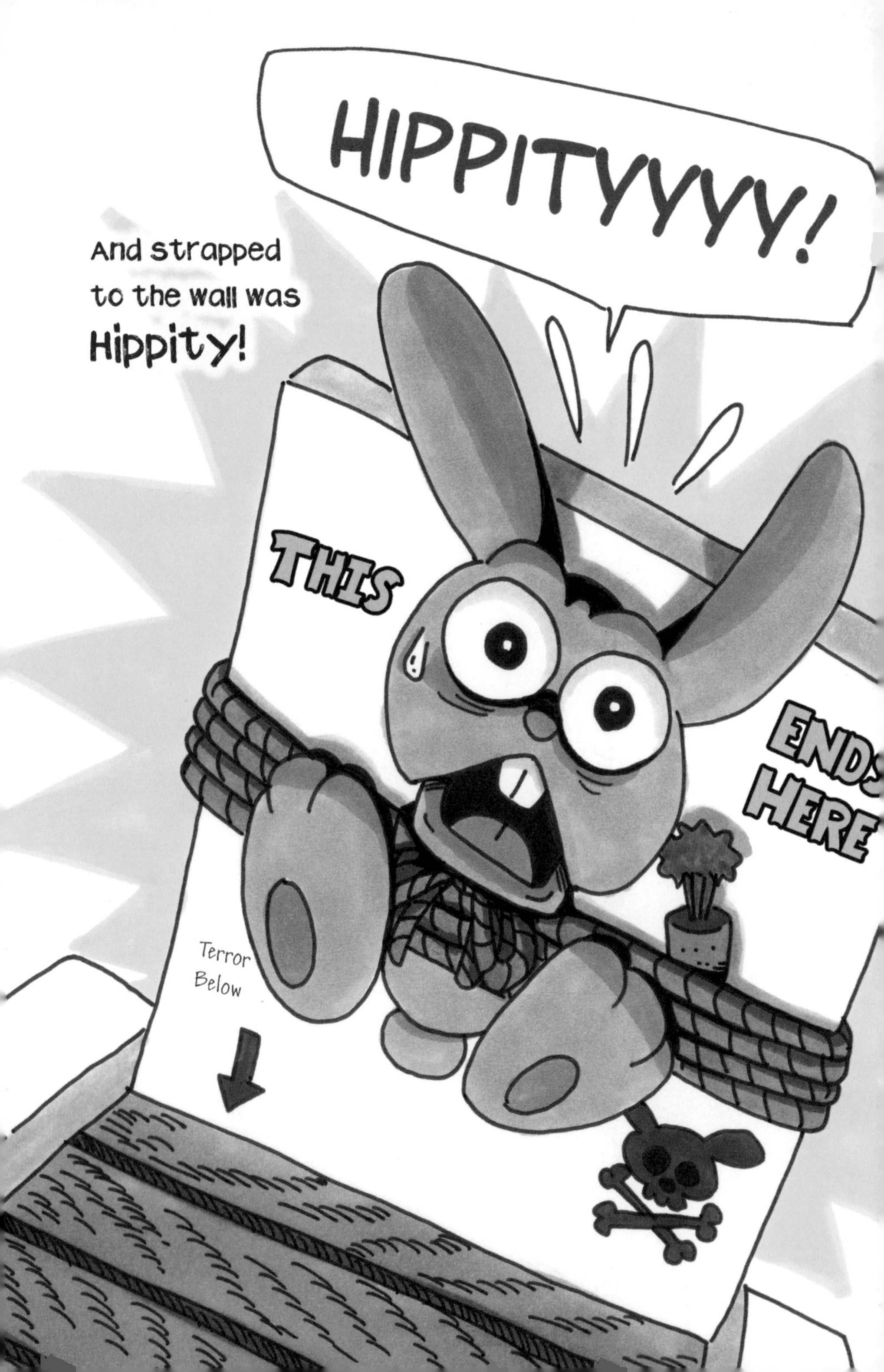
And strapped to the wall was Hippity!
HIPPITYYYY!
THIS
END
HERE
Terror Below

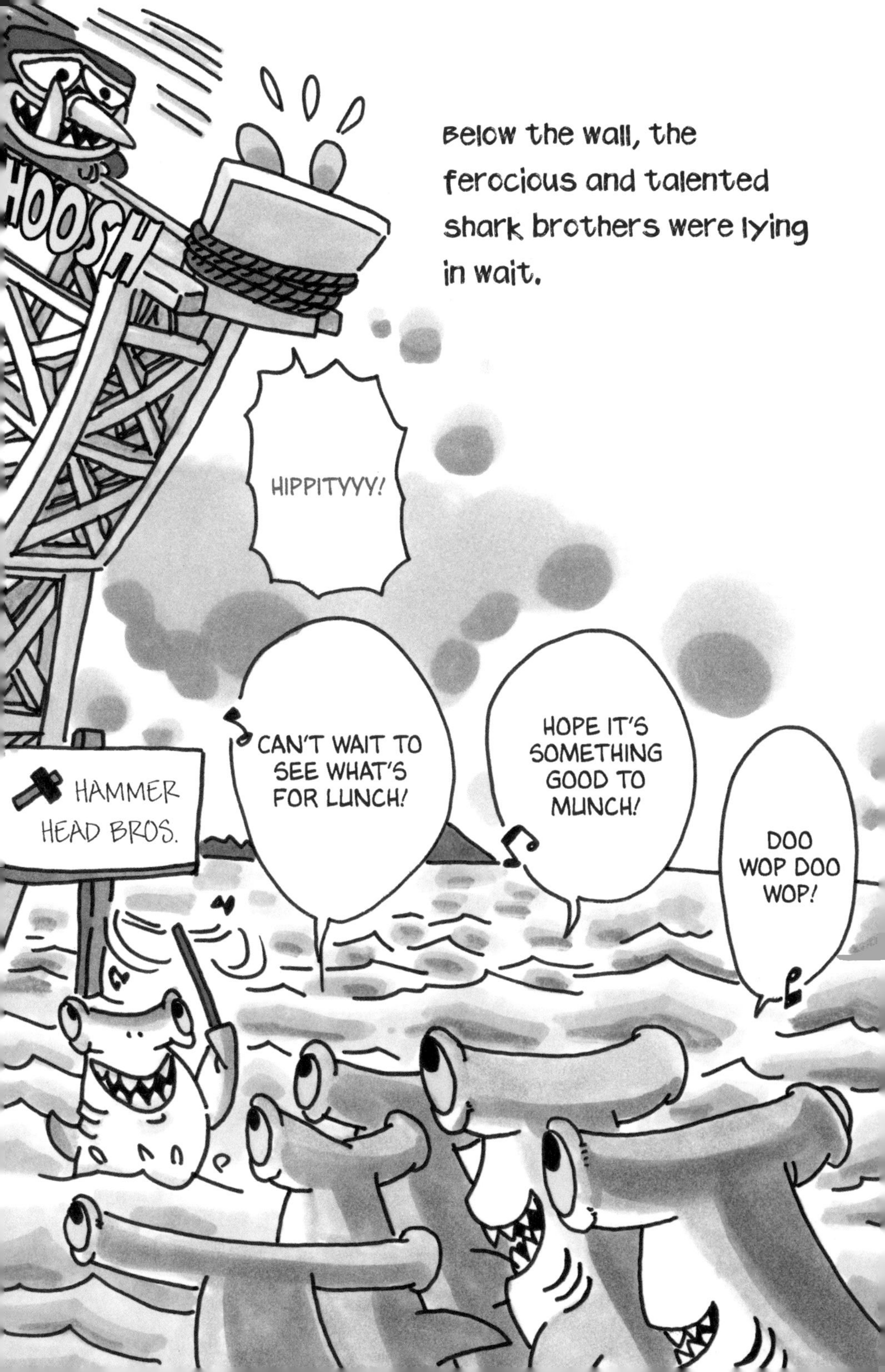
HOOSH
Below the wall, the ferocious and talented shark brothers were lying in wait.
HIPPITYYY!
HAMMER HEAD BROS.
CAN'T WAIT TO SEE WHAT'S FOR LUNCH!
HOPE IT'S SOMETHING GOOD TO MUNCH!
DOO WOP DOO WOP!

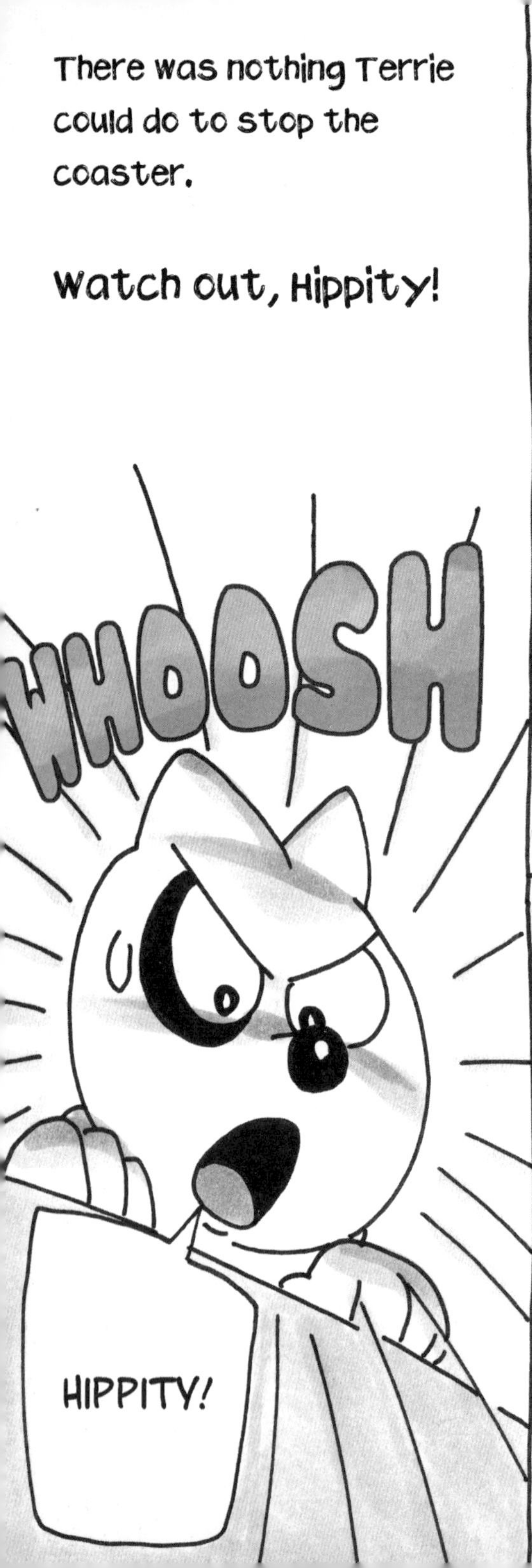
There was nothing Terrie could do to stop the coaster.
Watch out, Hippity!
WHOOSH
HIPPITY!

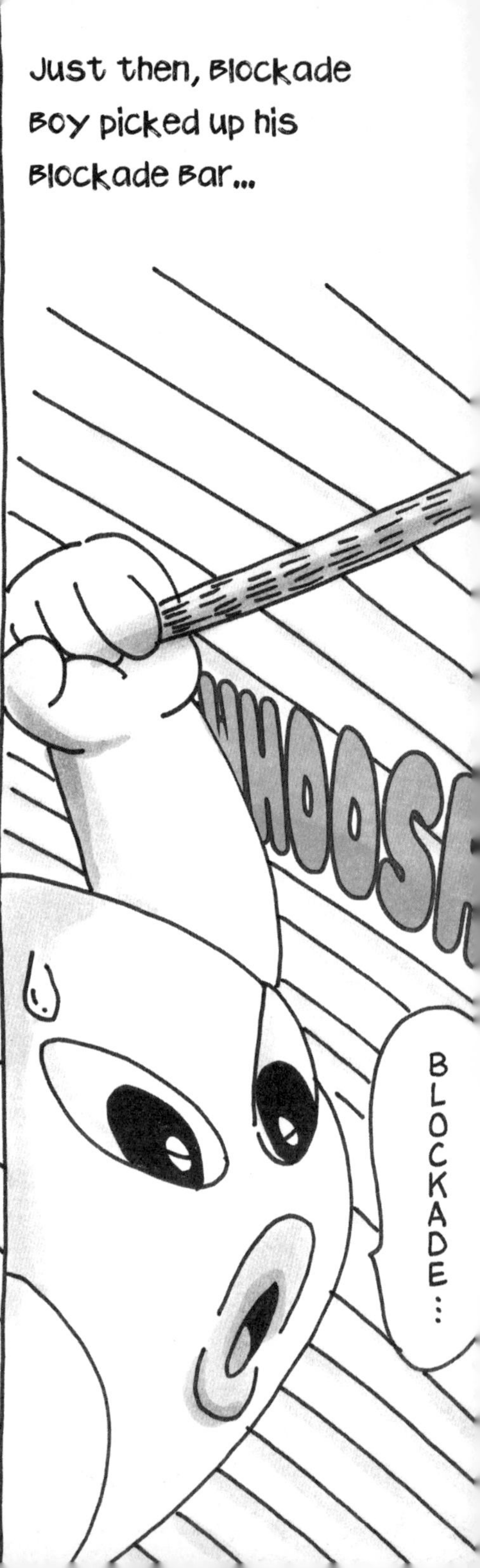
Just then, Blockade Boy picked up his Blockade Bar...
WHOOSH
BLOCKADE...

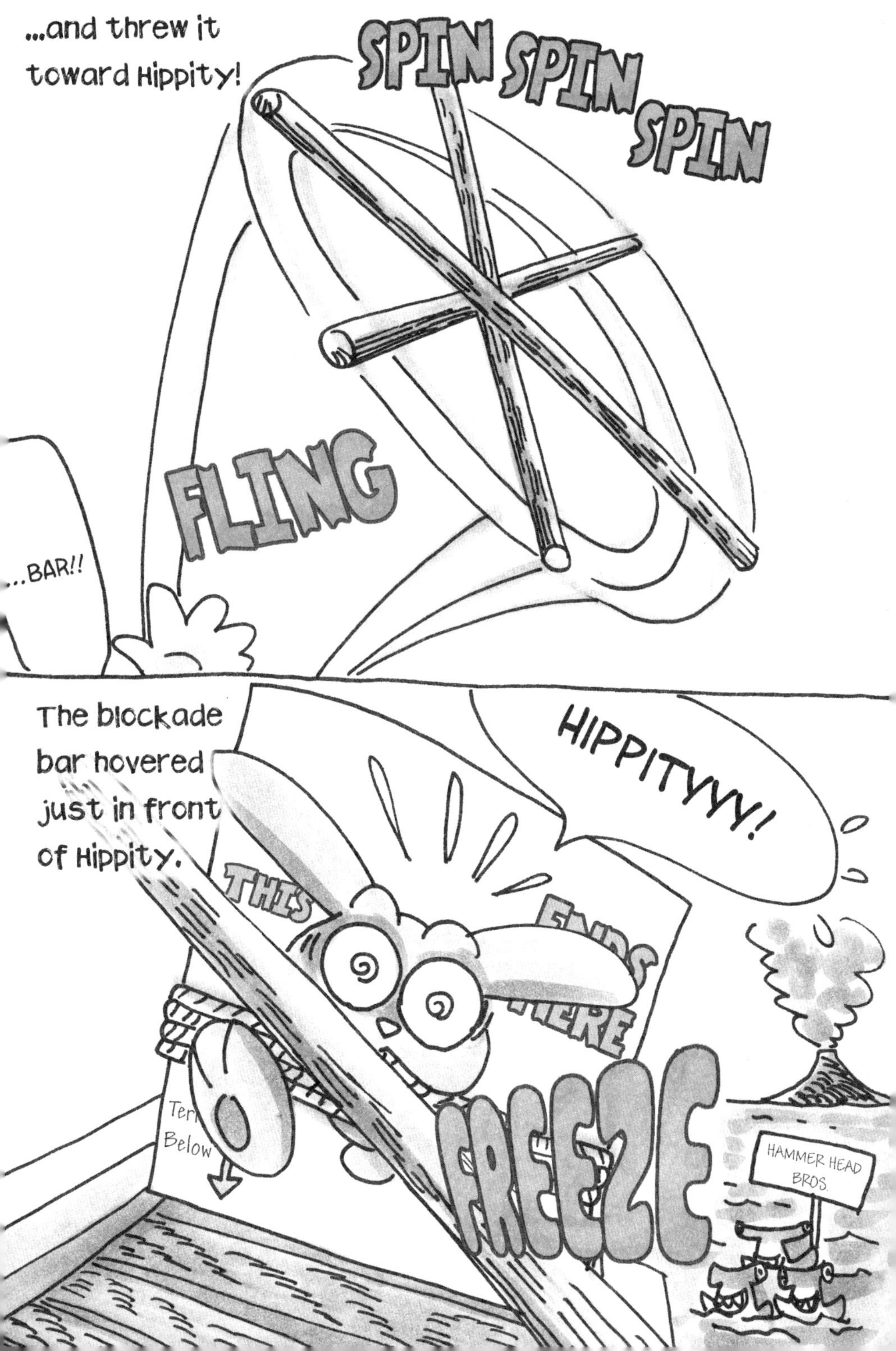
...and threw it toward Hippity!
SPIN SPIN SPIN
FLING
...BAR!!
The blockade bar hovered just in front of Hippity.
HIPPITYYY!
THIS
Below
FREEZE
HAMMER HEAD BROS.

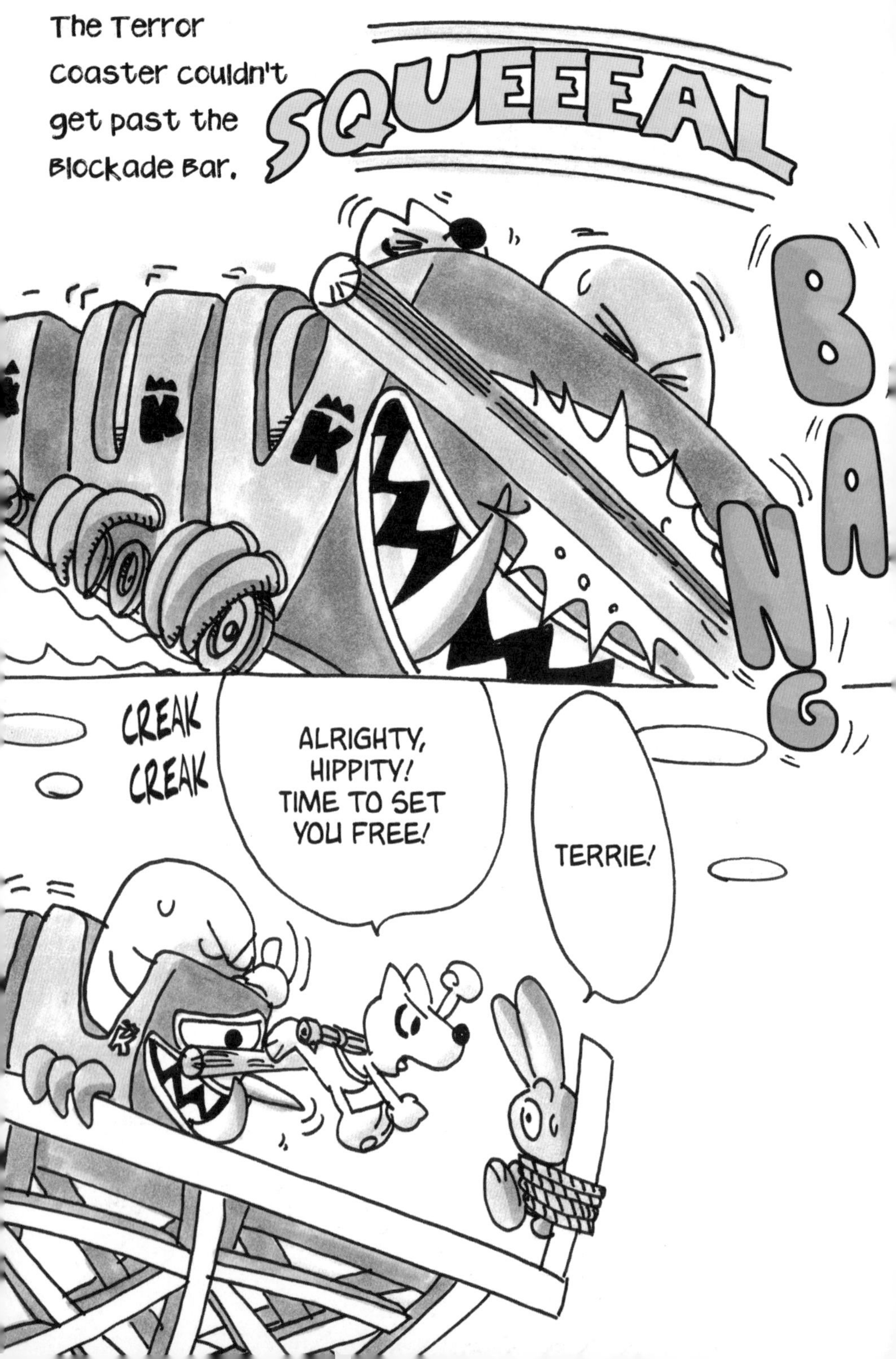

The Terror coaster couldn't get past the Blockade Bar.
SQUEEEAL
BANNG
CREAK CREAK
ALRIGHTY, HIPPITY! TIME TO SET YOU FREE!
TERRIE!

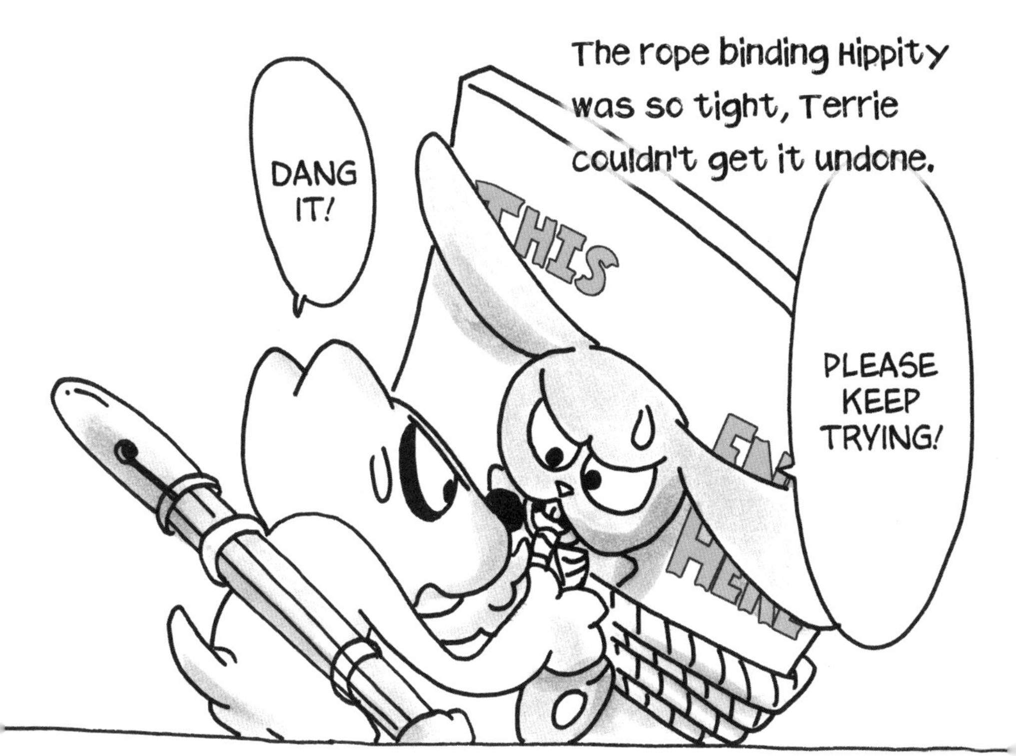
DANG IT!
The rope binding Hippity was so tight, Terrie couldn't get it undone.
PLEASE KEEP TRYING!

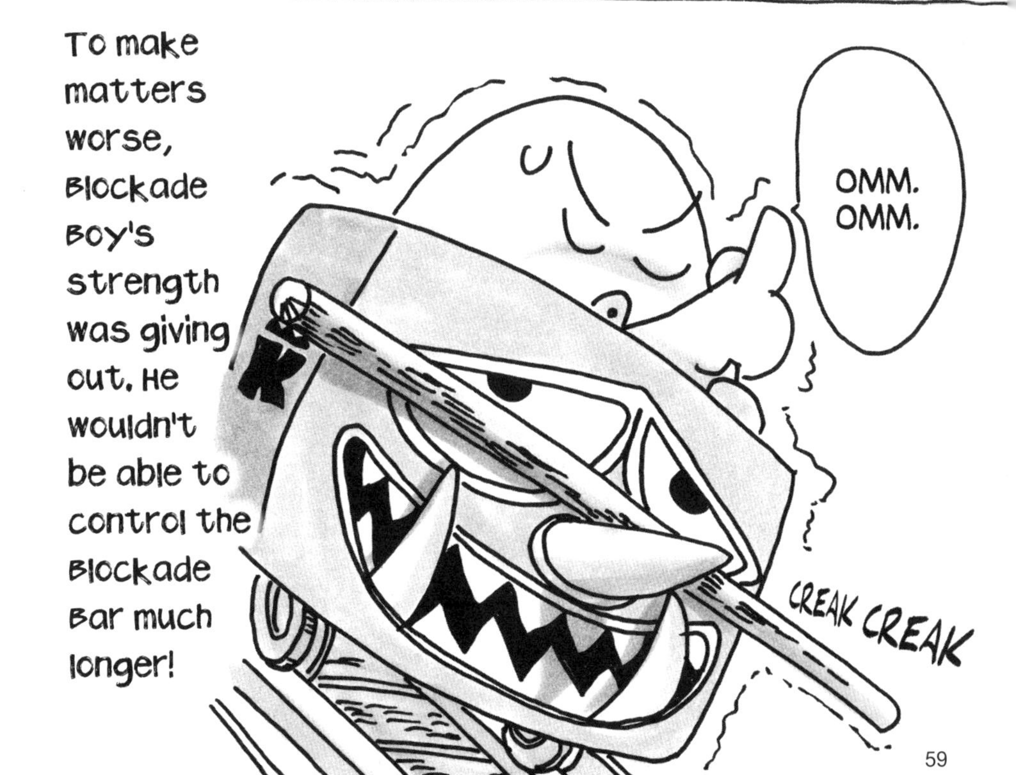
To make matters worse, Blockade Boy's strength was giving out. He wouldn't be able to control the Blockade Bar much longer!
OMM. OMM.
CREAK CREAK

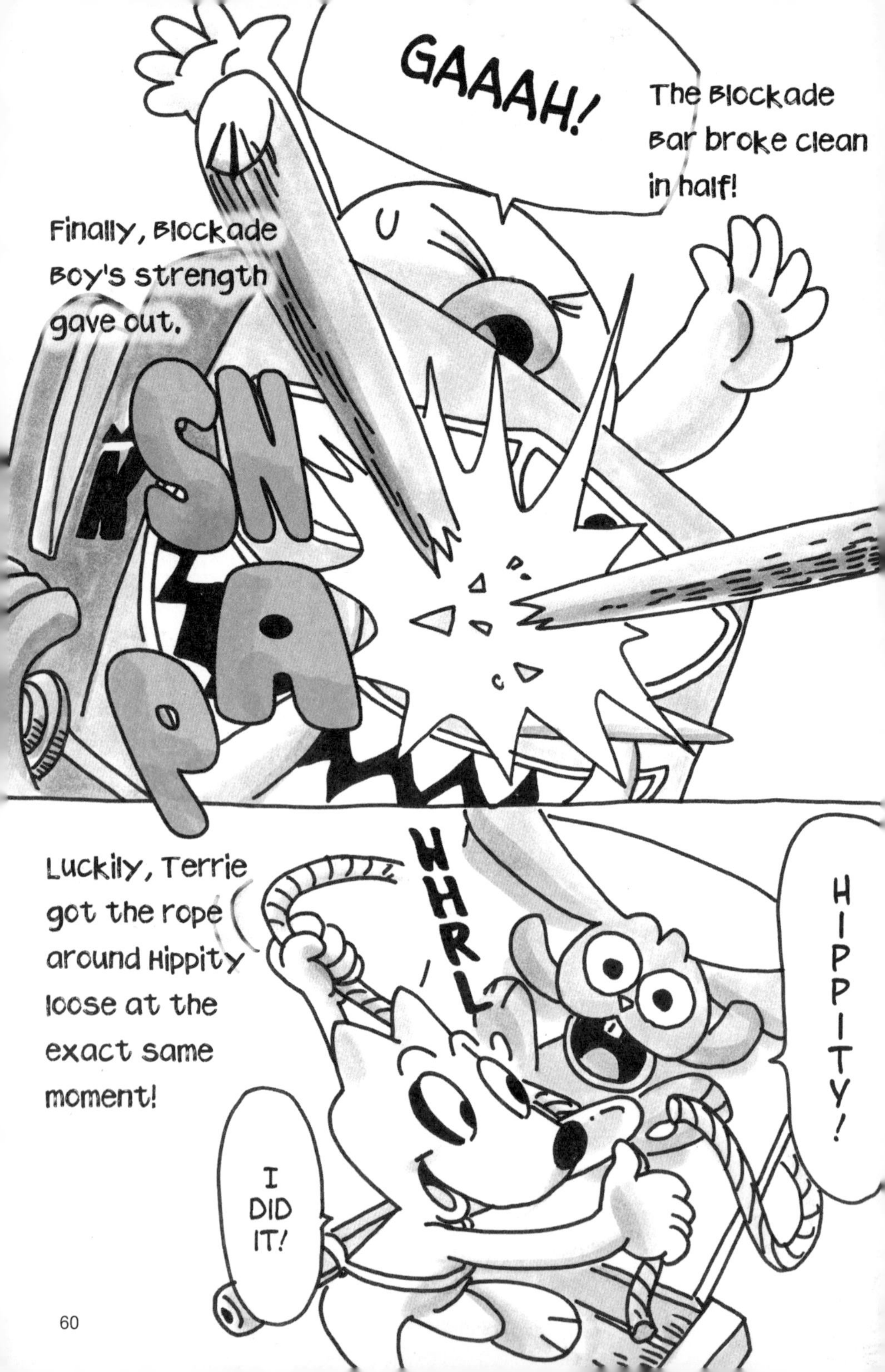
GAAAH!
The Blockade Bar broke clean in half!
Finally, Blockade Boy's strength gave out.
SNAP
Luckily, Terrie got the rope around Hippity loose at the exact same moment!
WHRL
HIPPITY!
I DID IT!

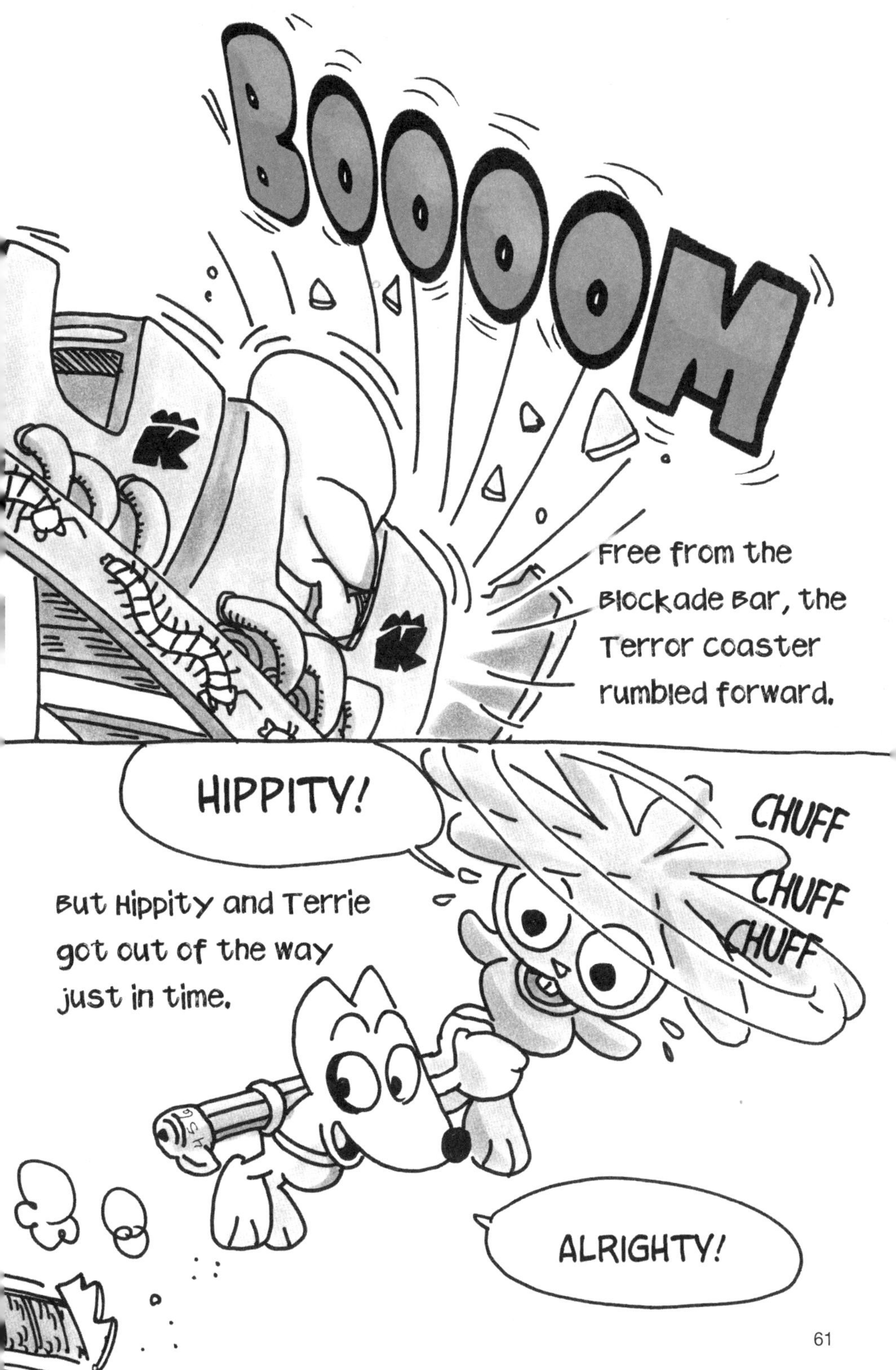
BOOOOOM
Free from the Blockade Bar, the Terror coaster rumbled forward.
HIPPITY!
CHUFF
CHUFF
CHUFF
But Hippity and Terrie got out of the way just in time.
ALRIGHTY!

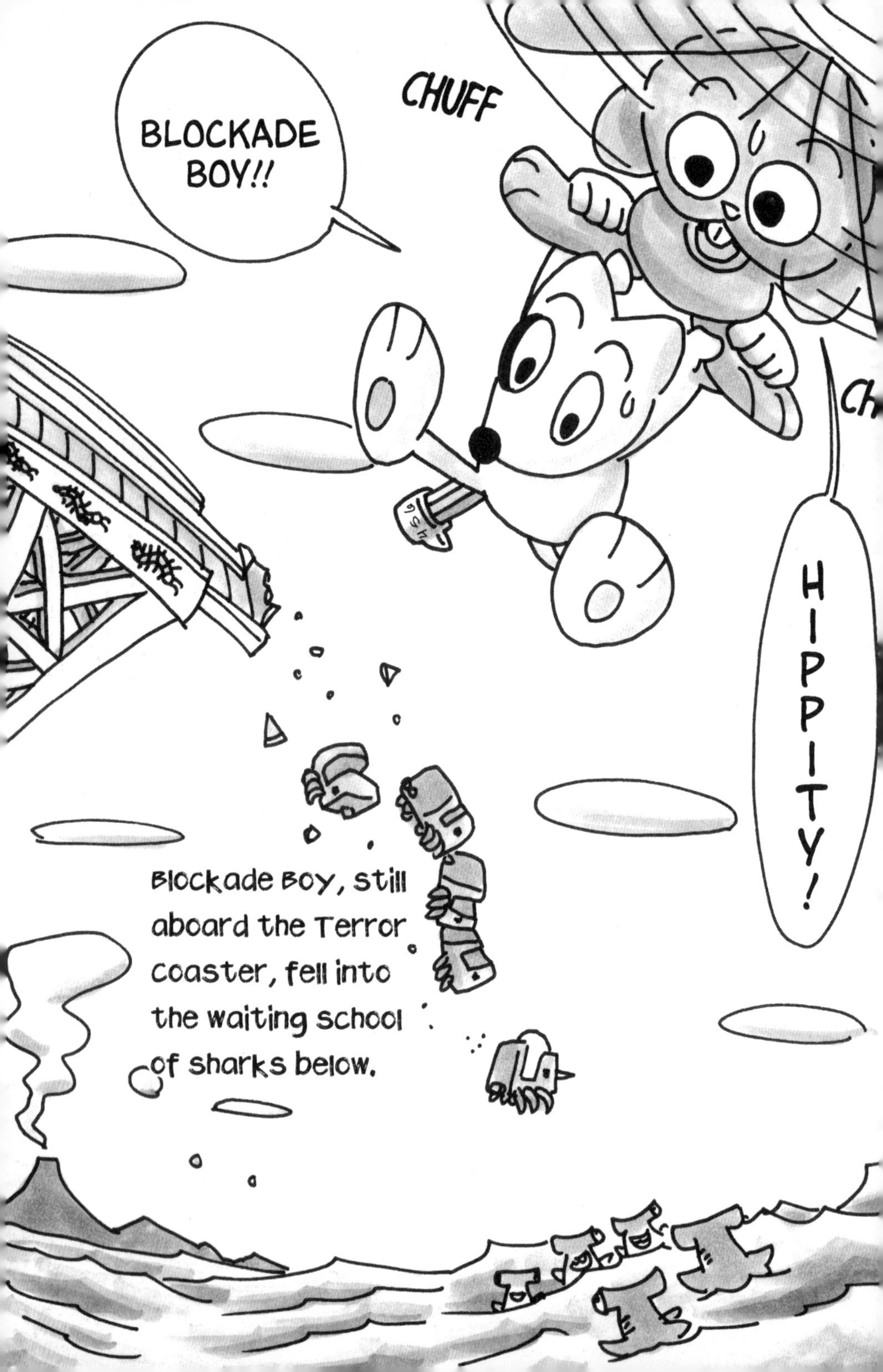
BLOCKADE BOY!!
CHUFF
HIPPITY!
Blockade Boy, still aboard the Terror coaster, fell into the waiting school of sharks below.

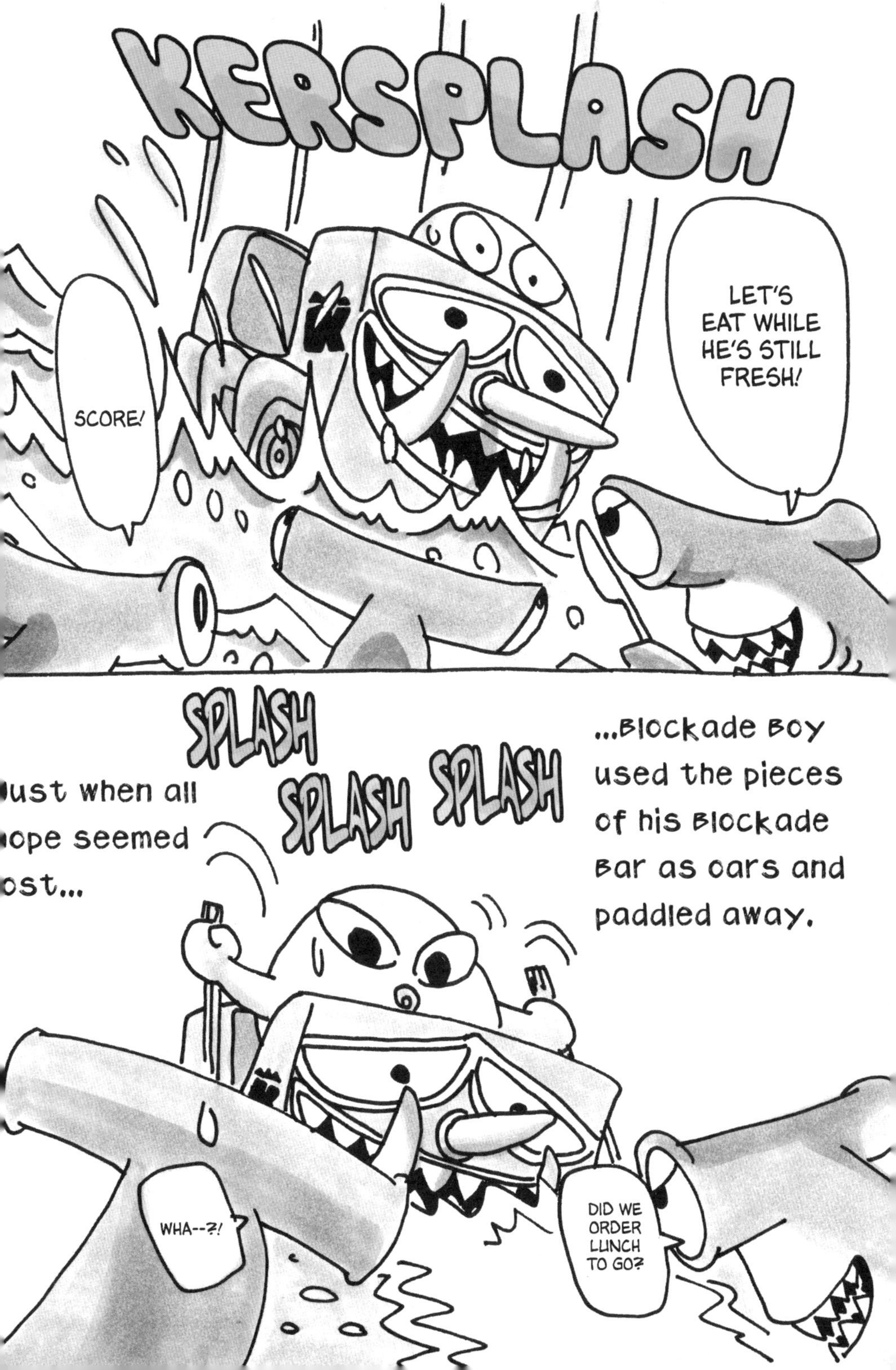
KERSPLASH
SCORE!
LET'S EAT WHILE HE'S STILL FRESH!
ust when all ope seemed ost...
SPLASH
SPLASH SPLASH
...Blockade Boy used the pieces of his Blockade Bar as oars and paddled away.
WHA--?!
DID WE ORDER LUNCH TO GO?

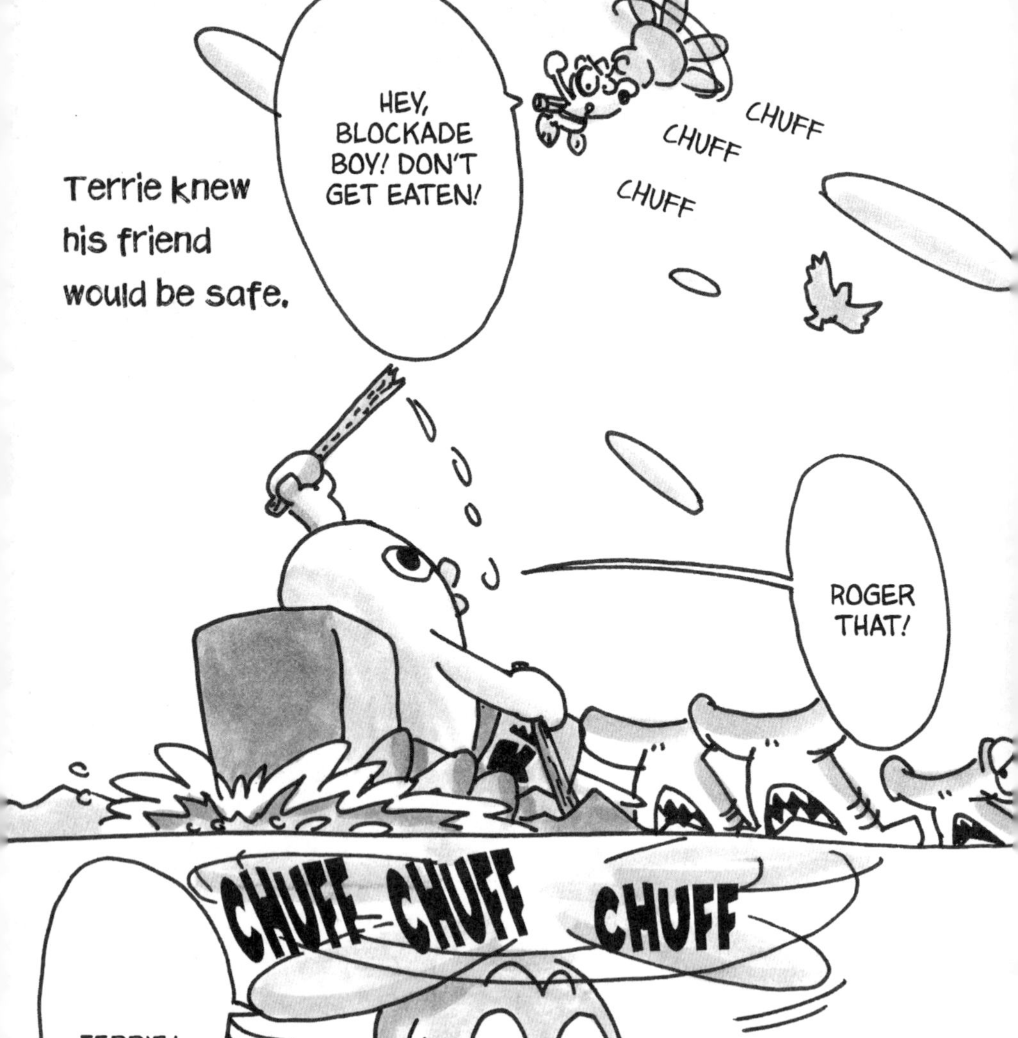
Terrie knew his friend would be safe.
HEY, BLOCKADE BOY! DON'T GET EATEN!
CHUFF
CHUFF
CHUFF
ROGER THAT!

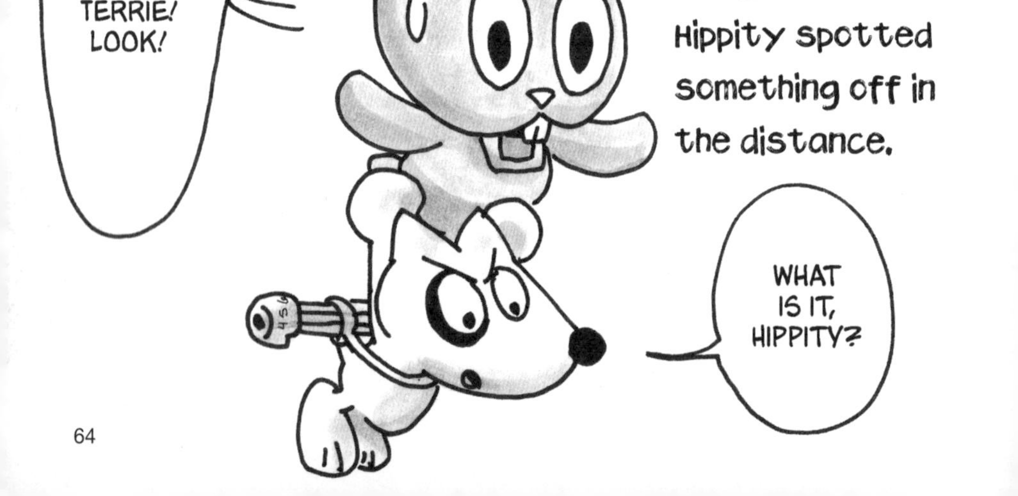
TERRIE! LOOK!
CHUFF CHUFF CHUFF
Hippity spotted something off in the distance.
WHAT IS IT, HIPPITY?

Having failed to defeat Terrie yet again, King Crossout fled to the haunted house.

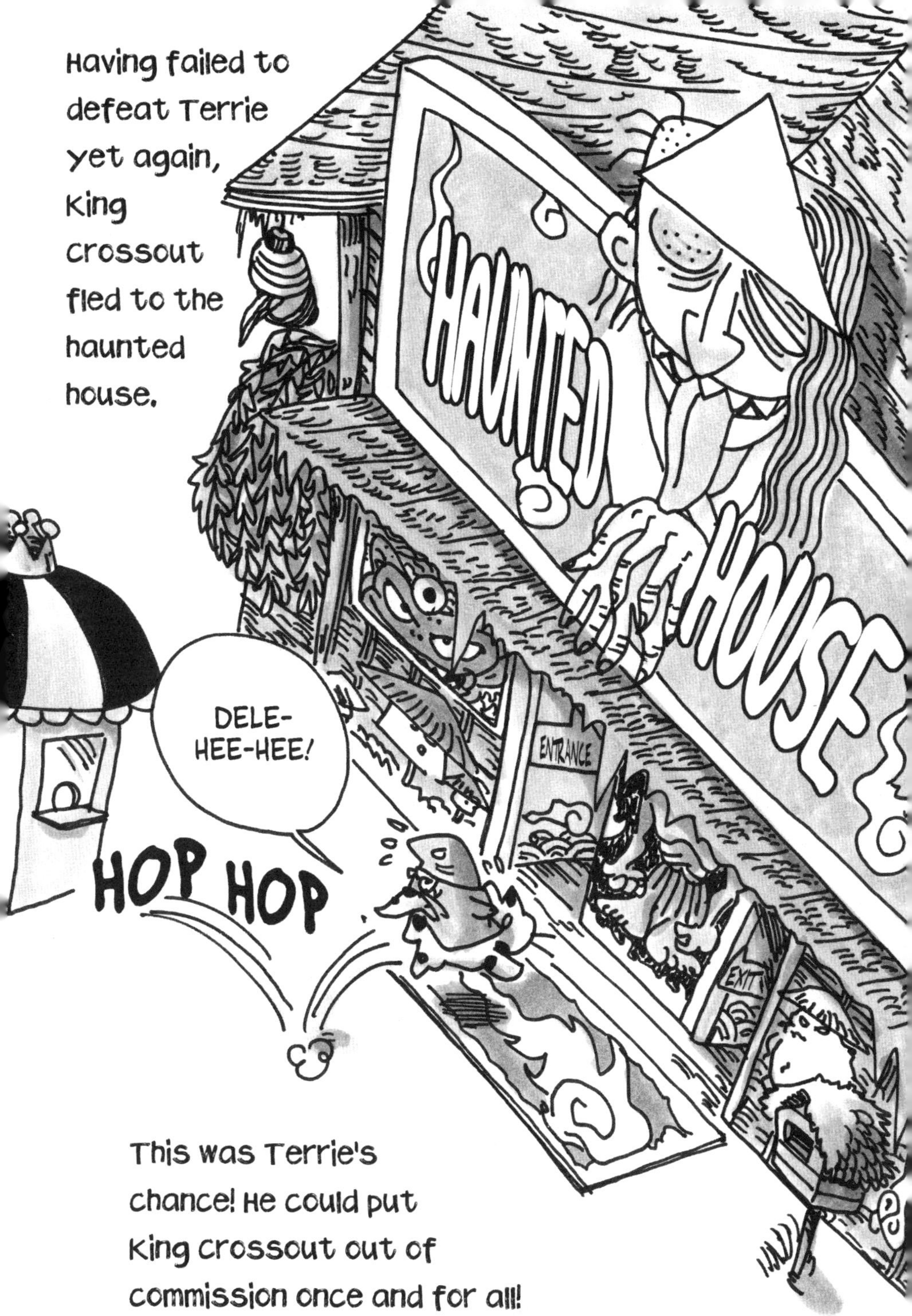
HAUNTED HOUSE
DELE-HEE-HEE!
ENTRANCE
HOP HOP
EXIT

This was Terrie's chance! He could put King Crossout out of commission once and for all!

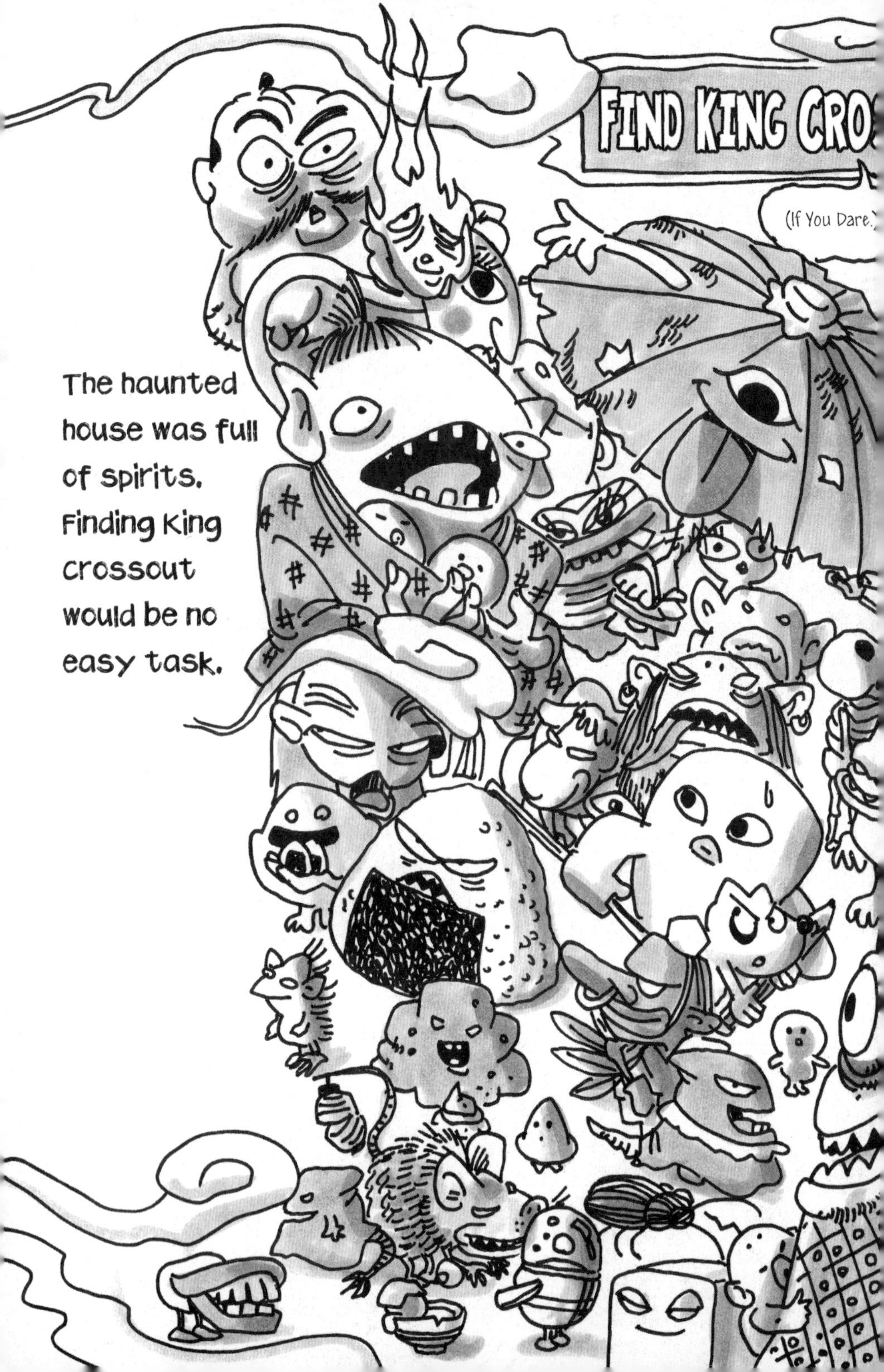
FIND KING CROS
(If You Dare.)
The haunted house was full of spirits. Finding King Crossout would be no easy task.

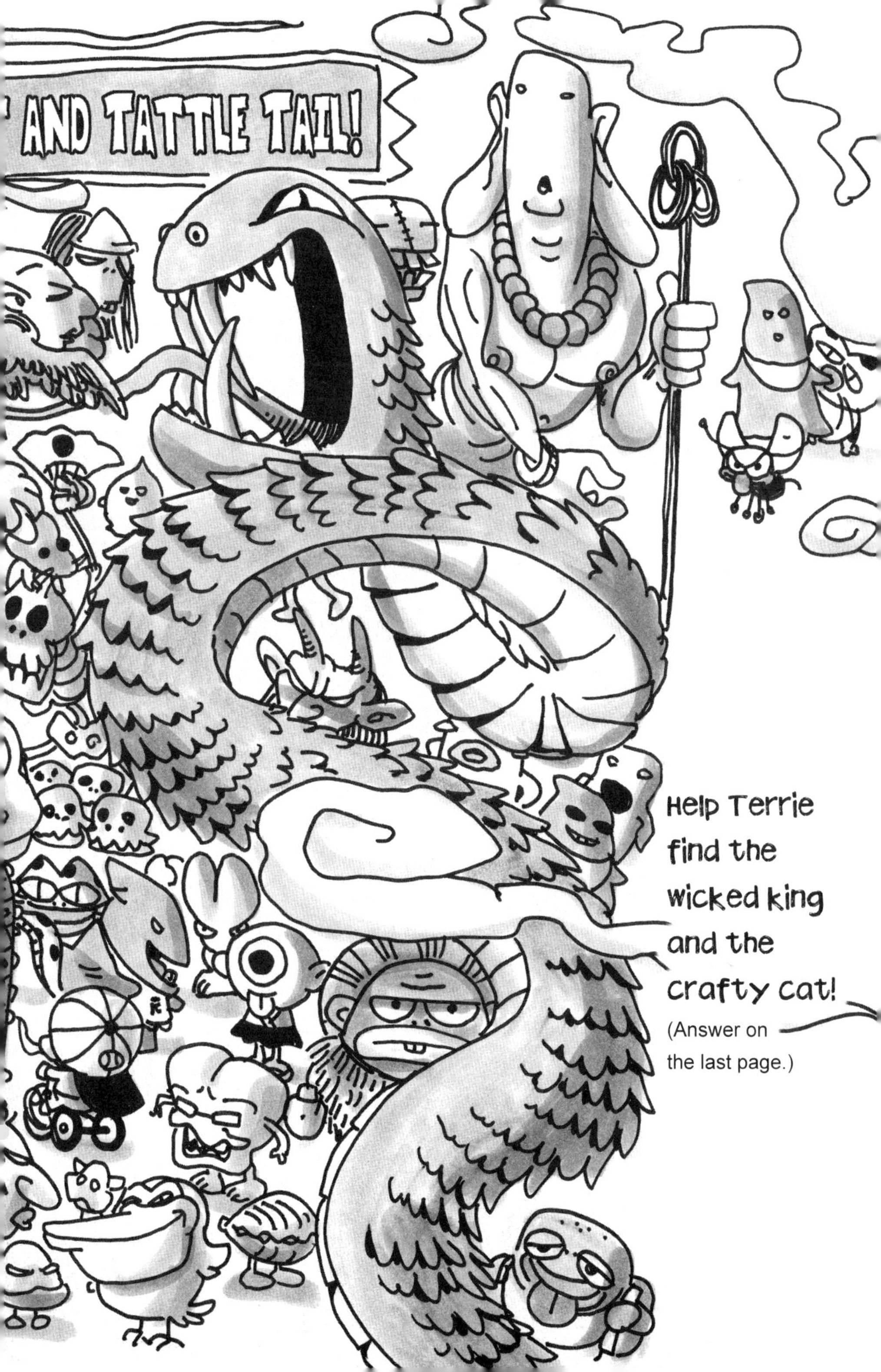
AND TATTLE TAIL!

Help Terrie find the wicked king and the crafty cat!

(Answer on the last page.)

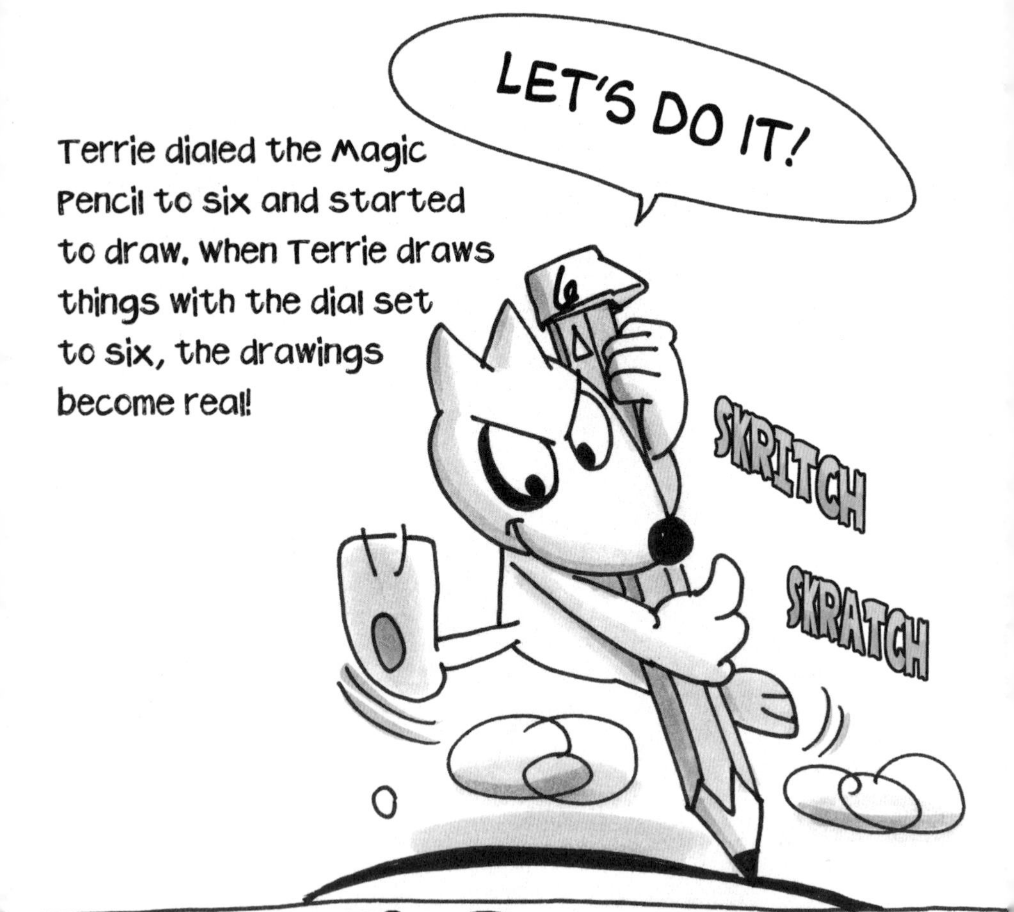
Terrie dialed the Magic Pencil to six and started to draw. When Terrie draws things with the dial set to six, the drawings become real!
LET'S DO IT!
SKRITCH
SKRATCH

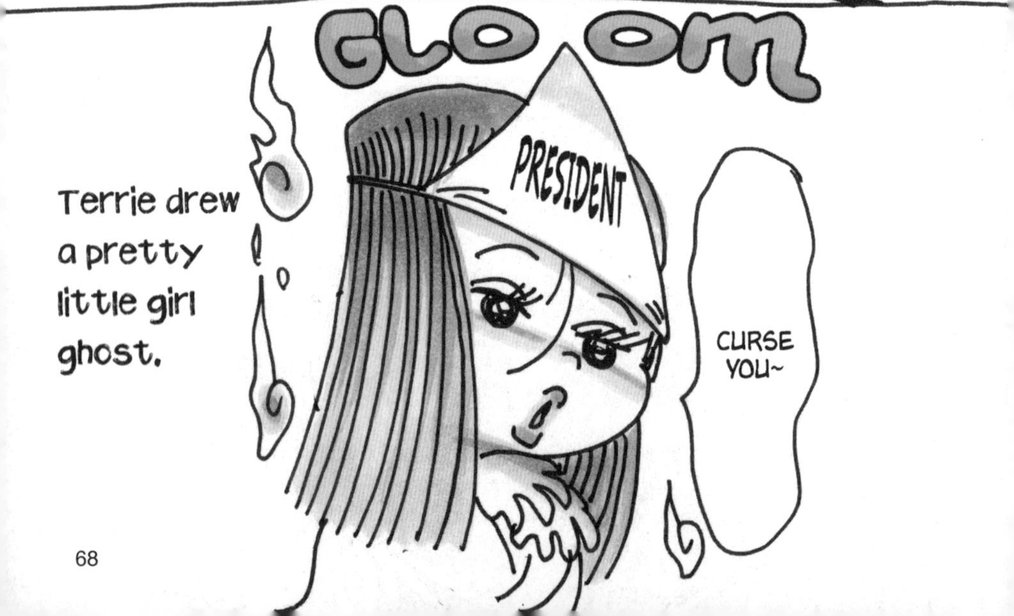
GLOOM
Terrie drew a pretty little girl ghost.
PRESIDENT
CURSE YOU~

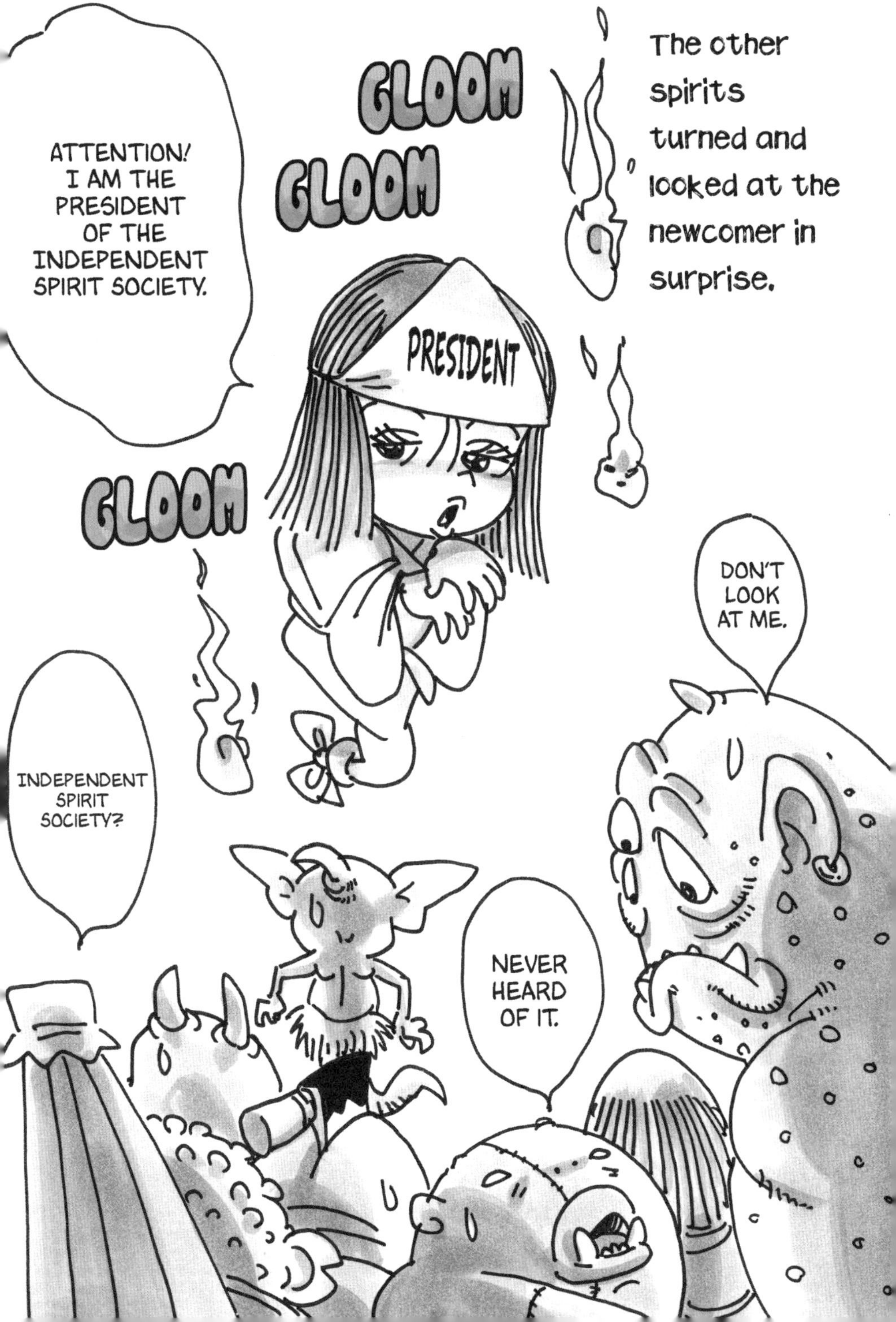

ATTENTION! I AM THE PRESIDENT OF THE INDEPENDENT SPIRIT SOCIETY.
GLOOM
GLOOM
The other spirits turned and looked at the newcomer in surprise.
PRESIDENT
GLOOM
DON'T LOOK AT ME.
INDEPENDENT SPIRIT SOCIETY?
NEVER HEARD OF IT.

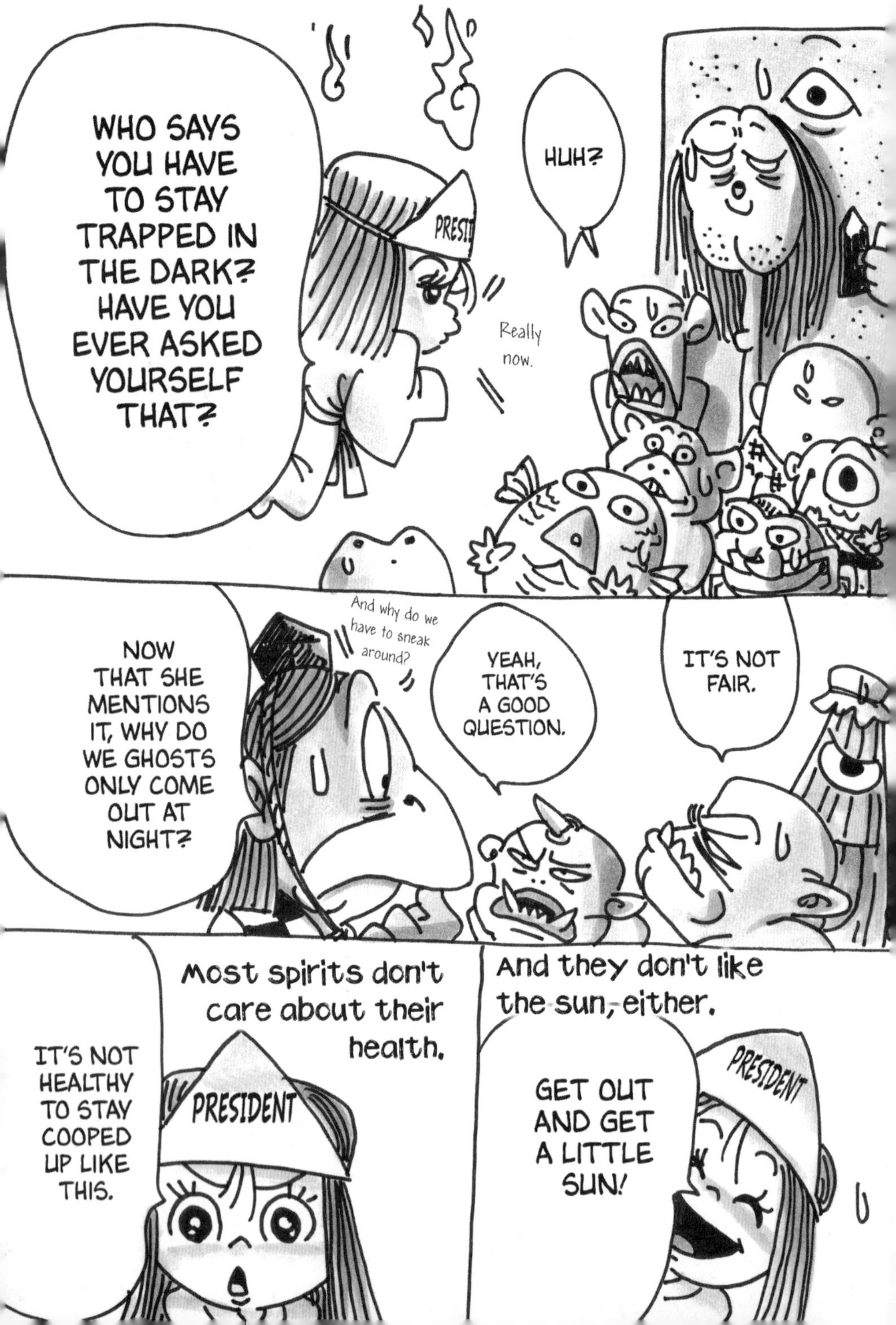
WHO SAYS YOU HAVE TO STAY TRAPPED IN THE DARK? HAVE YOU EVER ASKED YOURSELF THAT?
PRESI
HUH?
Really now.
NOW THAT SHE MENTIONS IT, WHY DO WE GHOSTS ONLY COME OUT AT NIGHT?
And why do we have to sneak around?
YEAH, THAT'S A GOOD QUESTION.
IT'S NOT FAIR.
Most spirits don't care about their health.
IT'S NOT HEALTHY TO STAY COOPED UP LIKE THIS.
PRESIDENT
And they don't like the sun, either.
PRESIDENT
GET OUT AND GET A LITTLE SUN!

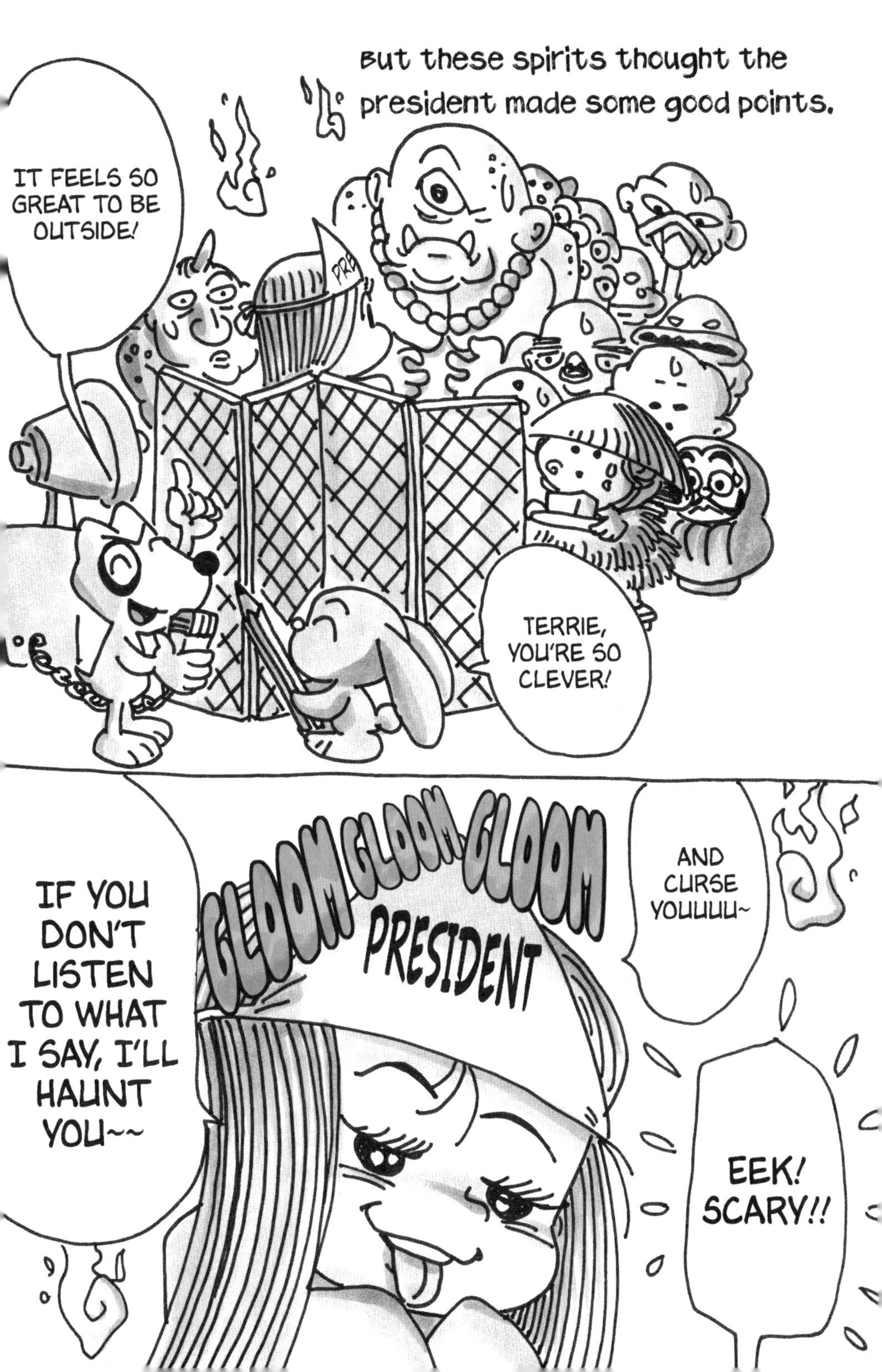
But these spirits thought the president made some good points.
IT FEELS SO GREAT TO BE OUTSIDE!
PRE
TERRIE, YOU'RE SO CLEVER!
GLOOM GLOOM GLOOM
PRESIDENT
AND CURSE YOUUUU~
IF YOU DON'T LISTEN TO WHAT I SAY, I'LL HAUNT YOU~~
EEK! SCARY!!

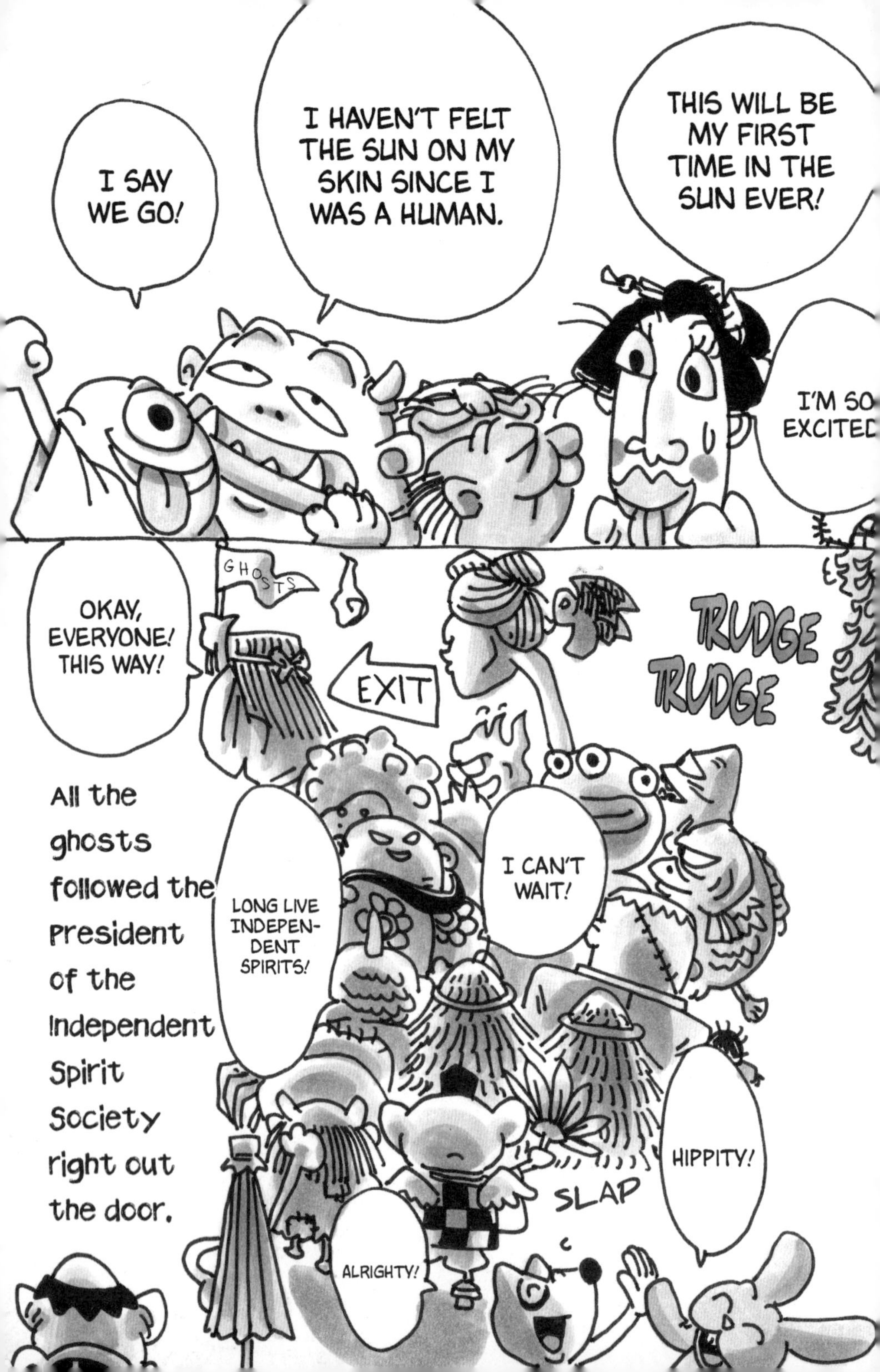

I SAY WE GO!
I HAVEN'T FELT THE SUN ON MY SKIN SINCE I WAS A HUMAN.
THIS WILL BE MY FIRST TIME IN THE SUN EVER!
I'M SO EXCITED
GHOSTS
OKAY, EVERYONE! THIS WAY!
EXIT
TRUDGE TRUDGE
All the ghosts followed the President of the Independent Spirit Society right out the door.
LONG LIVE INDEPEN-DENT SPIRITS!
I CAN'T WAIT!
HIPPITY!
SLAP
ALRIGHTY!

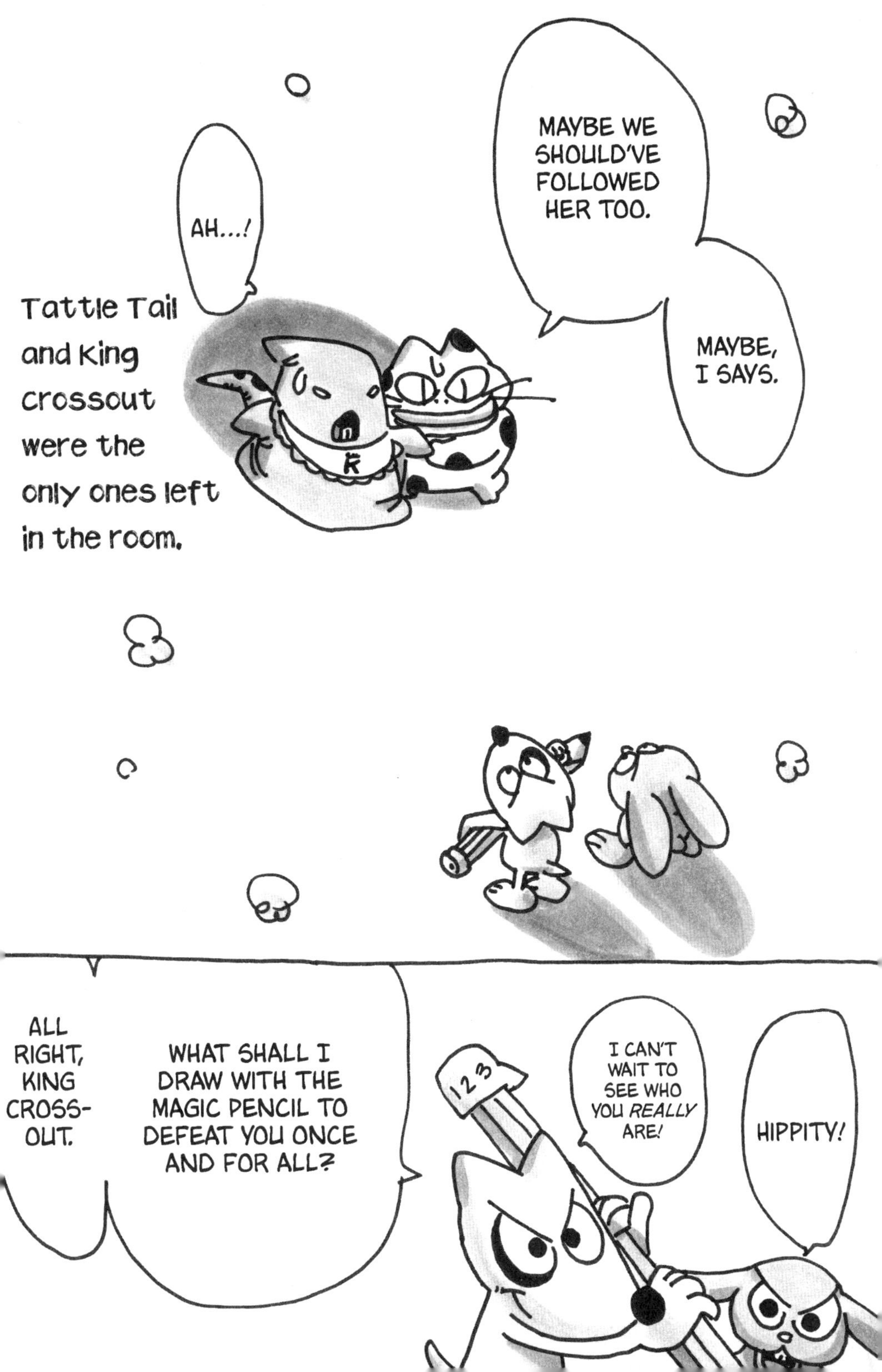
Tattle Tail and King crossout were the only ones left in the room.
AH...!
MAYBE WE SHOULD'VE FOLLOWED HER TOO.
MAYBE, I SAYS.
ALL RIGHT, KING CROSS-OUT.
WHAT SHALL I DRAW WITH THE MAGIC PENCIL TO DEFEAT YOU ONCE AND FOR ALL?
I CAN'T WAIT TO SEE WHO YOU *REALLY* ARE!
HIPPITY!

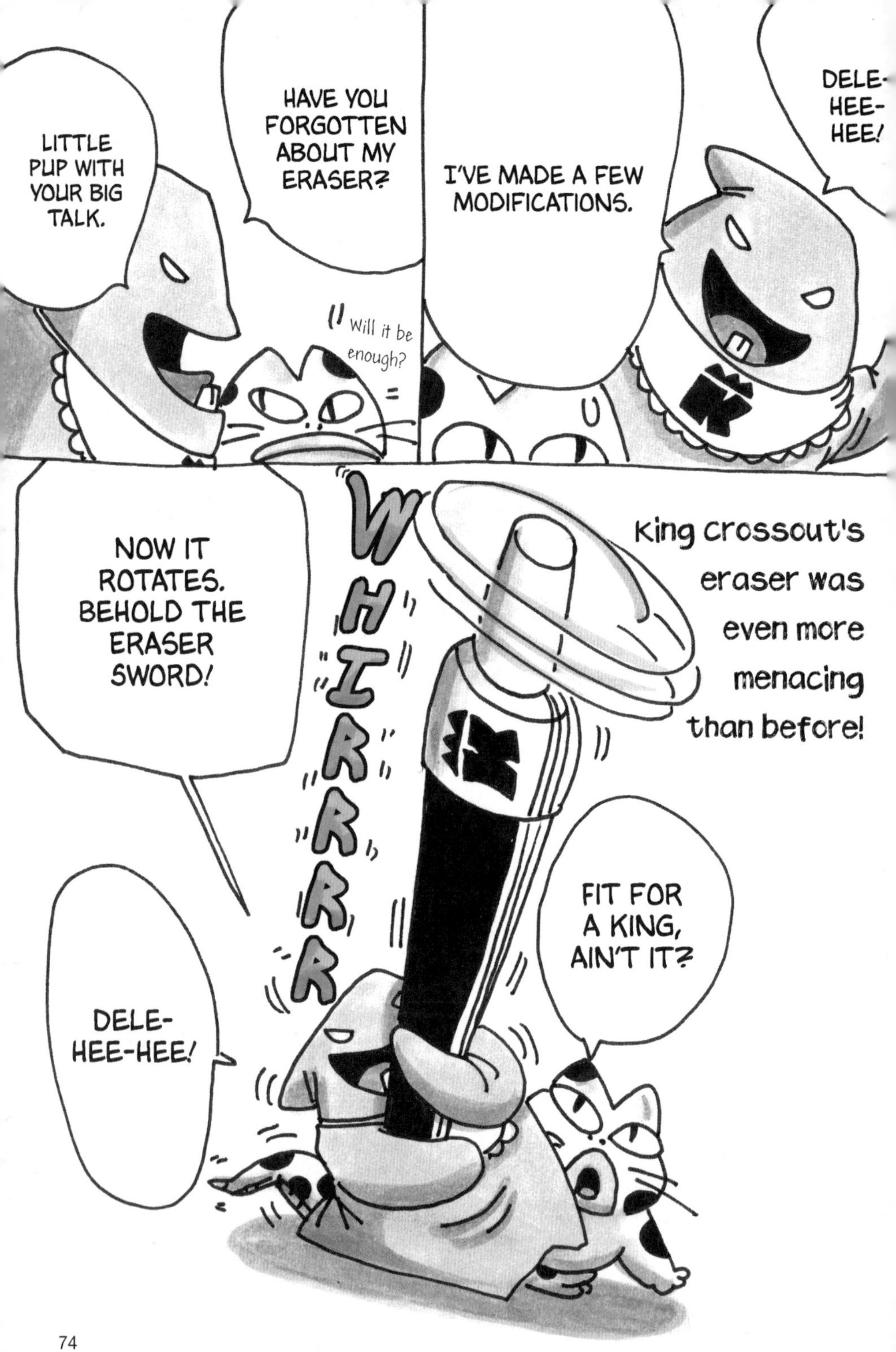

LITTLE PUP WITH YOUR BIG TALK.
HAVE YOU FORGOTTEN ABOUT MY ERASER?
Will it be enough?
I'VE MADE A FEW MODIFICATIONS.
DELE-HEE-HEE!
NOW IT ROTATES. BEHOLD THE ERASER SWORD!
WHIRRRRR
King Crossout's eraser was even more menacing than before!
FIT FOR A KING, AIN'T IT?
DELE-HEE-HEE!

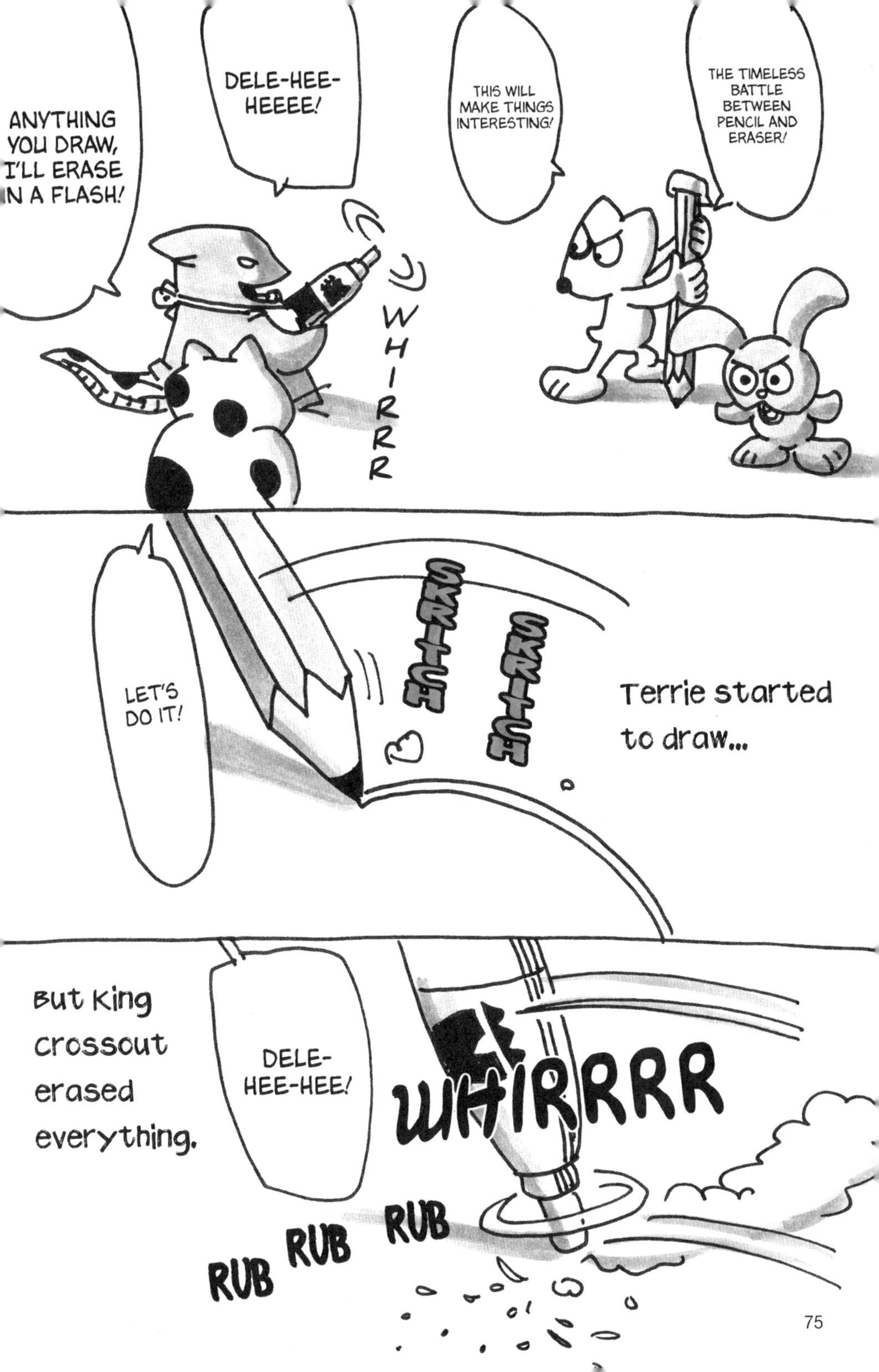
ANYTHING YOU DRAW, I'LL ERASE IN A FLASH!
DELE-HEE-HEEEE!
WHIRRR
THIS WILL MAKE THINGS INTERESTING!
THE TIMELESS BATTLE BETWEEN PENCIL AND ERASER!
LET'S DO IT!
SKRITCH
SKRITCH
Terrie started to draw...
But King crossout erased everything.
DELE-HEE-HEE!
WHIRRRR
RUB
RUB
RUB

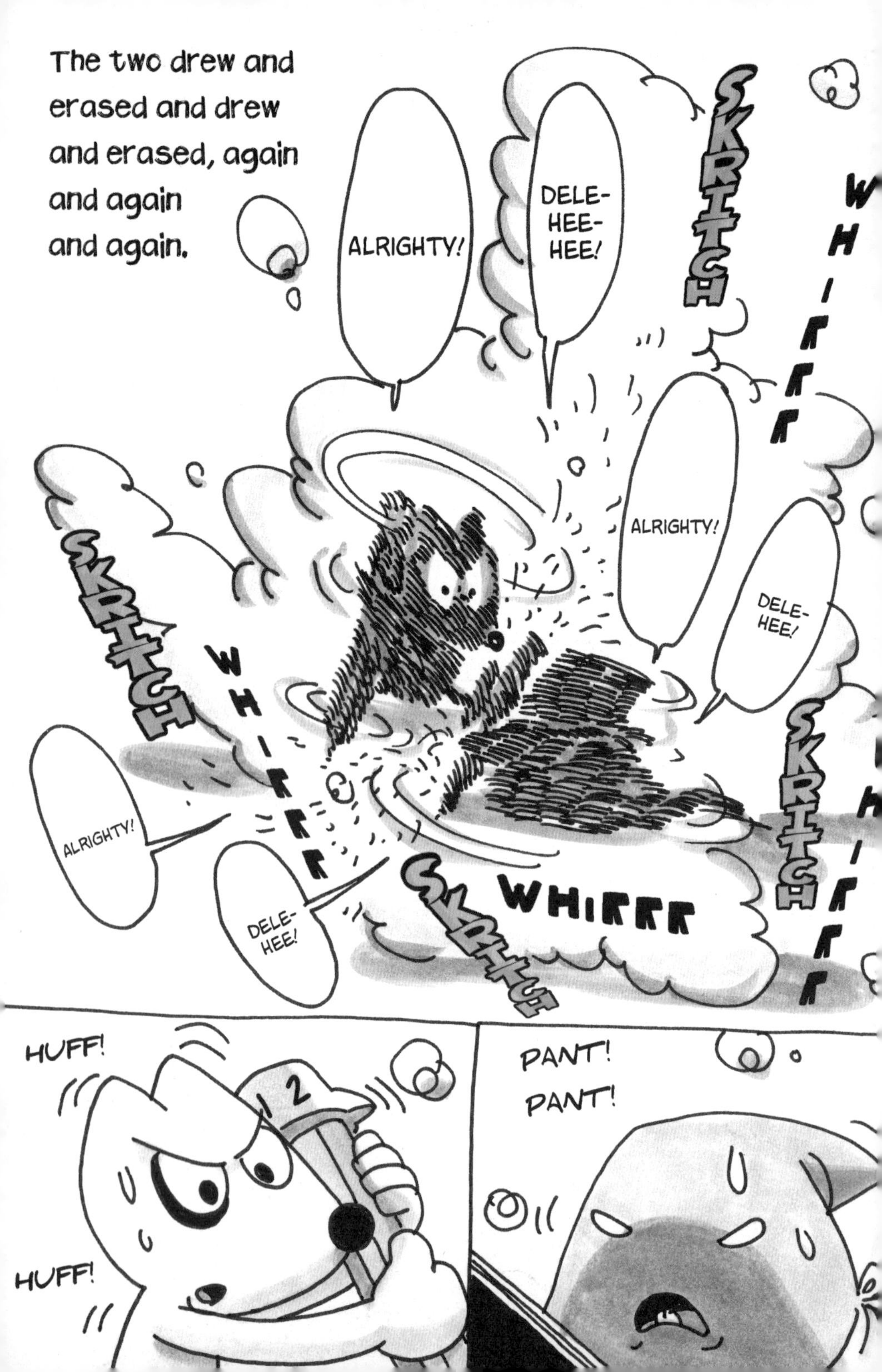
The two drew and erased and drew and erased, again and again and again.
ALRIGHTY!
DELE-HEE-HEE!
SKRITCH
WHIRRR
ALRIGHTY!
DELE-HEE!
SKRITCH
WHIRRR
ALRIGHTY!
DELE-HEE!
SKRITCH
WHIRRR
SKRITCH
WHIRRRR
HUFF!
HUFF!
PANT!
PANT!

The two had fought hard, and both the Magic Pencil and King Crossout's rotating eraser were worn to nubs.

Once the tip of the Magic Pencil was gone, Terrie would have to go back to the real world. Once the eraser was gone, King Crossout would lose all of his power.

OH WELL, TERRIE. HEH. HEH. I'LL LET YOU GO FOR TODAY.

SUCH A COWARD. A COWARD, I SAYS.

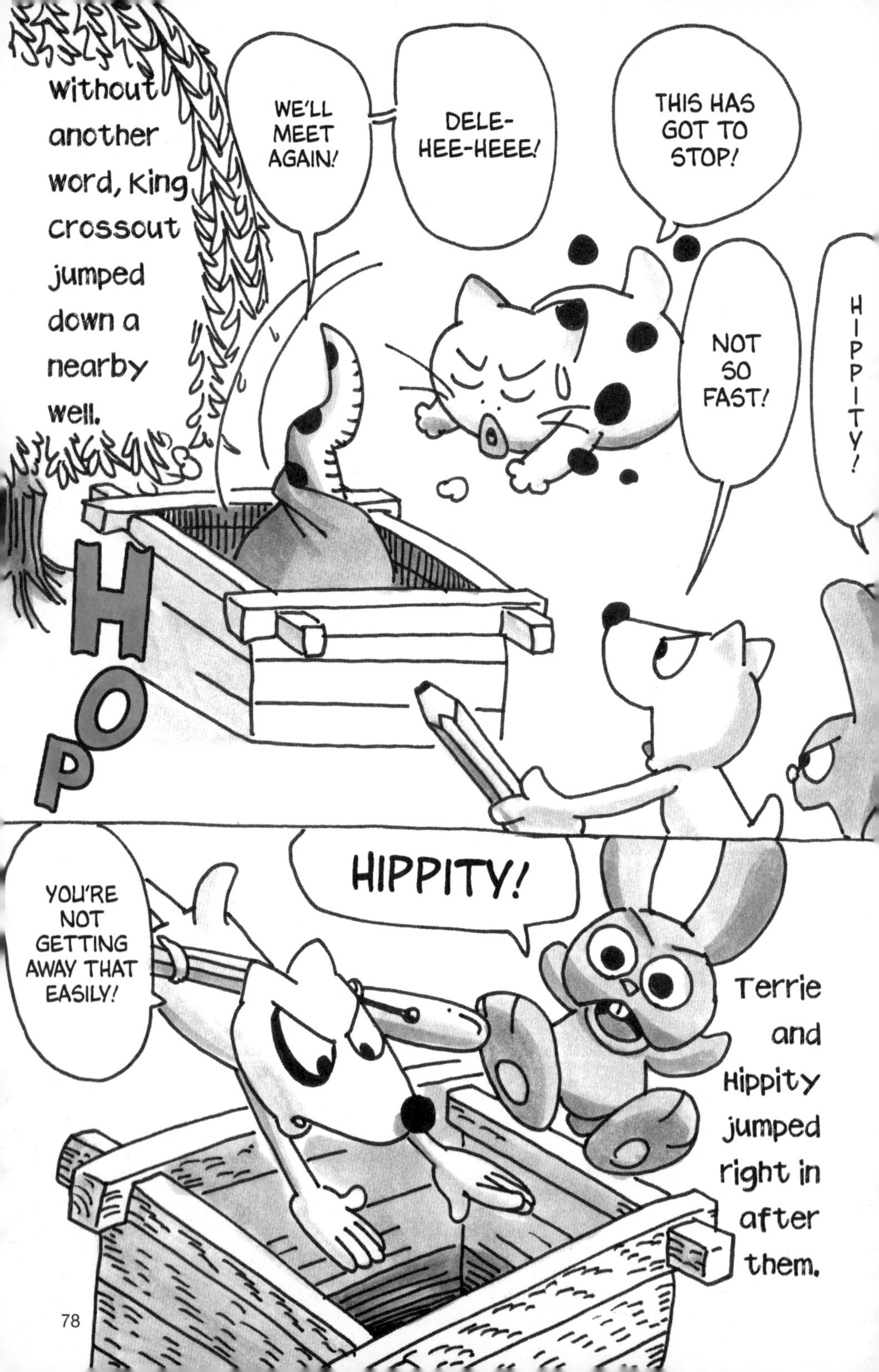
without another word, King crossout jumped down a nearby well.
WE'LL MEET AGAIN!
DELE-HEE-HEEE!
THIS HAS GOT TO STOP!
NOT SO FAST!
HIPPITY!
HOP
YOU'RE NOT GETTING AWAY THAT EASILY!
HIPPITY!
Terrie and Hippity jumped right in after them.

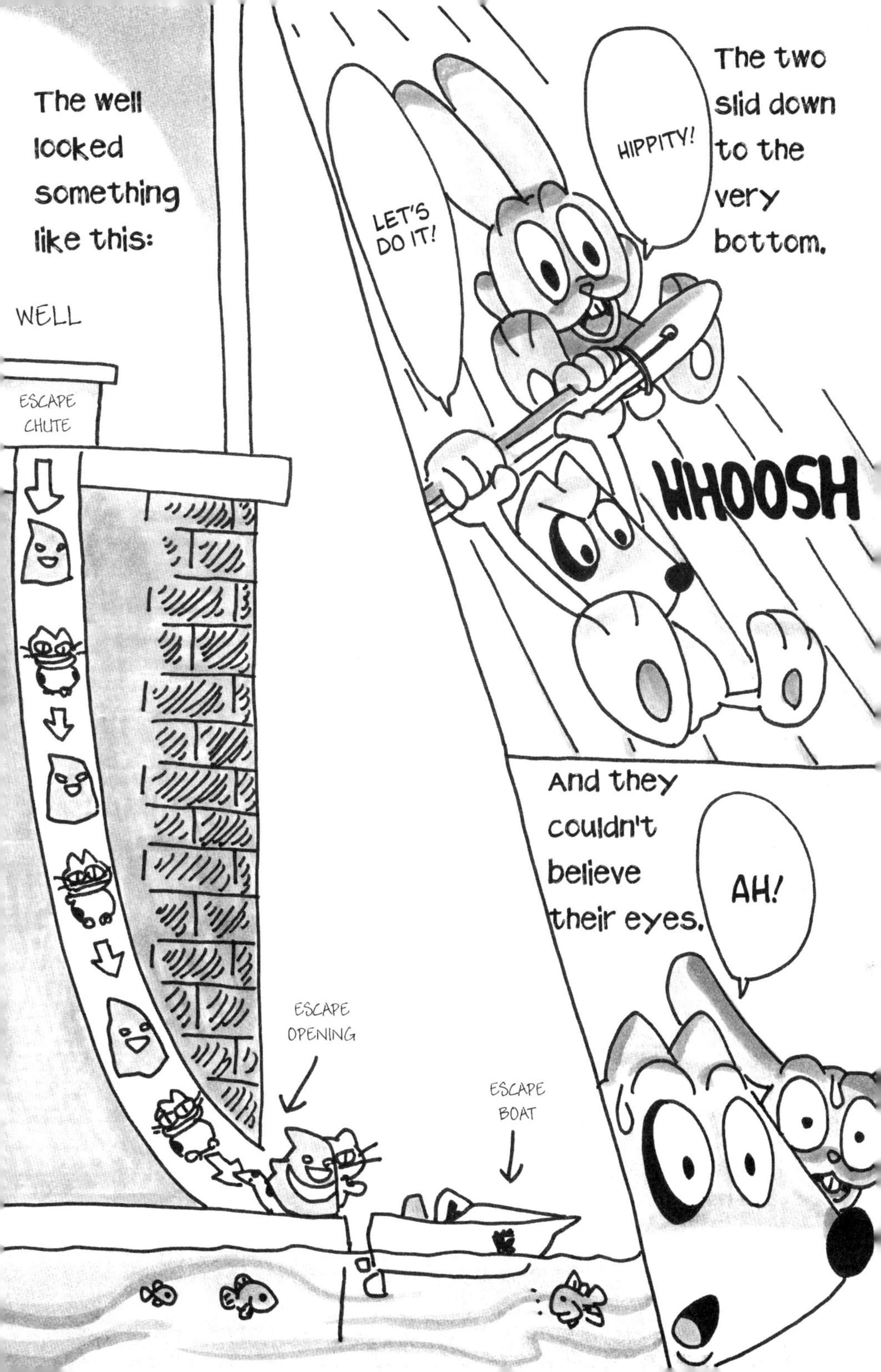
The well looked something like this:
WELL
ESCAPE CHUTE
ESCAPE OPENING
ESCAPE BOAT
The two slid down to the very bottom.
LET'S DO IT!
HIPPITY!
WHOOSH
And they couldn't believe their eyes.
AH!

King crossout and Tattle Tail were completely surrounded by the shark brothers. They were stuck.

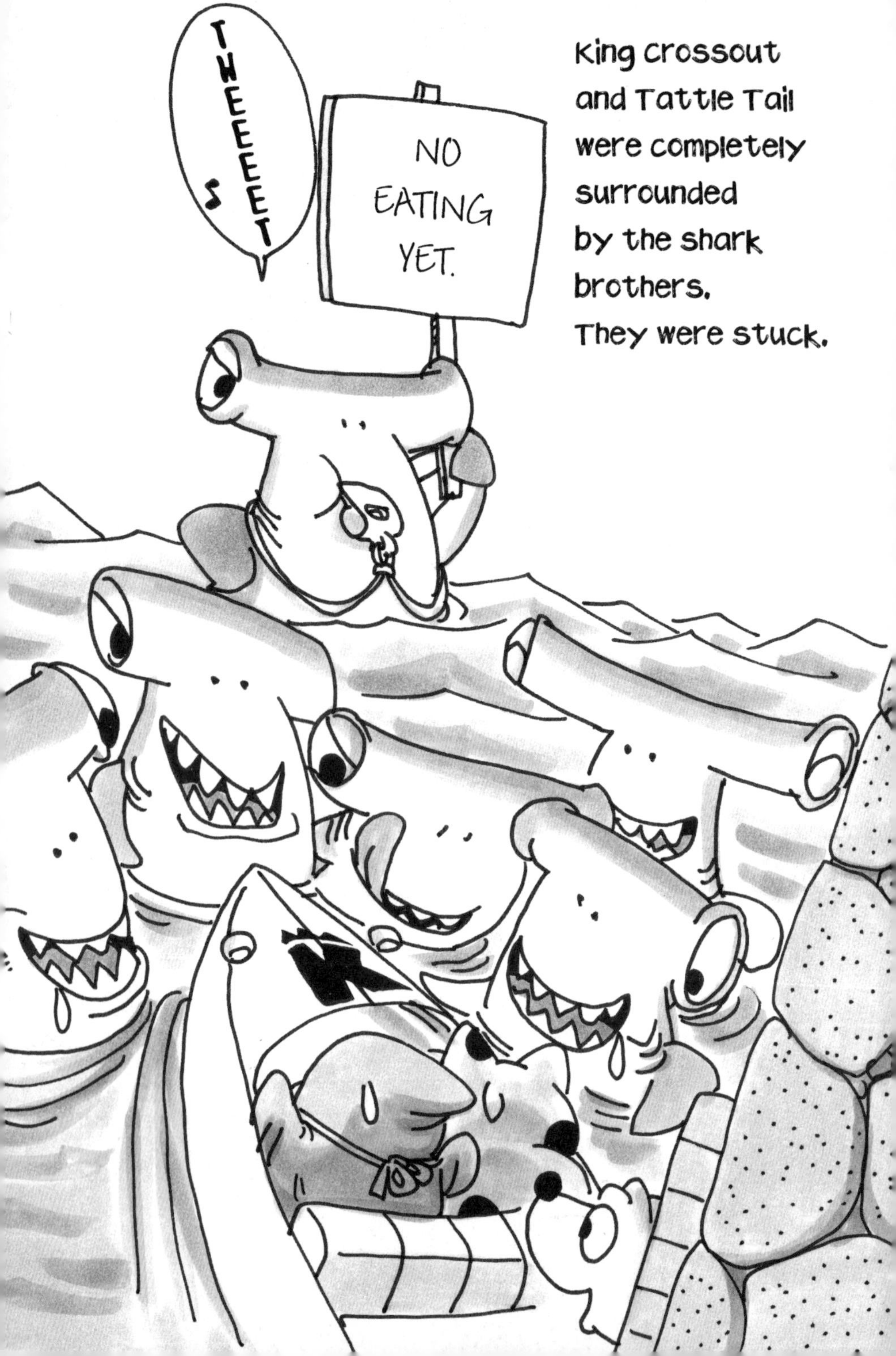
TWEEEET
NO EATING YET.

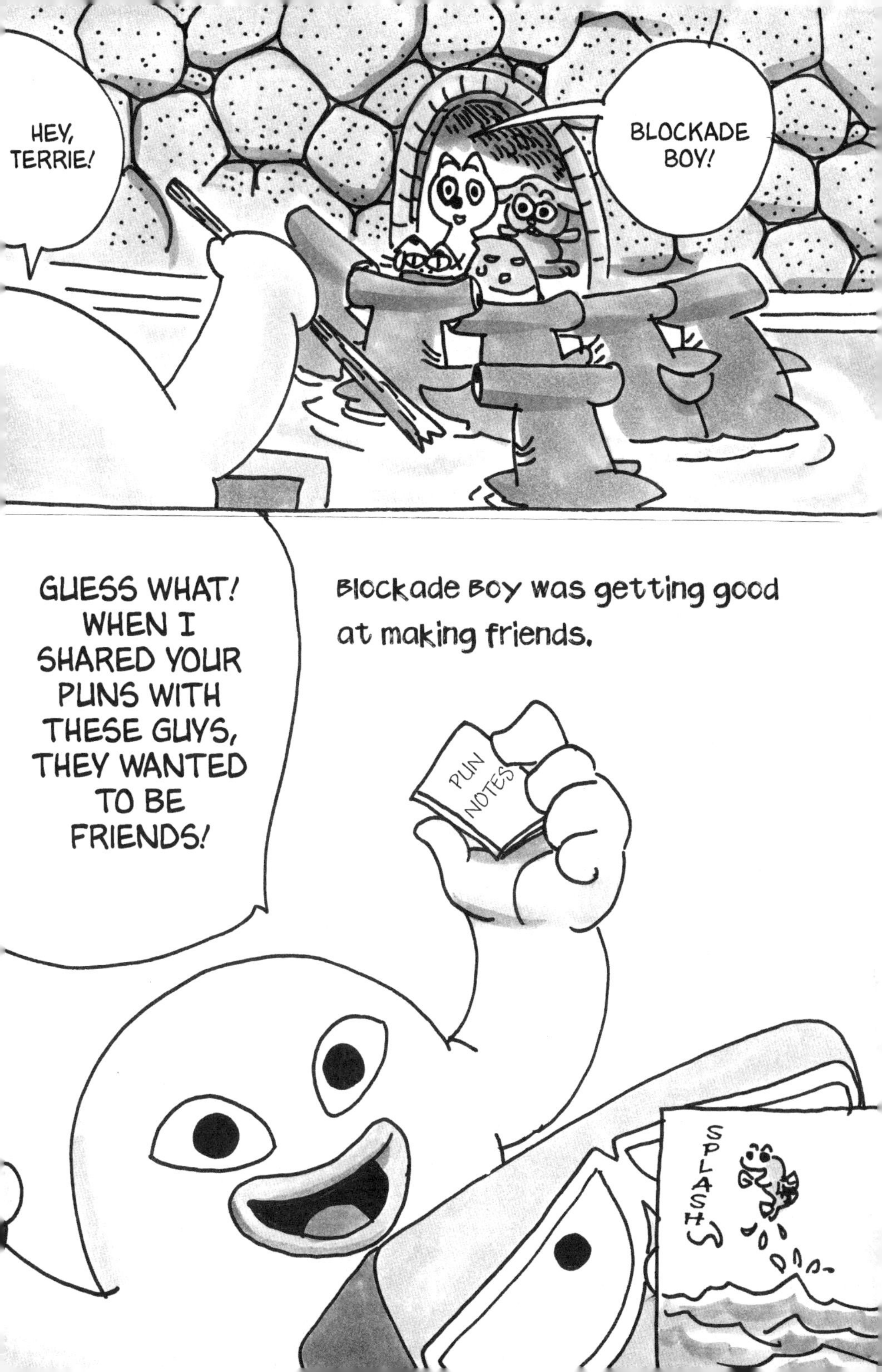
HEY, TERRIE!
BLOCKADE BOY!
GUESS WHAT! WHEN I SHARED YOUR PUNS WITH THESE GUYS, THEY WANTED TO BE FRIENDS!
Blockade Boy was getting good at making friends.
PUN NOTES
SPLASH

Terrie took away King Crossout's eraser and tied him and Tattle Tail tight.

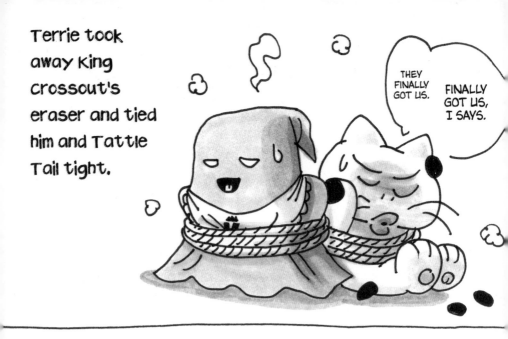

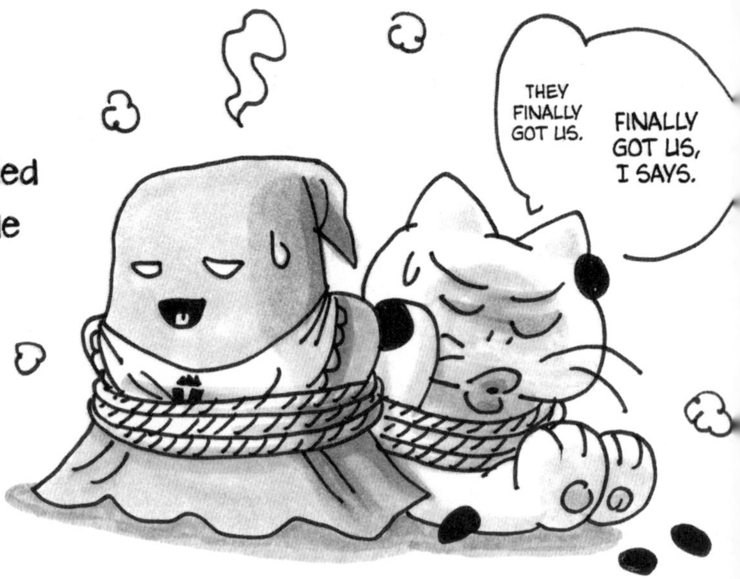
THEY FINALLY GOT US.
FINALLY GOT US, I SAYS.

At long last, King Crossout's true identity would be revealed.

What horrible face was beneath Crossout's cloak?

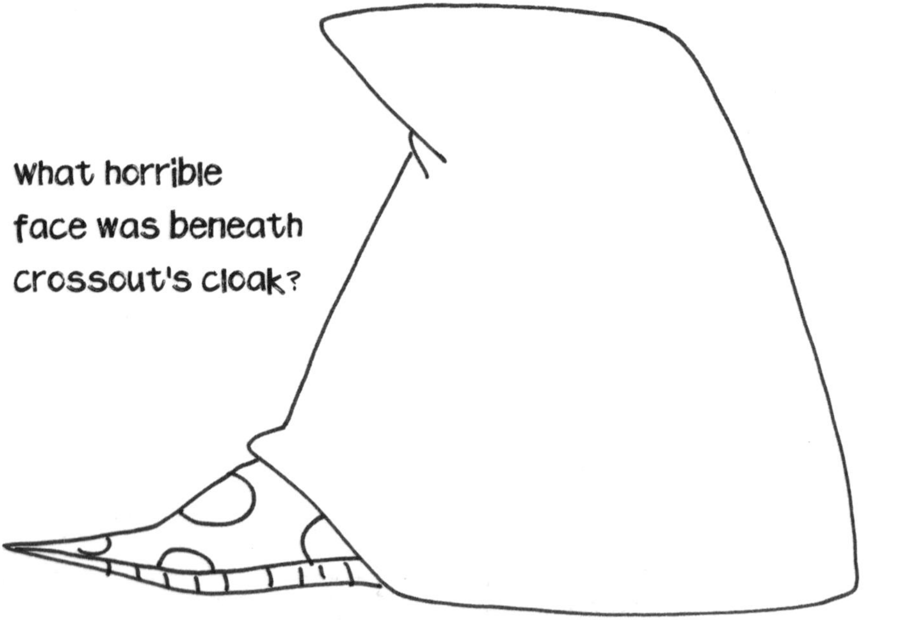

What do you think King Crossout looks like?
(Draw your own King Crossout above!)

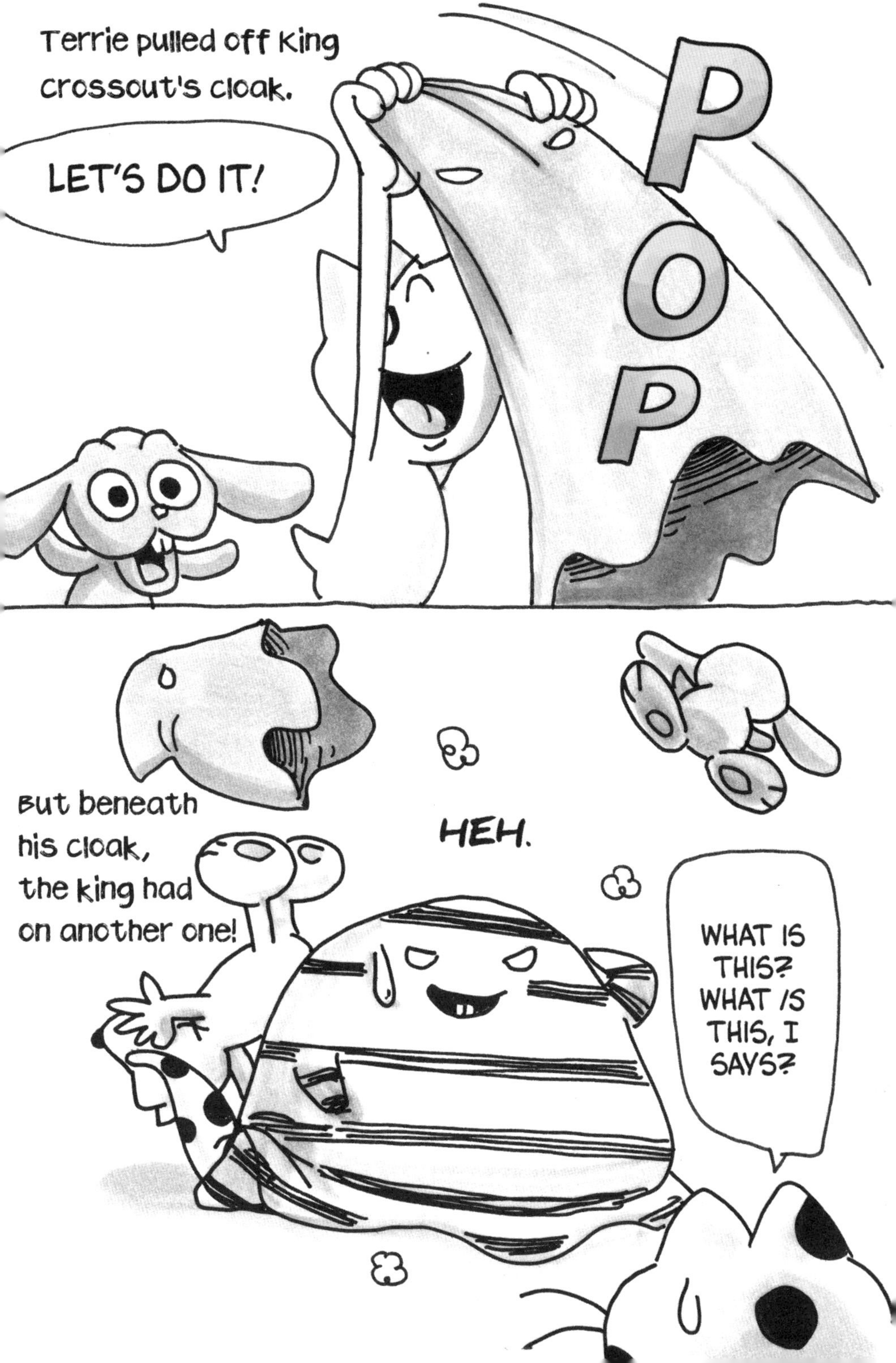
Terrie pulled off King Crossout's cloak.
LET'S DO IT!
POP
But beneath his cloak, the king had on another one!
HEH.
WHAT IS THIS? WHAT IS THIS, I SAYS?

KING CROSSOUT'S SEVEN COSTUME CHANGES

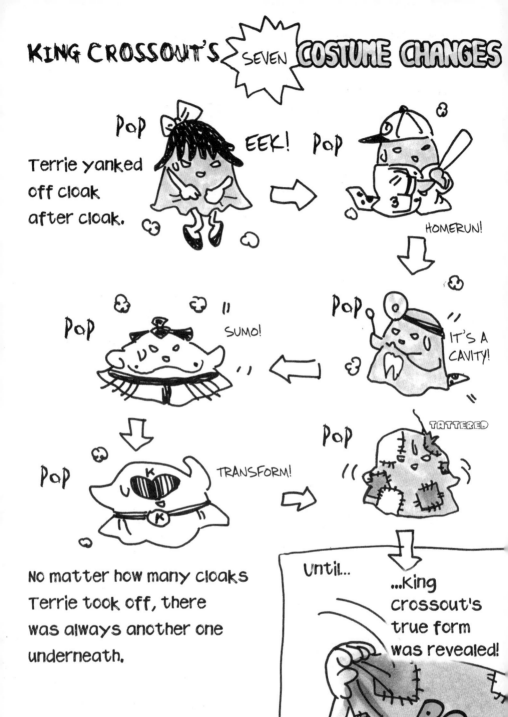

POP

EEK! POP

Terrie yanked off cloak after cloak.

HOMERUN!

POP

SUMO!

POP

IT'S A CAVITY!

POP

TRANSFORM!

POP

TATTERED

No matter how many cloaks Terrie took off, there was always another one underneath.

Until...

...King crossout's true form was revealed!

POP

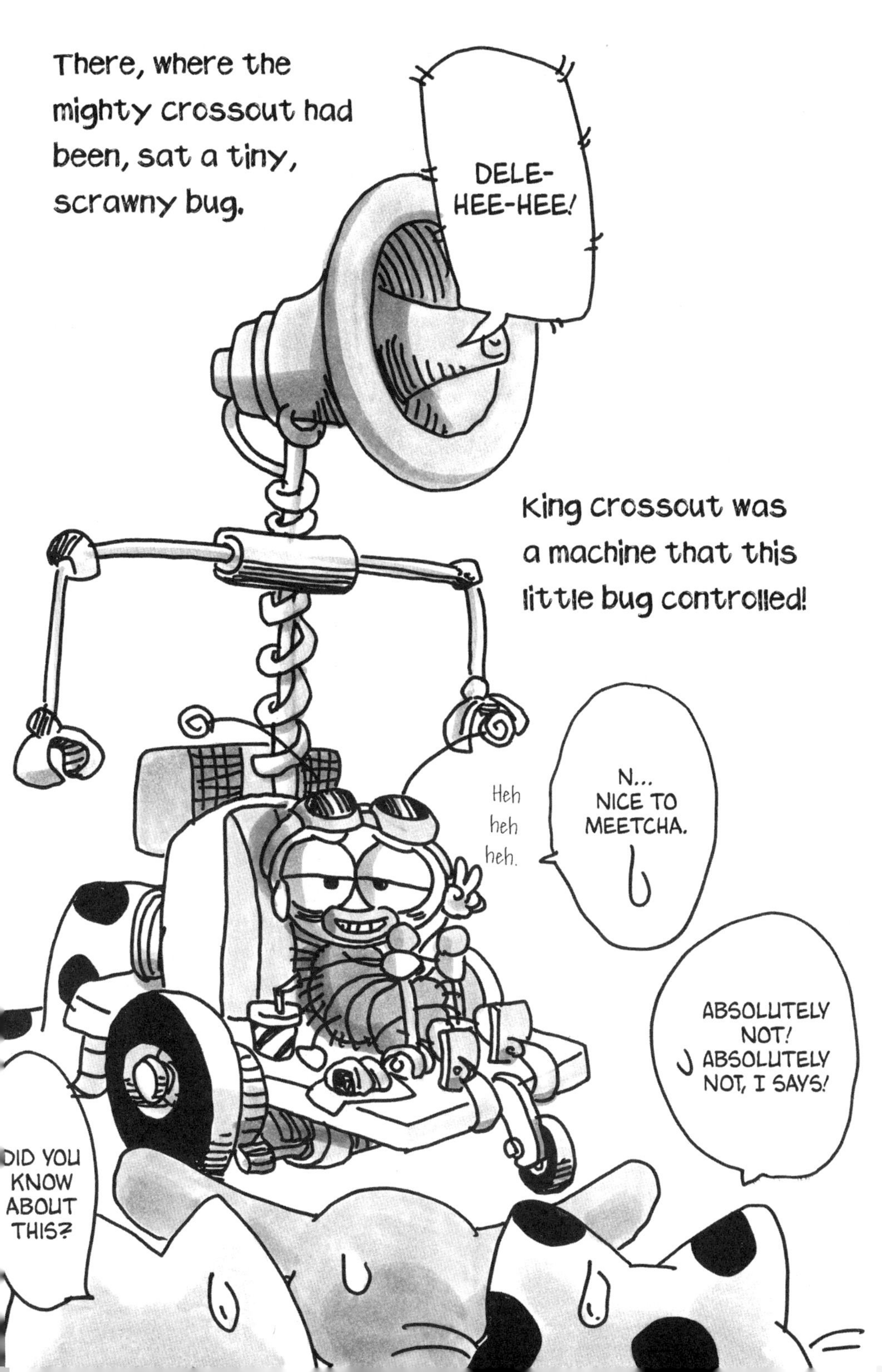
There, where the mighty crossout had been, sat a tiny, scrawny bug.
DELE-HEE-HEE!
King crossout was a machine that this little bug controlled!
Heh heh heh.
N... NICE TO MEETCHA.
ABSOLUTELY NOT! ABSOLUTELY NOT, I SAYS!
DID YOU KNOW ABOUT THIS?

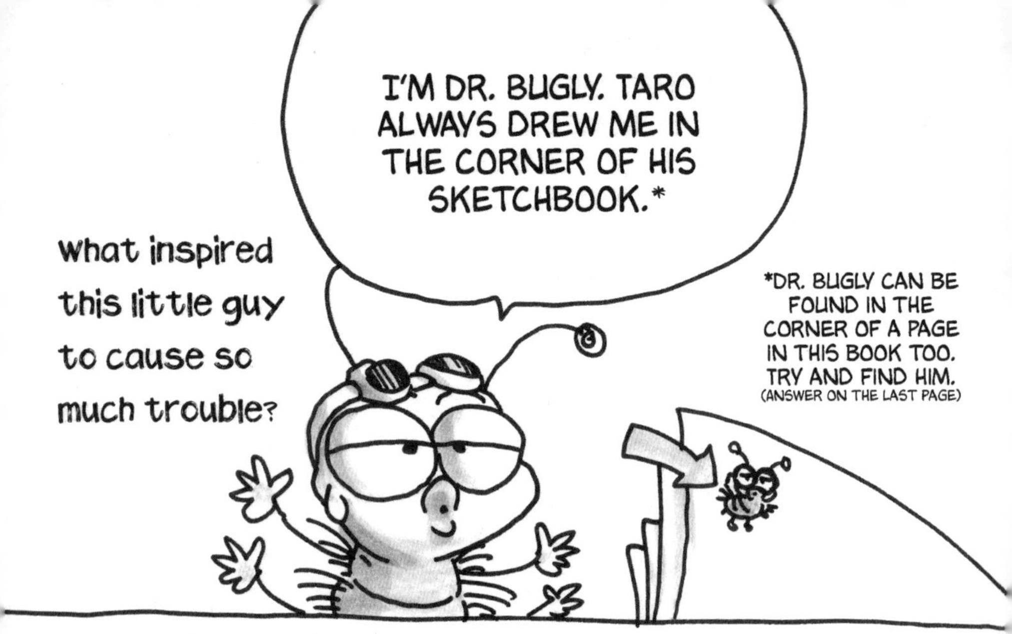
what inspired this little guy to cause so much trouble?
I'M DR. BUGLY. TARO ALWAYS DREW ME IN THE CORNER OF HIS SKETCHBOOK.*
*DR. BUGLY CAN BE FOUND IN THE CORNER OF A PAGE IN THIS BOOK TOO. TRY AND FIND HIM.
(ANSWER ON THE LAST PAGE)

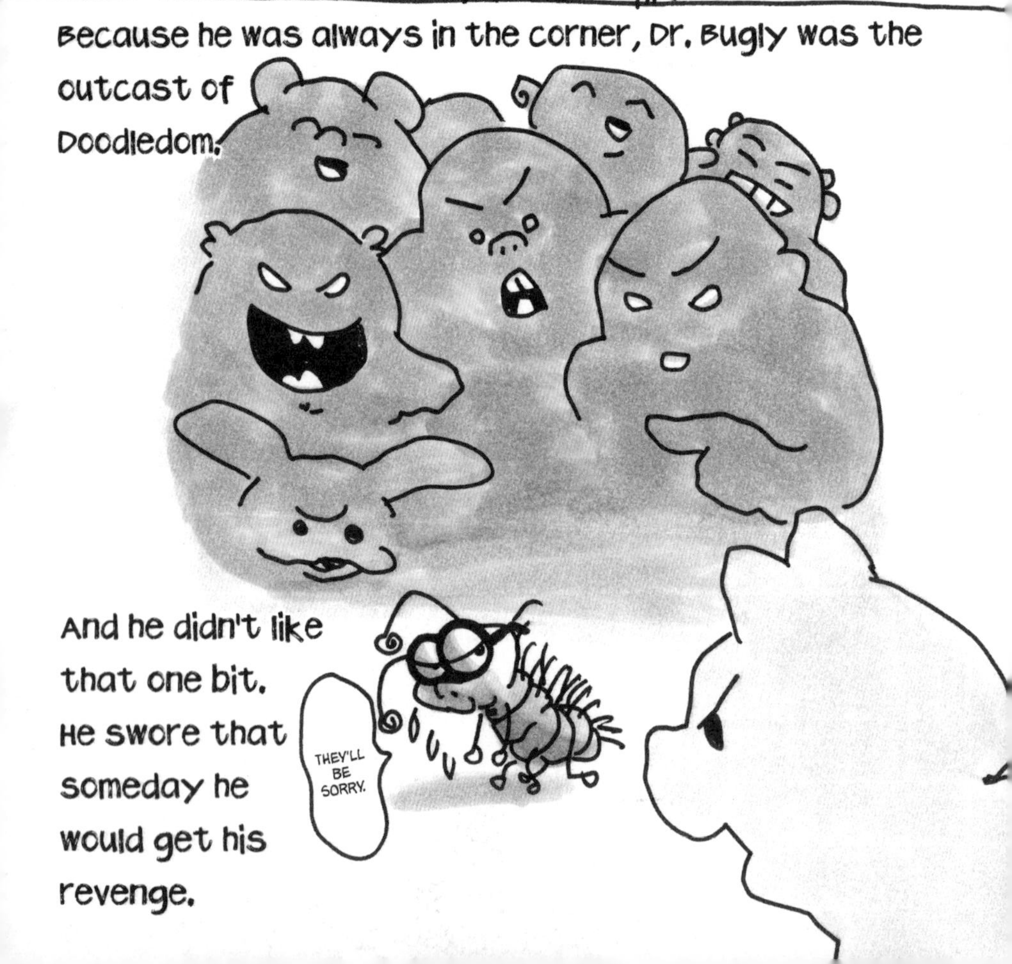
Because he was always in the corner, Dr. Bugly was the outcast of Doodledom.
And he didn't like that one bit. He swore that someday he would get his revenge.
THEY'LL BE SORRY.

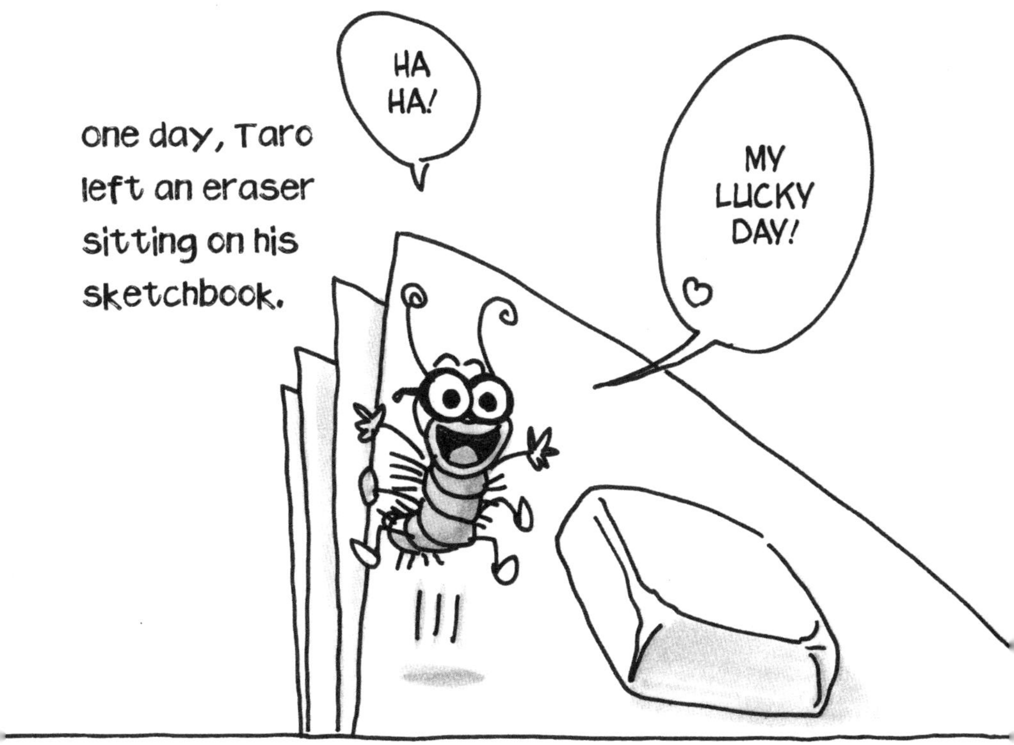
one day, Taro left an eraser sitting on his sketchbook.
HA HA!
MY LUCKY DAY!

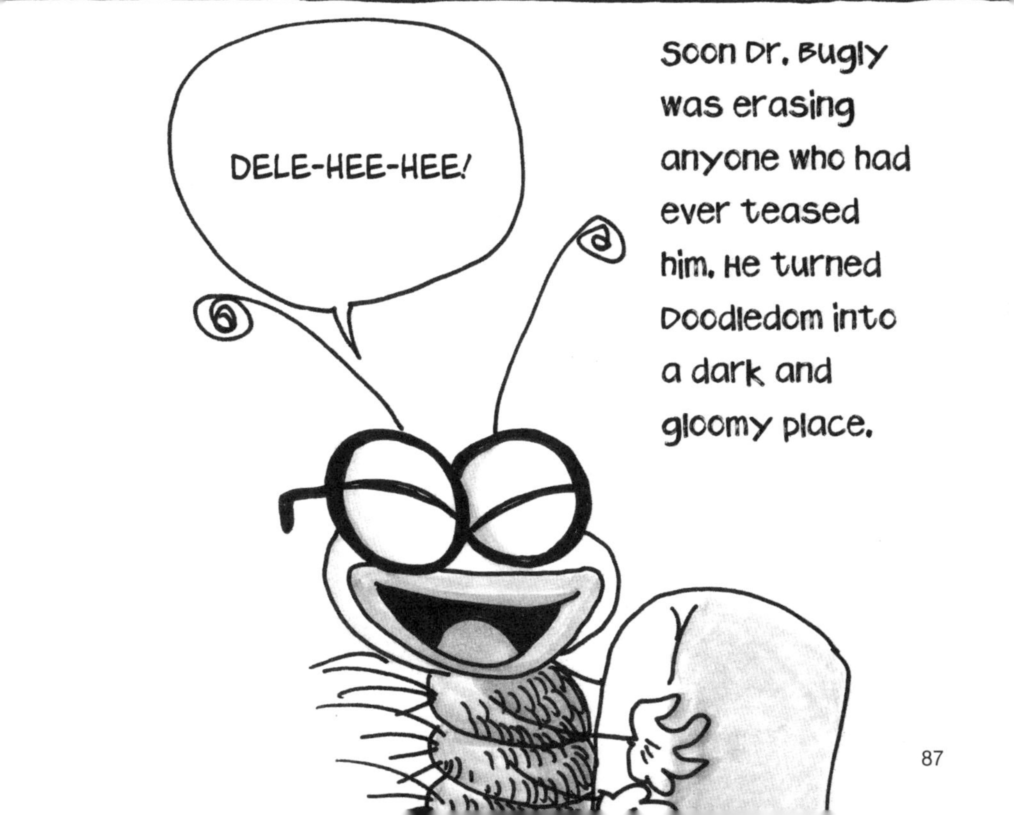
DELE-HEE-HEE!
Soon Dr. Bugly was erasing anyone who had ever teased him. He turned Doodledom into a dark and gloomy place.

Now that he was back to his buggy little self, he promised never to cause trouble again. As King Crossout, Dr. Bugly had invented a lot of things. Now he promised that he would use them for good. The bitty bug seemed so sorry that Terrie forgave him on the spot.

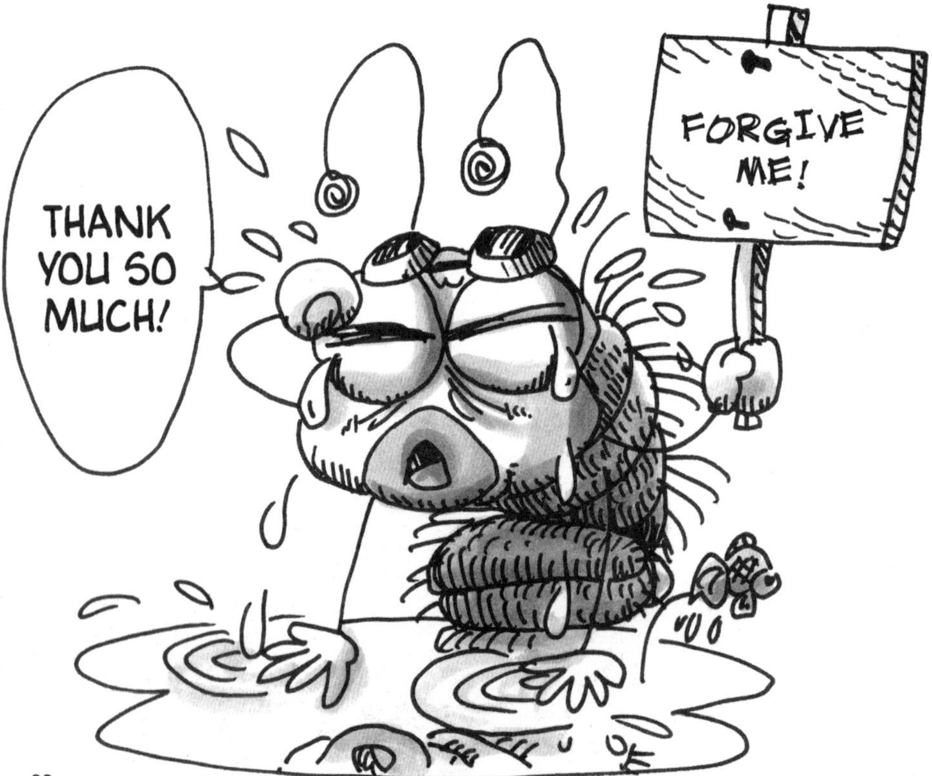
THANK YOU SO MUCH!
FORGIVE ME!

Dr. Bugly's first order of business was to turn Carnival Crossout into an amusement park for everyone in Doodledom to enjoy.

Tattle-Tail gave up his wicked ways too! He got a job taking tickets at the new amusement park.

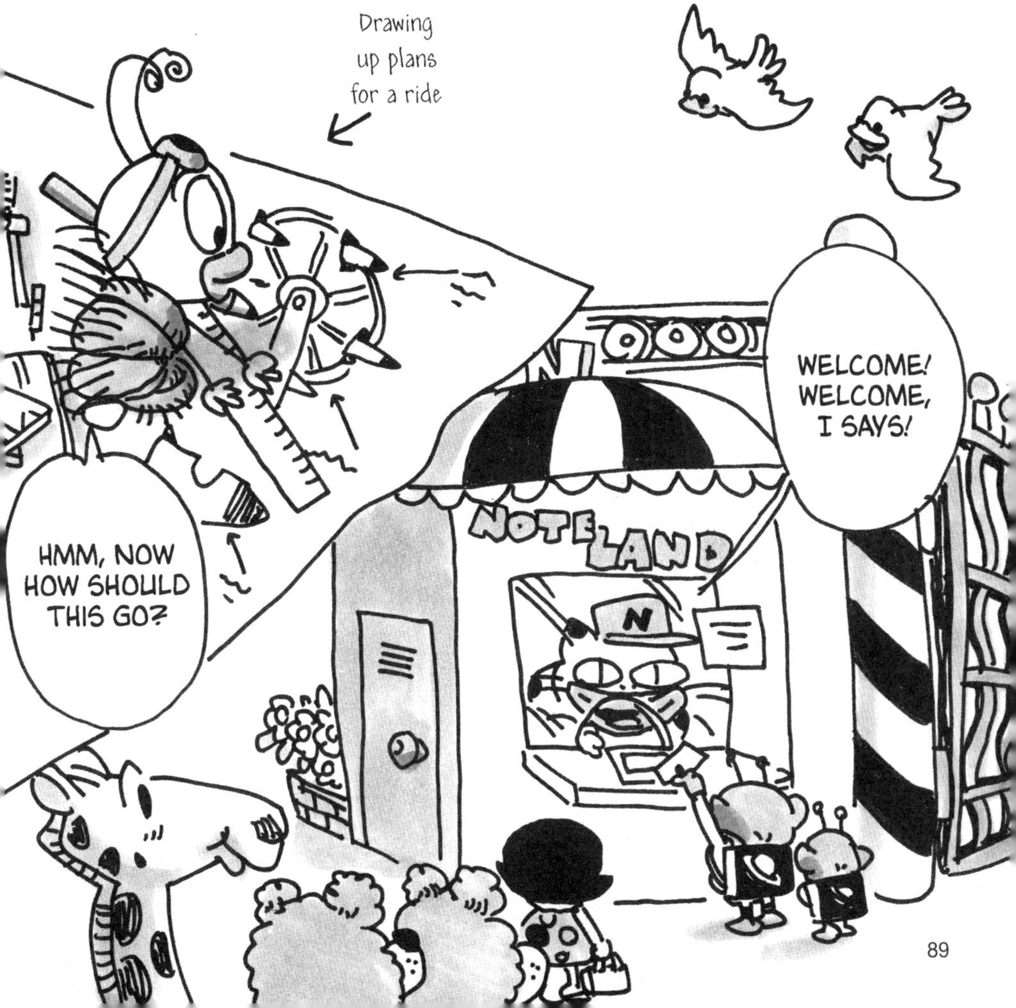
Drawing up plans for a ride
HMM, NOW HOW SHOULD THIS GO?
NOTELAND
WELCOME! WELCOME, I SAYS!

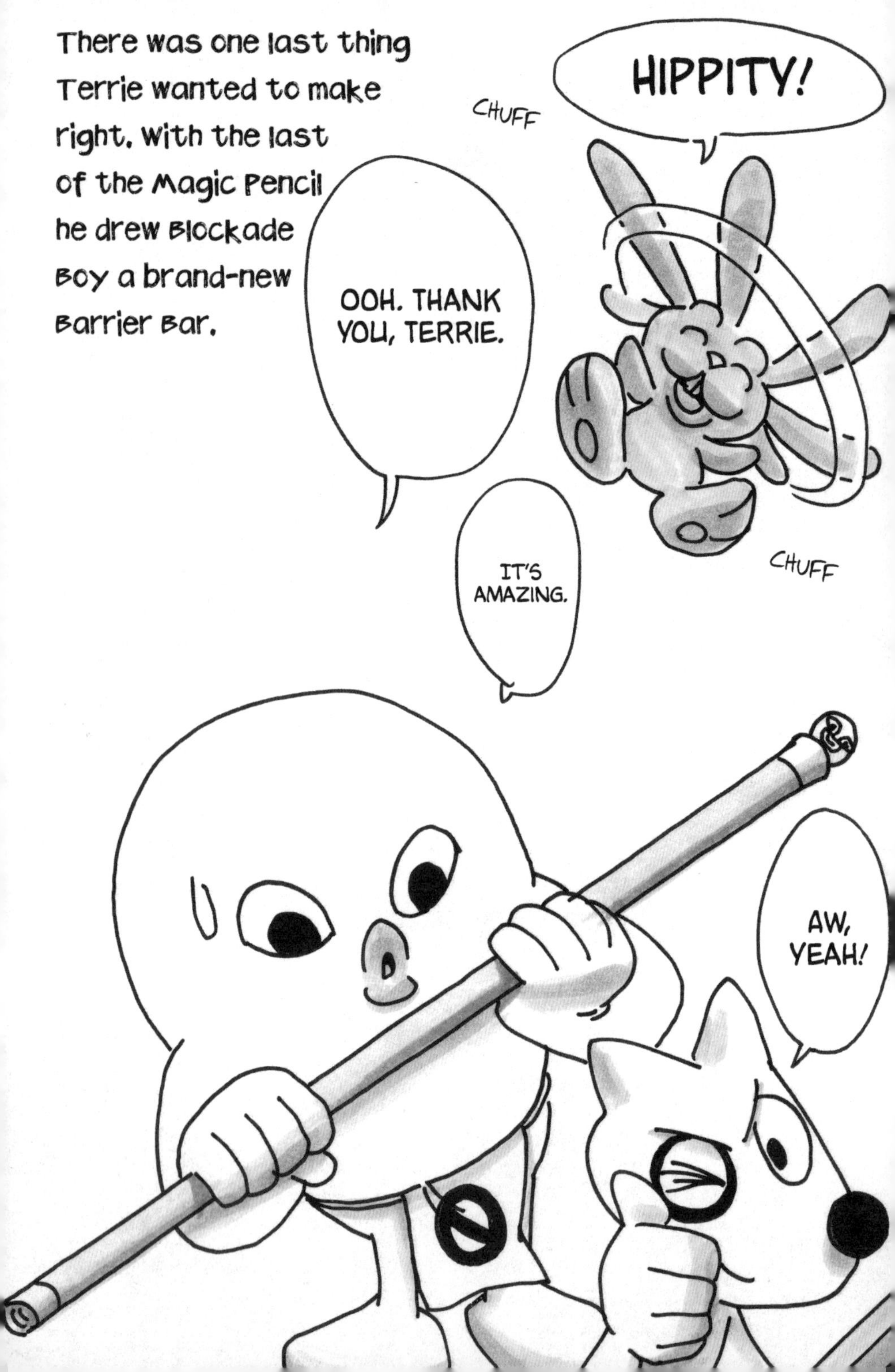
There was one last thing Terrie wanted to make right. With the last of the Magic Pencil he drew Blockade Boy a brand-new Barrier Bar.
CHUFF
HIPPITY!
OOH. THANK YOU, TERRIE.
IT'S AMAZING.
CHUFF
AW, YEAH!

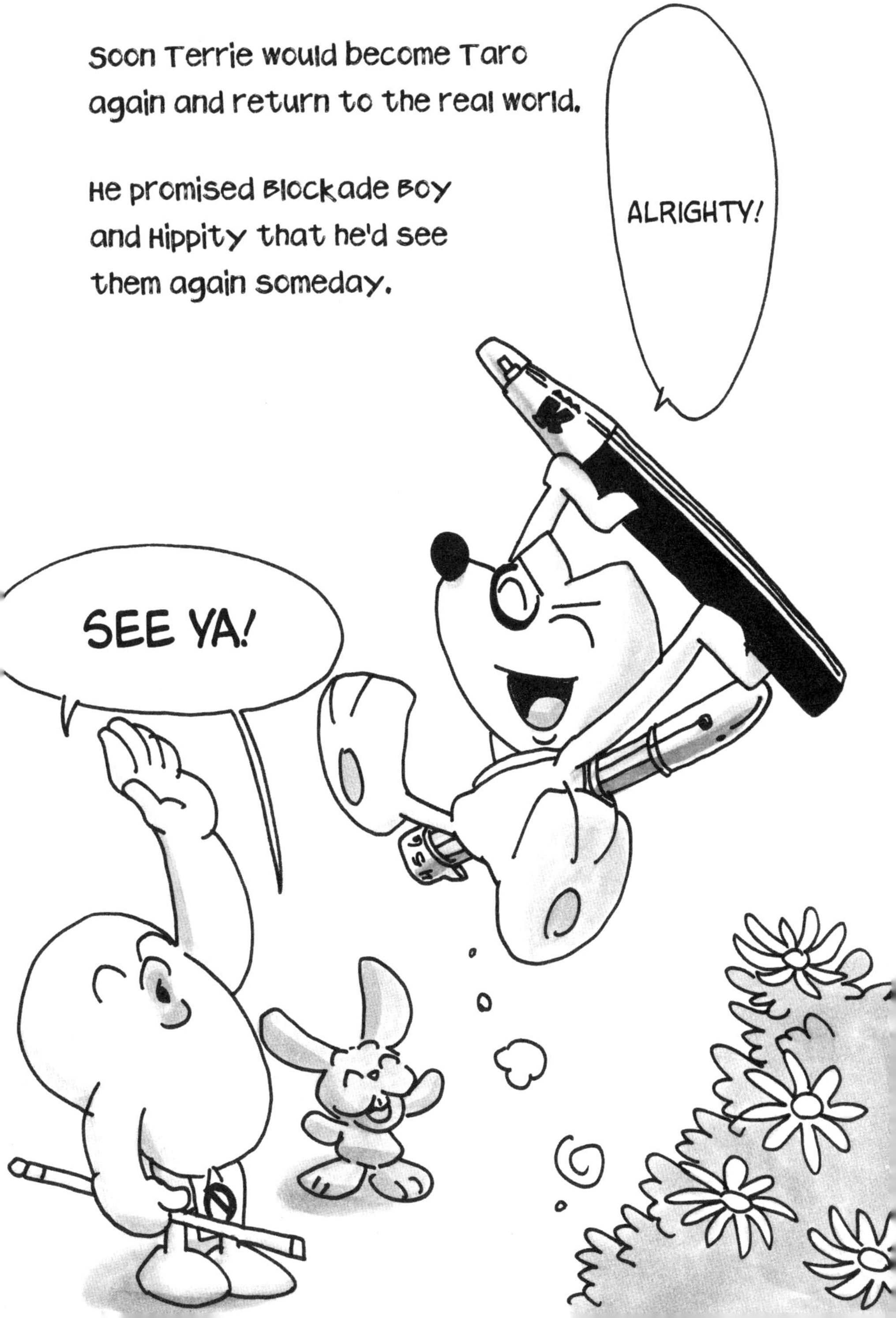
Soon Terrie would become Taro again and return to the real world.
He promised Blockade Boy and Hippity that he'd see them again someday.
ALRIGHTY!
SEE YA!

This time, Terrie took a different way home—he floated straight up into the sky.

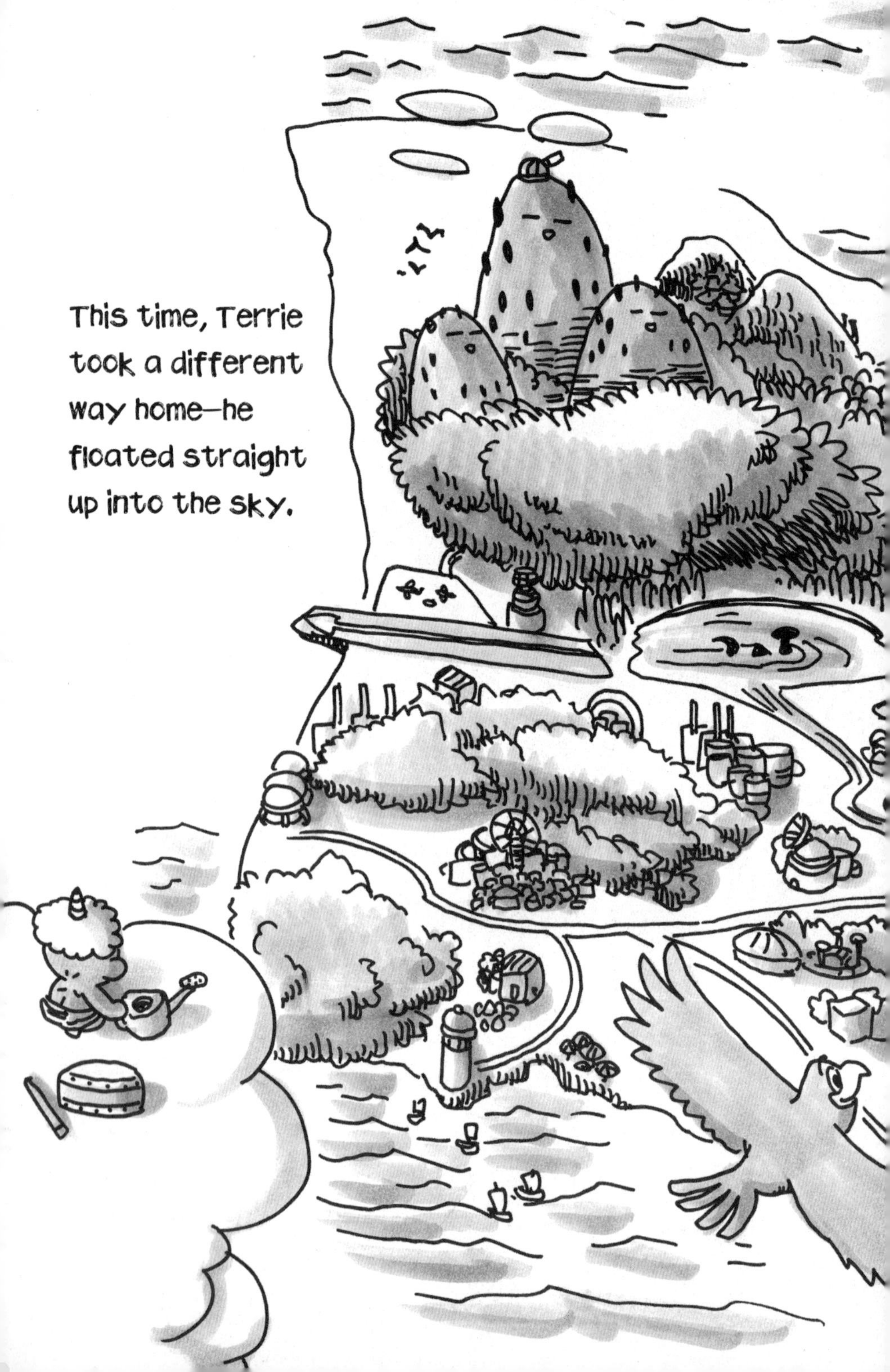

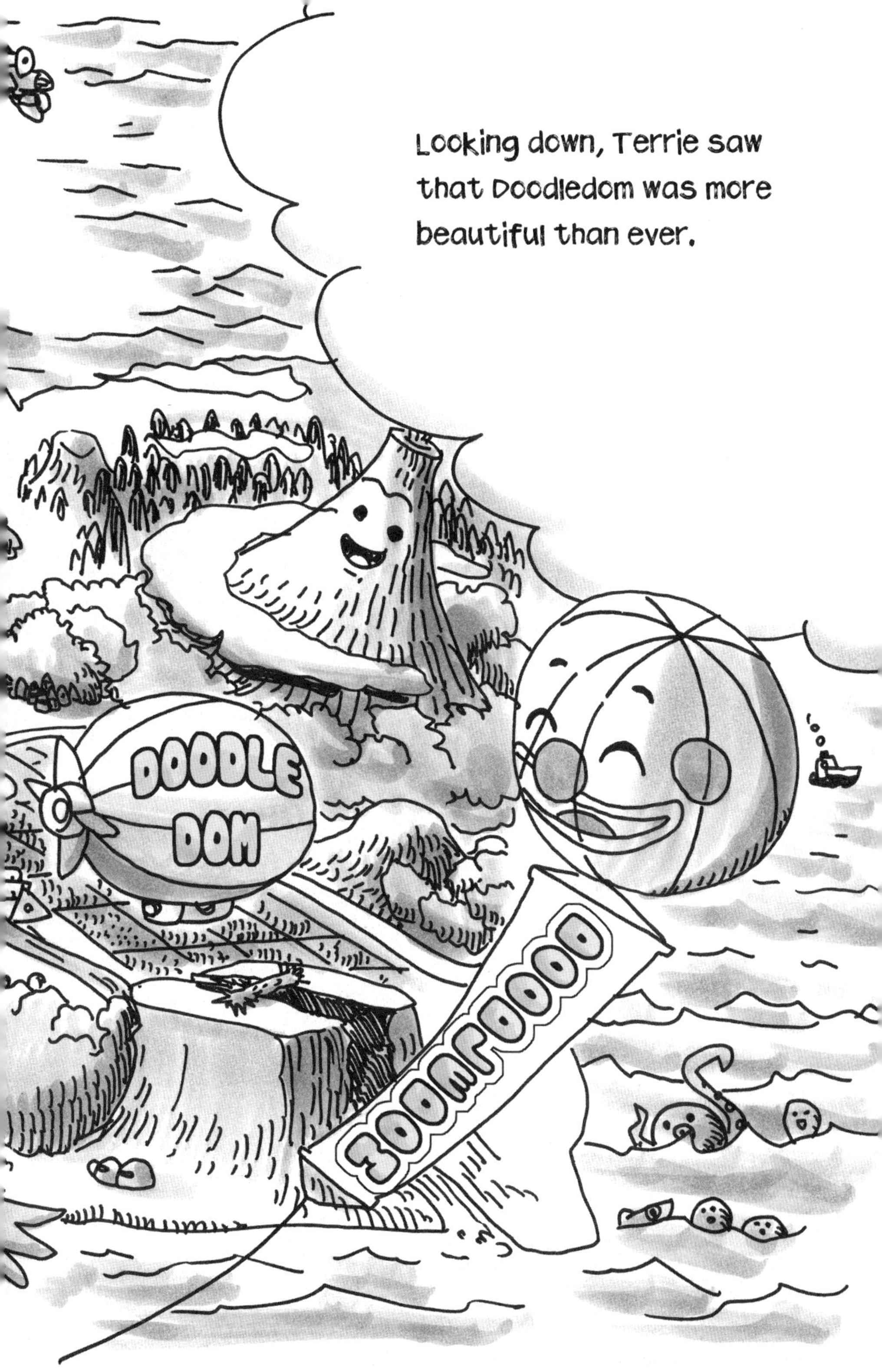
Looking down, Terrie saw that Doodledom was more beautiful than ever.
DOODLE DOM

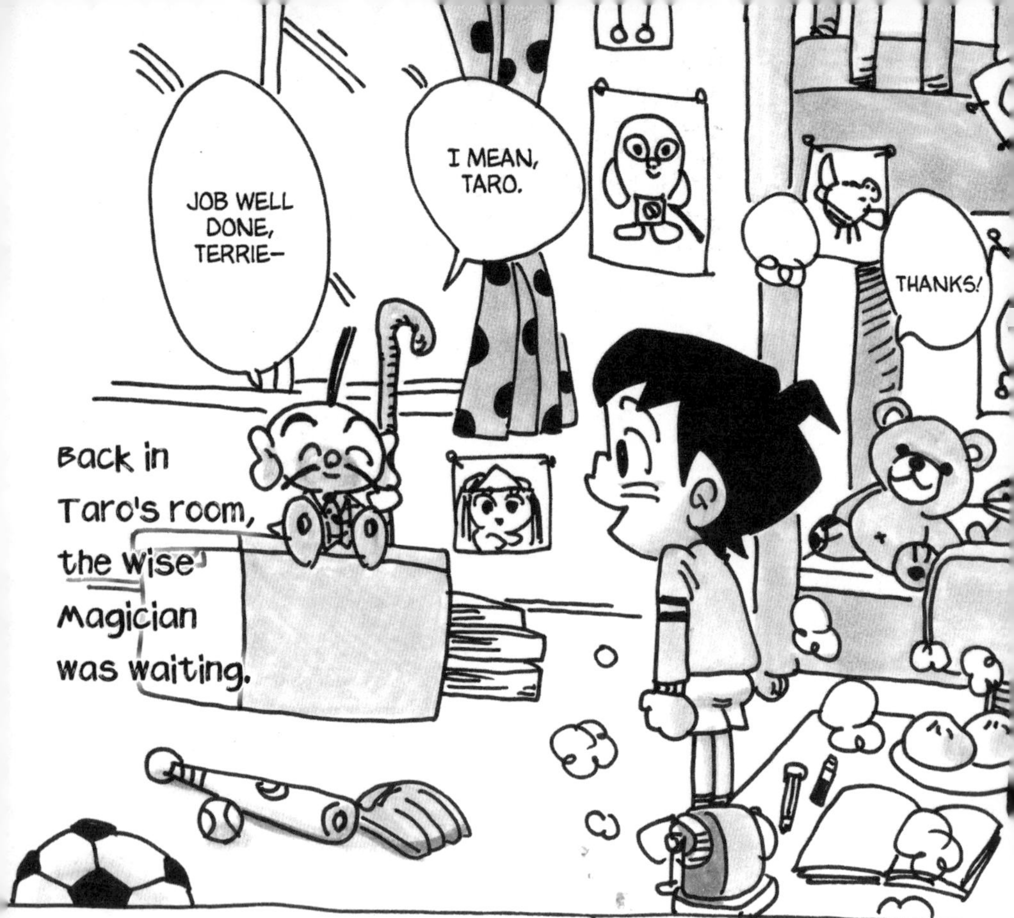
Back in Taro's room, the wise Magician was waiting.
JOB WELL DONE, TERRIE—
I MEAN, TARO.
THANKS!

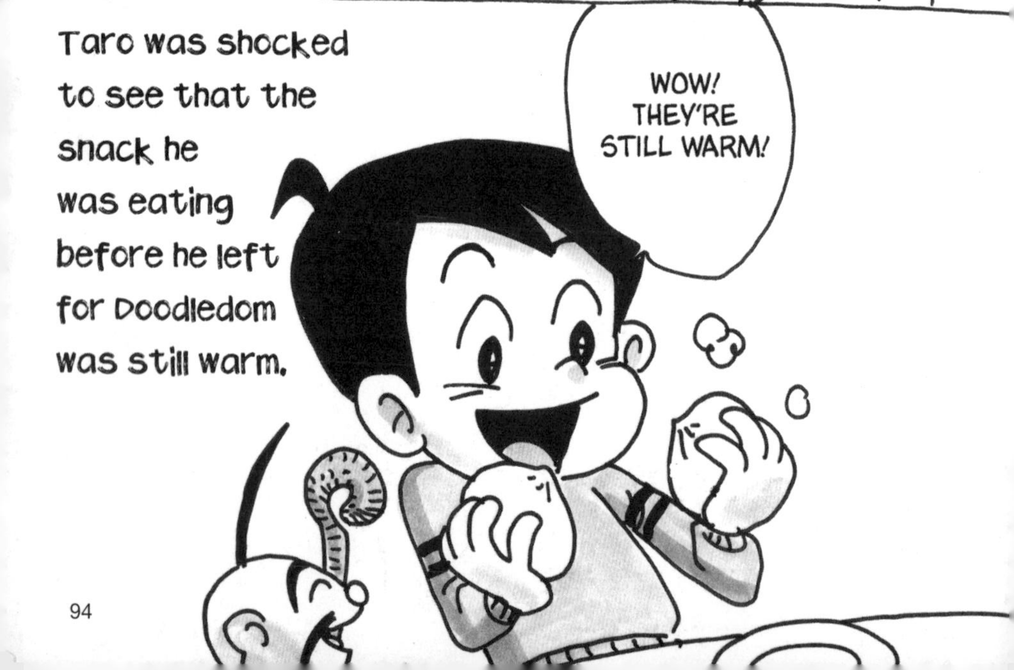
Taro was shocked to see that the snack he was eating before he left for Doodledom was still warm.
WOW! THEY'RE STILL WARM!